KATE'S LAKE

David Odle

Black Rose Writing | Texas

The author grants the final approval for this literary material.

First printing

This is a work of fiction. Names, characters, businesses, places, events, and incidents are either the products of the author's imagination or used in a fictitious manner. Any resemblance to actual persons, living or dead, or actual events is purely coincidental.

ISBN: 978-1-68433-519-0
PUBLISHED BY BLACK ROSE WRITING
www.blackrosewriting.com

Printed in the United States of America
Suggested Retail Price (SRP) $18.95

Kate's Lake is printed in Baskerville

*As a planet-friendly publisher, Black Rose Writing does its best to eliminate unnecessary waste to reduce paper usage and energy costs, while never compromising the reading experience. As a result, the final word count vs. page count may not meet common expectations.

For those who had to burn shit in the desert.
Semper Fi

And for JT.

KATE'S LAKE

PART I
THE BOTTOMS

CHAPTER 1

I blame my wife for what happened.

That's a bullshit thing to say, I know. I hate myself for even thinking it.

But it's true.

The day I left for Harry's funeral, Amy leaned against the kitchen counter and glared at me with narrowed eyes and lips pursed to a thin, red line. Our daughters were still at school. Thank god for that little circumstance.

"You're not even going to talk to me about it?" She drummed her fingers on the countertop.

"No." I stood my ground. I'd made this decision. "I'm going."

A bitter smile crossed her face. "That's great. Real nice." Her voice hitched. Difficult conversations weren't easy for her.

She flipped a hand at me in a gesture that always made me feel wrong. Despite the facts or my reasons why, when she did that, I felt like a complete horse's ass.

I scraped my tongue against the back of my teeth and said, "This is crap. How can you expect me to miss his funeral? It's Harry."

Her fists clenched, but the anger never touched her eyes. The crack in her armor. She'd known Harry. She knew what he'd meant to me. "I get that it's Harry. But how long's it been, Mick, since you spoke to him? Three years? Four?"

"Four," I said. I couldn't believe it'd been so long.

"Four years." She strolled across the kitchen to a drawer at the far end of the counter, pulled out something small, and then marched right up to me. She slapped a coin onto the table and I flinched. "You didn't have *that* four years ago, did you?"

My eyes crawled down to my sobriety coin gleaming silver on the table. Three years. She'd made her point. She'd stuck with me through the bad years.

"Look." I locked onto her glare. "It's two days. I probably won't even talk to anyone. Hell, I don't know anyone. I sure as hell ain't planning to drink anything. Harry's gone, sweetheart. It'll just be me."

Her eyes darted down and she shook her head. She didn't trust me and I understood. But three years was a long time. Surely that meant something. The ghost of a life I'd left behind years ago whispered faintly in my ear like drifting images of nightmares struggling to stay alive.

I placed my hands gently on her shoulders. "His dad called and asked me to come. His dad, sweetie. And you know how we were, Harry and me."

"Oh yeah," a deep chuckle. I loved it when she chuckled like that. "I know."

"I don't mean the partying. He was my best friend." Those words echoed in my brain as they rolled off my tongue. *My best friend*. So many firsts we'd experienced together.

The thought of him dead still didn't resonate, like watching the news about a shooting death in a faraway city.

Amy reached up and delicately grasped my forearms. She gazed into my eyes and I anticipated her warm kiss. Instead, she pulled my hands off of her and twisted away. "Go then," she said as she trudged out of the kitchen. She stopped in the archway and looked back at me. Her expression bore betrayal, one of relenting to the inevitable. "Don't do anything stupid, Mick. Promise me that, please?"

"Of course." She had no faith in me whatsoever. "What the hell am I gonna do out there, babe? Seriously?"

Her eyes found mine and a sad smile curled the corners of her mouth. "I know it's Harry. I know you have to go. But I can't go through it again, Mick. I won't."

I opened my mouth to say *Give me a break, here. It's been three years*, but she was gone. I hurt for her, I really did. I understood. But at some point, we needed to move on. *She* needed to move on.

The past was the past. We'd both changed so much in the last few years. We'd grown stronger. We were totally devoted to our daughters. We even went to church sometimes.

I had a fleeting urge to go after her right then. Give up on this whole notion of attending Harry's funeral. I lived in Denver. Indiana sat halfway across the country. Harry would understand. *Wouldn't you, Harry?*

Of course he would.

If he were standing right here and I said, *hey man, I can't risk things with Amy and the girls.* He'd smile and say, *I get it. Don't risk a good thing, dipshit.*

Darn right, he would. He knew me. He knew my demons. He knew what haunted me. He knew that I'd be dead now if it weren't for him. No one else tried to save me when I needed it most.

I couldn't skip his funeral. We'd been brothers. We'd been to war. I'd have to fix this thing with Amy when I got back. Two days from now, when I come strolling back through that front door, and she learns that there'd been nothing to worry about, it'll all be good.

Amy and I were stronger than that. Because Harry *made* us stronger than that.

Harry Darnell. *Semper Fi, brother.*

▪ ▪ ▪ ▪ ▪

My flight to Indianapolis departed that afternoon. The argument with Amy lingered with me the entire drive to the airport. I even re-enacted it in the car, talking aloud, and of course, in these solo conversations, my points were always profound and inarguable. By the time I parked the car and started my long stroll to the ticket counter with my bag slung over my shoulder, I felt better. I felt right.

During the flight, my thoughts shifted from Amy to Harry. My dead friend. My brother in the Corps. After everything, he was no more. His dad said he'd died in a car accident. Even sitting in that airplane, the reality hadn't completely sunk in. People like Harry didn't just up and die.

But of course, I knew that wasn't true. I'd seen it happen too many times in a shit-hole country a million miles from here. A small flutter rippled my chest at the thought of him no longer existing in this world. I plugged my earbuds into my ears and let the music consume me.

It didn't take long to find the rental car lot after we landed. Thank goodness, the Indianapolis Airport was nothing like Denver. I drove straight to Harry's house from the airport. His dad mentioned on the phone that's where everyone planned to gather today. I drummed my fingers nervously on the steering wheel as I followed my phone's navigation. Would his mom recognize me? I'd met her twice and neither time for very long. I hoped it wouldn't be too awkward.

I parked along the street and gazed at the house. Cars stuffed the driveway. Two little kids chased each other around in the yard. The sun drifted low and I wished it was dark. Not sure why, other than the night made it easier to be inconspicuous. I remembered this house. I'd stayed here with Harry when Amy and I separated. Good times, we'd had.

Going in there now didn't excite me.

I considered driving to my motel first. Check in, relax a little, and call Amy to see if her mood had lightened.

Stop it. Suck it up and get in there.

I pursed my lips, opened the door, and got out.

▪ ▪ ▪ ▪ ▪

The house smelled like flowers and food. People loitered throughout and I didn't know any of them. I stopped and asked a younger guy if he knew where I might find Mrs. Darnell. He pointed me to the dining room. Mrs. Darnell recognized me, but speaking to her was a fiasco about as comfortable as swearing in church. My palms sweat, my heart thudded, and she told me that Harry never stopped talking about me.

She told me that Harry's older sister, Arlene, was there somewhere and that I should find her. I smiled sympathetically, patted her hand, and told her I'd go find her right away.

I lied. I wanted out of that house.

Outside on the back patio, while standing with my hands shoved in my pockets and gazing at the sunset, I met a guy I didn't recognize; old with deep lines in his face and thinning gray hair. He looked tired. He asked me if Harry had mentioned anything about what he'd been up to lately. I had no idea what *up to* meant, and I'm not sure I cared at the time.

Looking back, there were a lot of things I should've paid more attention to, this old man being one of them.

He asked if I'd spoken to Harry recently.

"No," I said. We lingered in the back yard, off by ourselves, away from where Harry's family and friends congregated on the back patio. "I haven't talked to him in..." I shrugged, "a while." Four years slipping by embarrassed me. Time gets away.

"Never mentioned anything about the lake or the Bottoms?" The old guy asked. I detected something in the way he asked it. Surprise. Confusion.

"Lake? Why would he mention a lake? You mean the reservoir?" I knew Harry liked to fish out there sometimes, I remembered him talking about it when we were in the Marine Corps. We talked about so many things then.

"No." The old man frowned, as if about to say something else, then didn't.

He nodded and then left with a quick goodbye. Apparently, he'd only stopped by to ask me that one, strange question. Weirdo.

. . . . .

I hung around uncomfortably for about another half hour before bailing out. I stopped at a little bar in Harry's hometown called the Golden Nugget. We'd gone here many times back in the day. I toasted to my late, great friend with a Coca-Cola (years ago, it would have been a *Jim Beam* and Coke) and then headed to my motel out on highway 41, close to the interstate.

I checked in and dropped my bag on the end of the bed. Blessed quiet. Not a single person on earth to bug me. I fumbled through my bag and found my boarding pass for the next day. It felt good to touch it, to know it was there. My plane was scheduled to depart from Indianapolis at 5 PM, shortly after the funeral. No way I'd risk that.

I crawled into bed knowing that I should call Amy, but I had no idea what kind of mood she'd be in. Plus, I'd bet she was busy getting the girls to bed. I'd call her in the morning. The room's air conditioner hummed and it soothed me to sleep.

The day had taken its toll.

. . . . .

I awoke late to the rattle of the doorknob wiggling back and forth. My eyes snapped open. Still nighttime. I glanced at the clock on the nightstand. 3:13 in the morning. *What the shit?* Goose bumps pebbled my arms. I propped myself up on one elbow and gawked at the door.

Darkness shrouded the room except for the light of an outside streetlamp fighting through the slats of the closed blinds. I pictured Harry's corpse standing out there, drooping with sagging skin and wet clothes. God knows where *that* image came from.

I held my breath for fear that the lurid thing might hear me and that somehow me being awake would cause it to do something horrible. I laid there hoping it would go away.

"Mr. Smith?" A voice called.

The voice sounded familiar. As I swung my legs off the bed, a shiver raced over my skin. I wondered, *why was his corpse soaking wet?*

My phone lay on the nightstand next to me. I plucked it up and considered calling 911. The guy tried to break into my room for Christ's sake.

I slipped over to the door and peeked through the eyehole. Holy shit. There stood that strange, old guy who I'd met briefly in Harry's backyard. He had one hand shoved deep in his pocket while the other touched the doorknob. *Jesus, didn't he know how to knock?*

I yelled, "Just a sec." I must be crazy to even consider talking to this old coot. I pulled on a pair of jeans, squirmed into a T-shirt, and opened the door. The guy stood there and stared at me. His eyes were piercing, almost crystalline.

"Need to talk to ya," he said.

"Why didn't you knock?"

"Figured you was sleepin'," he answered, as if any fool should have known that.

An awkward pause fell between us. Finally, I asked, "So what do you want?" If the guy so much as looked at me wrong, I'd drop him. I didn't care how old he was.

"Told ya, I need to talk. Mind goin' across the road and gettin' some coffee?"

He'd asked about a lake earlier and if I knew what Harry was up to. This old man *knew* things. I rubbed a hand through my hair and glanced at the clock one more time. Was I seriously going to do this? I looked back at the old man clenching his jaw and shifting his weight nervously from foot to foot. I shook my head and said, "Sure. Let me get my shoes on."

Humidity hung heavy in the night air, not like the crisp evenings back home. It had an oily smell which I blamed on a gas station perched next to the motel. As we strolled across the deserted highway to a 24-hour Denny's restaurant, I thought, *I can't believe I'm out here at 3 in the morning talking to this weirdo*. Yet something gnawed at me, like knowing someone's about to tell you a juicy secret, and the gnawing compelled me to talk to him, that I *needed* to talk to him.

Our shoes scraping asphalt disrupted the night's stillness as we meandered across the road. Thank goodness for the streetlights.

In hindsight, this is where it all started.

CHAPTER 2

One other guy was in the restaurant and he sat far enough away that he couldn't hear us. A skinny, black-haired waitress, I'd guess early twenties, carried a pot of coffee, ready to fill up a cup if anyone so much as took a sip. Place was dead.

Sitting there with my coffee cup full, my forefinger curled into the small, porcelain handle, I glanced toward a row of barstools across the room where the other guy sat. He appeared drunk, swaying back and forth, like he'd just woken up from a roadside ditch. I smiled inwardly because I knew what that felt like. Demons haunt us wherever we go. The thing I always found the most peculiar about Denny's is how the place always looked jarringly yellow inside.

The old guy sat directly across from me. He asked, "How'd ya know that guy that died?"

"Harry?"

He nodded.

Funny, I assumed he knew. "He was a friend of mine from the military."

"Military, huh?" He sipped from his coffee, running his tongue against his upper lip when he finished drinking. "What branch?"

"Marine Corps."

He nodded as if I'd told him I could bench press 300 pounds. "Never went to the military, m'self; I'd 'a gone to Nam. Didn't want none of that shit."

It wasn't uncommon for people, once they found out I'd been in the military, to say they wished they'd gone or that they'd tried and some medical condition prevented it. But this guy gave no such insinuation.

"It's not for everyone," I said and took a slow slurp of my coffee. It tasted good, but I'd never get back to sleep.

"Name's Bob," the man said.

"Mick…"

"Mickey Smith," Bob finished for me. "Yeah… I've heard your name before. Heard that fella that died sayin' it."

"You knew Harry?"

"Didn't use to. I'd seen him a lot out there to the lake. I found him." Bob glanced toward the large window next to us, as if he expected someone to be standing out there.

"Found him?" I adjusted my foot under the table, suddenly not comfortable.

Bob nodded and shifted his gaze from the window, back to me. "The night they say he died. I found him."

"In the car wreck." I scrunched my eyebrows and shot him a crooked smile. "You found the car wreck?"

"Nope. No car wreck." Bob placed his hand on the table and lightly tapped his thumb, as if music played in his head.

He was either a total loon or the old man, good 'ole Bob, was trying to screw with my head. "All right." I held up a hand. "I don't know who you are or what you're trying to do here, but Harry died in a car wreck and I'm here for the funeral at his father's request." For some unknown reason right then I pictured my wife and two daughters at home, sleeping in their beds. A bead of cold sweat dripped down my side out of my armpit. I scratched it.

"Uh, yeah, his father," the old man said.

"Yep." I cleared my throat. "He called me night before last and told me what happened… asked me to come here." I watched Bob's eyes trail to the window again and his eyebrows curled. An uneasiness settled on me and I asked, "Who are you?" My turn to ask questions.

The feather of a smile touched Bob's lips. Hard to read. I maintained my gaze, even though he wasn't looking at me, and drank my coffee. To hell with this guy if he thought I'd sit here and put up with being told a bunch of crap.

"I live in the Bottoms, close to the lake," Bob said.

"The reservoir," I clarified. "You're talking about the reservoir." I knew about the reservoir. Harry always talked about fishing there. I'd gone out there with him years ago.

"Nah." He scratched his chin. "The lake. Kate's Lake. It's about forty or so miles down Highway 41. You gotta turn off the highway and take a dirt road about 10 or so miles back in the woods. It's back in there."

"Never heard of it." I thought of the conversation we'd had in Harry's backyard earlier. *Yesterday*, my mind corrected, *that conversation happened yesterday... it's three o'clock in the damn morning!*

"It's back in there quite a ways," Bob said, "off the highway and down a dirt road. There ain't many people that know 'bout it."

"Hmmm." My eyes drifted down at my coffee cup. Half empty. I glanced around for the black-haired waitress. *Black-haired and scrawny*, as Harry might've called her. He was a dick sometimes.

She sat by the cash register peering down at something in her hand, it looked like a stack of receipts. I wondered why a girl so young worked in here so late. I'd never let my own daughter do that. "So." I turned my attention back to Bob and decided to humor him, not yet ready to admit my own dark curiosity. "How did Harry die then, if it wasn't a car wreck?"

"He didn't." The old man's voice dropped to a whisper and his eyes darted around the restaurant as if he feared hidden spies lurked below the tables. 'Ole Bob might be bat-shit crazy. A real loon. I considered calling the police.

"Look," I'd had about enough of this. Time for me to be on my merry way back to my room, go to the funeral tomorrow, and then get the hell back home where I belonged. Not sitting at Denny's talking to this nutcase. "I'm not saying you're wrong, but I'm not sure we're talking about the same person."

"We are." Bob's jaw clenched and softened.

"His dad said he died in a car wreck." I'd already said that, but it seemed prudent to mention again, as if my mission changed from one of curiosity, to compassion for the mentally ill.

"That's what he told you."

"Why would he lie?"

"Don't know, I ain't met 'im. But, have you seen the body?"

I damn near said *yes* to get him off my case. But something inside me said that to lie about this would be wrong. "I haven't seen the body, no. But I've known his family a long time and don't know why they'd lie about it."

"They're not lyin'," Bob said. "They think he's dead."

I sighed. Black haired and scrawny finally sauntered over with a full pot of coffee to give me a refill. I looked at Bob, mustered an intense stare, but he never changed course. He just sat there tapping his thumb. A long silence fell between us as the waitress refilled my cup. She asked if we were fine. I told her we were. Bob didn't answer.

When she was out of ear-shot, I leaned forward and said, "Look, Bob, I'm not sure what the hell you're tryin' to do here, but I'll say this... I got a call two days ago that Harry had died in a car wreck. I'm no one *that* special… just a friend. Harry's older sister knows me, or at least she knows *of* me. Hell, I'm not even a pallbearer. I have a wife and two kids. I plan on leaving today, right after the funeral to head home and will probably never set foot in Indiana again. If there's something you need to explain about Harry, you should take it up with *his* family, not me."

Bob's mouth curled into a grimace and he leaned toward me, his eyes finding mine, locking on, explaining a profound truth. "I've lived out by that lake for thirty-two years. I know it like the back of my hand… but there is one thing I *don't* know, that I don't wanna know." He glanced around the inside of the restaurant again and then back at me. "That cottage your friend bought last year, it's been sitting out there empty for years, never been nobody live in it that I know of."

Cottage? Lake? Harry bought a cottage?

"Some time ago there was a fella from out east that owned it and he stayed out there a few times, but other than that, ain't no one lived in it." Bob strained to maintain a whisper, almost a hiss, and I caught the stench of old chewing tobacco on his breath. "Not 'till your friend moved in out there last year."

He hesitated, as if expecting me to interject something. Finally, I said, "I didn't even know he bought a place, other than his house in Gainesville. He never told me about it." I tried to recall if Harry had mentioned a cottage or lake the last time we'd spoken.

"Yep. He did. Him and that girlfriend of his," Bob said. *Girlfriend?* Didn't know about that either. I still wasn't convinced Bob wasn't full of shit. He kept talking, but I took it all with a grain of salt. "They moved in last fall. He told me he liked to fish. A few folks got cabins and cottages down in the Bottoms so they can fish." He'd used that term *Bottoms* a couple of times now.

"Yeah." The feather of a smile touched the corner of my mouth. Harry loved fishing. Even when we were in the Corps, stationed at Camp Pendleton, he'd pack up on the weekends and head out toward Big Bear Mountain or up to the La Jolla Reservation. Sometimes I joined him, but most times, I stayed put on base or drove into town, barhopping. That's when the drinking started, right after I got home from my second tour in Iraq.

Bob sipped his coffee and clanked the cup back onto the table. "I told him one day as we walked 'round the lake that fishin' ain't no good in there. He asked why and I asked him if he'd ever heard the rumors about this here place. I told him that Kate's Lake is bottomless. A bottomless lake."

"Bottomless, huh?" Even though I found the part about Harry buying a cottage and moving in with his girlfriend fairly interesting, for no other reason than the fact that I hadn't known, I found the rest of Bob's ramblings too bizarre to take seriously.

"Yep. Bottomless."

I needed to get out of there. "So, how does this affect me?" I asked.

Bob's gaze turned icy. "I think your friend lied to me… he knew exactly what that place was. You ain't supposed to drink the water no more and I told him that." The old man's eyes stayed fixed on me. A chill raced down my spine. "God as my witness, I told him that."

I nodded and for the first time in four years, I wanted a cigarette. More than wanted, I *craved* it, like an insatiable hunger swelling from the center of my chest, cruising through my veins like a ravenous worm. I licked my lips and sat back in my seat.

I pictured Amy, her beautiful face stoic as she watched me and read my mind. Guilt crept into me. *Don't do anything stupid*, she'd said. The weak man inside me wished she was here, right now, to slap the cigarette thought right out of my mind.

"He's still out there, ya know." Bob pressed his lips together.

I barely registered his words. My mind strayed away. "Who?"

"Your friend. The guy everyone thinks died. He's still out there."

"Where? At the cottage?"

Bob nodded in slow, deliberate movements. I gazed into his eyes and knew, in that instant, that he wasn't lying. Whether Harry was dead or not, this crazy old man believed his own bullshit. I wondered why he had singled me out. Why hadn't he gone to Harry's family? Or someone here in Indiana? Why me?

The waitress's voice caught me off guard and I nearly jumped. "You two need anything else?"

"No," I said. "We're done here."

Bob glared at me. The waitress reached into her apron and withdrew a small, black binder and plopped it down on our table. "I'll take that when you're ready," she said.

I stuffed my hand into my jeans pocket and fished until I found the soft paper of a five-dollar bill. I slapped it on top of the black binder that contained our check for the two coffees.

"I'm getting out of here, Bob, so tell me, what do you want from me? Why are you telling me this at three in the morning?"

Bob's stare creeped me out. He said, "I want ya to come out there. That guy, your friend, told me to find you. And I didn't want people gettin' nosy, that's why I'm out here so early."

Great, more weirdness. "Was this before or after he died?" I tried not to sound sarcastic again. Pretty sure I failed miserably.

"Well," Bob cocked his head, seriously considering it, and said, "It'd be before all this." He looked down at the table as if he were considering his answer, making sure he was right.

"Yeah." I glanced around again and noticed no one else had come in. "All right, Bob, I have to go. I have to attend a funeral tomorrow for a very dear friend of mine. After that, I'm heading home. I honestly have no clue what you're talking about, but I wish you the best of luck resolving your issues."

Bob didn't answer.

I slid out of the booth seat and stood by the table, debating on saying something else to him. It seemed wrong leaving him sit there by himself, but it would be even more ludicrous to keep entertaining this conversation.

I tapped the table and said, "Take care." I headed toward the front doors. I didn't look back, but sensed Bob's eyes following me, searing into the back of my head. I opened the door and stepped out into the morning air. Early darkness greeted me and the deserted parking lot slept.

Chalk that up to one of the weirdest conversations ever.

I hurried across the highway. Other than my motel and Denny's, only a gas station stood out here, one of those highway-stop stations selling everything from milk to Harley Davidson clocks. Floodlights from the motel shined like lonely vestiges for a guy wishing like hell he was asleep in a warm bed.

Bob's words echoed in my head. Cottage. Kate's Lake. Harry's girlfriend. A bottomless lake. What the hell? I mean, Christ, I came out to Indiana for a funeral. Now I had this weirdo following me around.

Still, crazy as it sounds, what if Harry *was* still alive?

I shook the thought away. I needed to get through today and go home.

CHAPTER 3

By the time I got back to my motel room, it was after 4 AM; my alarm was set to go off at six. I stripped off my clothes and climbed into bed, but falling back to sleep was as likely as hitting the lottery. The two cups of coffee I drank ensured that. I lay there, staring up at the ceiling, playing the conversation with Bob over in my mind and wishing like hell I could forget it.

It didn't even make sense, the stuff he talked about. Did some dark conspiracy exist here in Indiana? I smiled. Hardly seemed possible.

I considered calling Amy, but she'd be irritated to receive a 3 AM call about a conversation I'd with an old man named Bob. *Mick*, I heard her saying in a groggy voice, *why don't you call me about this later. I have to get up early to take the girls to school.*

I wished stuff like that didn't bother her, and she'd get up, concerned about *me*, pushing a strand of hair behind her ear and asking me to tell her about it. Nope, not Amy. She'd get pissed at me for using the salt-shaker wrong. But that's regular married stuff, I guess. Not sure why it bugged right then.

I contemplated jumping in my rental car and catching the next plane out of there. I pictured myself driving through the early morning darkness and stopping and picking up a pack of cigarettes to have one on the drive. No big deal, only one, two at the most, and then I'd throw the pack away before my plane left. Get this ridiculous craving out of my system.

I wondered if there were any Starbucks along the way, I'd had plenty of coffee already, but Starbucks always sounded good.

How would Harry's mom react when I didn't show up at the funeral? She might be upset, or not miss me at all. In the end, it didn't matter to me. I'd never see these people again. Of course, there was Harry to think of.

Harry.

My brother, as we'd referred to each other in the Corps; especially after Iraq. I pictured him sitting on the end of his rack, next to mine, writing a letter or polishing a boot while bobbing his head up and down to music through dangly earbuds. Harry stood taller than me, skinny, with a few acne potholes in his cheeks; adolescent war wounds.

He never had problems hooking up with women on our weekend excursions to the bars or heading to Tijuana. *You know the secret to women*, he'd told me once while we were driving down Oceanside Boulevard, *you have to learn not to give a shit about them. For some reason, if you do that, they're all yours. See that's your problem, Mickey, you care too much.* I didn't completely agree with him on anything, but you gotta respect a guy who's that honest and still gets laid like clockwork.

Except, of course, the time he got pissed off because he ended up with dick-warts. I rode with him to sickbay. He'd gone inside for like an hour; then came out carrying a little brown paper bag and mad as hell. *Girl gave me dick-warts,* he'd said climbing into the car. *Remember when Smitty had that shit?* Smitty was another guy in our platoon who seemed prone to the clap or dick-warts. *Yeah,* I'd said, *took him a goddamn month to get rid of it.* Harry slapped the steering wheel and said, *Son-of-a-bitch*. And then I'd started laughing. We'd both laughed and when we got back to the barracks that day, I announced it to the platoon and we all laughed our asses off while Harry, being the good sport, put up with it: *Fucked Suzy-rotten-crotch, huh Harry? Dippin' the dick in the sludge there buddy? You ain't burnin' are ya?*

Damn, we'd laughed. Twelve-years ago and it seemed like yesterday. So often I wished for those days again, sometimes going as far as to tell Amy I was considering re-enlisting in the Corps. I was talking shit, of course, but part of me wished for those days when being rowdy was acceptable; normal even.

As long as you picked up a rifle, prepared to do your business, no one gave a shit if you got trashed in Mexico, woke up in L.A., and then hitch-hiked home along I-5 – be in formation come Monday morning or your ass was grass. That's why it paid to have good friends like Harry. When you're an alcoholic, especially in the early days, you have no idea how much you count on other people to save you. And Harry had saved me so many times. Hauled me out of bars, dragged me to my bed, and had even picked me up once when the MPs had me at the front gate of Pendleton.

"Hell yeah, Harry." My own voice comforted me in the stillness of the motel room. "I ain't bailin' out on ya now." I'd see my old friend put to rest before leaving; I made that promise right then and there.

But *after* the funeral, it'd be hasta la vista, baby.

▪ ▪ ▪ ▪ ▪

I called Amy around nine in the morning, Indiana time. Thank god she was more pleasant today. I didn't bring up our parting argument from the day before and I hoped she wouldn't either.

"What time is it there?" I asked while sitting on the edge of the bed, staring absently at the window where the blinds were still drawn.

"Six in the morning," Amy said. "Didn't you bring your watch?"

Damn. She and the kids bought me a watch for Christmas that I didn't like. I didn't have the heart to share *that* tidbit of information, not after hearing that my seven-year-old daughter picked it out. And of course, the icing on the cake... *we wanted to get you a nice watch.* Now, Mick 'ole buddy, why don't you tell the people who love you most how much you like it. Sure thing. And paint the words 'I'm a jackass' on my forehead for the entire world to see. I decided right then, that as soon as I got home, I'd put that watch on.

"You know I only like to wear that watch to work," I lied, and quite convincingly if I did say so myself. "If I wear it all the time, the band'll end up breaking and I'll lose it."

"That's true," Amy said. We'd been married a long time and even though most of the amazing parts of marriage passed by me without so much as a second look, there were times when I caught little gems. She'd substantiated my lie because she knew I lacked the competence to take care of any watch (I'd broken many watches in my time). These were the subtleties of our marriage that the world didn't know, which made it all the more ours.

"Kids up?" I asked.

"They're getting up." She must have put the phone on her shoulder, because I heard her yell, "Are you girls brushing your teeth?"

I heard two tiny voices answer, "Yeah." I smiled.

"They're moving slow this morning," Amy said.

"Hopefully, I'll be back before they go to bed tonight," I stood up, walked to the blinds, and opened them.

"That'd be nice," Amy said, "How are things there?"

Amy had been to Gainesville once, about six years earlier when I'd come to visit Harry. I'm sure she remembered it vaguely, and I wasn't lying when I said, "Hardly anything has changed around here."

"I figured," she sounded as if she were concentrating on something besides our conversation. As childish as it sounds, I hated it when she did that.

"I'm staying at a motel along the highway, so I'm not even close to Harry's house this time." I gazed down at the parking lot noticing the large SHELL sign across the way. The building aged in the daylight with faded white paint. Grass climbed tall and weedy along the sides. I wondered if they sold KOOL Superlongs in there - the cigarettes I used to smoke.

"Have you talked with Harry's mom yet?" Amy asked.

"I did for a little bit, but didn't say much." The image of Bob sitting across from me in the Denny's restaurant popped into my head as I stared across the street at the yellow sign with DENNYS written in crooked, red letters. I remembered the smell of Bob's old chewing tobacco. "I don't ever know what to say in those situations."

"She probably has a lot of other things on her mind," Amy said and I agreed with that. I doubted Mrs. Darnell cared much about me and what I'd said.

I wasn't sure if I should tell her about Bob, but decided what the hell. That bizarre conversation still bugged me and though I wouldn't admit it, Amy was my foundation and how I got past things like that. "You know one thing really weird?"

"What's that?"

"I got woke up this morning at like 3 AM by this old guy who said Harry'd bought a cottage out on a lake or something. Guy was a freakin' loon." The words *he said Harry wasn't dead* popped into my head, but I decided to build up to that. I moved away from the window to my suitcase, which lay open on the bed, and peered inside. My eyes settled on my plane ticket tucked safely into a side pocket.

"Why did he tell *you*?" She seemed genuinely interested, so I kept going. Once I start talking to her about something, I'm like a faucet, it pours out.

"I don't know. To be honest, he scared the crap out of me."

"What'd he say?"

"That's the weird part; he didn't tell me anything that made any sense. He said Harry bought a cottage and that he had a girlfriend." I took a breath. "Here's the really freaky part… he said he found Harry and that Harry was still alive out at this lake."

"Girls! Come get your lunches." Her voice cut into my ear and I yanked the phone away while clenching my jaw. Goddamn it.

And she wasn't listening to me again. I hate it when she's on the phone with me and talking to someone else in the room. I know, it's immature and makes me sound like a dick, but it is what it is.

I pressed the phone back against my ear with an exasperated breath.

"Weird guy," I said, pressing on. "He said Harry didn't die in a car wreck and then he asked me to come out to the lake… said Harry asked for me." I remembered Bob saying something about the water. The thought nagged at me.

"Hmmm." Her mind wasn't on our conversation. I wondered if she listened to a word I'd said.

I considered hanging up.

She asked, "You didn't know him?"

"No." Then I remembered I'd seen him at Harry's house. "Actually, right after I got here yesterday, I went straight to Harry's house; I guess a bunch of people are helping to clear out his things, and that old guy was there… I forgot about that. His name's Bob. He asked if I knew what Harry had been doing and if I knew about the lake. Isn't that freaky?"

"I don't know. I guess. His name was Bob?"

"Yeah."

"Figures. Probably some old white guy. Bob." She chuckled and my anger cooled.

"Well hopefully I won't bump into him again. I could go the rest of my life without seeing him again."

A brief pause settled in and Amy asked the girls if they had their backpacks ready. I stood there listening and wondering if Bob would be at the funeral today. Surely not. He hadn't acted like he knew Harry or his family, which was strange in and of itself. I should ask Harry's mom if she knows the guy. But, how rude would that be? She's mourning the loss of her son and I'm asking about some old man.

Maybe one of Harry's sisters would know him.

I met Harry's older sister once before, years ago, the one named Arlene. Overweight, married young, divorced, had three kids and no husband. A real winner. She was nice enough, though.

I'd only seen a picture of his younger sister, Britney, when Harry and I were in Iraq. Funny thing, Harry planned to set me up with her right after Iraq and I admit that I'd been excited. In the picture, she was pretty, *damn* pretty, with long brown hair, a nice tan, and dark brown eyes – downright dangerous those eyes had been. That picture carried me through many long, sleepless nights at Camp Baharia. When we got back from Iraq my dreams of her died; she'd moved to North Carolina with her boyfriend. Just my luck. I met Amy a few months after that, so it all worked out.

I heard yesterday that Britney was in town and that she'd divorced the dude from North Carolina a few years ago. Not that I cared. Iraq was years ago. That picture was years ago. Still, I found myself thinking about it, remembering it, and wondering where the photo had ever gone.

"Well," Amy said and I forgot who I'd been talking to. I still saw Britney's tanned leg from that old pic on Harry's phone. She'd stood with her hands on her hips wearing white shorts with one leg thrust forward as if she were posing for a fitness ad. "I'd better get the girls to school. Give me a call when you're on your way to the airport."

"Yeah, I'll give you a shout." My mouth suddenly dried. "Should be around one or two."

"All right. Give Harry my love," she said.

I pictured Amy standing in the kitchen of our house in Colorado, her hand on the receiver and her hair pulled back in a clippie. Harry always had a thing for Amy too. But we'd all been friends. The best of friends. And she mourned him as I did.

"I will."

We said our goodbyes and then hung up. I zipped my suitcase closed and as I did, I realized how much I missed home and how much I wanted to get back there. Amy's constant presence grounded me and without her, my world felt strangely askew. I spent my first night away from my little girls last night. What had Amy told them? She probably made it fun for them. That's the type of mother she was.

My Amy.

It had been only yesterday that I'd walked out the front door carrying this old suitcase, heading for my truck. I'd left in a hurry and glanced back once to wave, but she hadn't come out to say goodbye.

CHAPTER 4

I parked the rental car across the street from the funeral home and climbed out into the warm air. The building looked immaculate, like a finely manicured hand. Even the trees lining the parking lot had the right amount of leaves and symmetrical branches in all the right places. I remembered this from the last time I visited in Gainesville. A quaint little town, tucked away and lagging twenty-years behind the big cities.

But it wasn't all a Norman Rockwell image.

Harry had taken me around the last time I visited, about five-years ago, and shown me the real town, the night-time town, the ugly town. We hung out in bars where married women picked up married men; men who usually turned out to be some drunk or unemployed schmuck blowing his last twenty bucks on Budweiser. I still drank back then, so I noticed shit like that.

We'd driven through the historic downtown district, where in the daytime it represented the fabled town of Mayberry with the remodeled buildings, the fancy 150-year-old courthouse, and the well-maintained wooden platform built over Fall Creek where love-struck teenagers watched the majestic waterfall.

But at night, Gainesville slipped off its mask.

We drove through at 2 AM, and the people we saw were not folks you'd want watching your nieces and nephews. They hung out in clusters, two or three in a bunch, normally with long hair, dirty baseball caps, and flannel shirts. Most of them appeared stoned and they'd watch you as you drove past like a male Baboon watches for danger as it licks its six-inch claws. *Fuck with me*, that look said, *and I'll rip your goddamn guts out.*

Still, the daytime serenity worked here, despite the darker side that I had witnessed with Harry. Gainesville on its worst day didn't hold a candle to Tijuana or Bangkok. I think Amy liked it here too. She was from Denver, born and raised, but had enjoyed our last visit here. She'd said it was a little backward, but cute. She'd used the word *cute* to describe the town – I told her to shoot me in the head if I ever called a town cute.

Now here I stood outside a funeral home and shocked at how bad I *still* wanted a cigarette. The craving lingered. I'm not talking about something that just sounds good, like a Dr. Pepper or a Taco, I mean a yearning that spreads like an invisible mist into your arms, and causes your fingers and toes to buzz with anticipation. No way to ignore it, no way at all.

I glanced around the parking lot. I saw a church, tall and old, across the street. A McDonalds stood about two blocks away, only half of the big, yellow 'M' visible around the trees between here and there. Looking the other way… *jackpot.* Large, red letters of the TEXACO gas station gleamed in the sun and my mouth tingled.

I visualized the Kool cigarettes tucked snuggly in their little trays behind the counter, waiting there like lollipops for a young girl who did well on her report card.

I knew, even before I started walking, that I was going over there to buy a pack. I tried to convince myself not to, but that did no good. Smoking, for those who love it, is more than just a habit. It's a state of mind, a comfort found only in the feel of the thin, round tobacco-stuffed paper between your fingers; the relief that sweeps through you as the smoke is sucked through the filter and into your lungs, wrapping you in comfort and familiarity.

Three years, my mind screamed as auto-pilot kicked in, *you're going to throw away three years?*

Yep, I think I am. I had no intention to keep smoking after I left Gainesville, but I needed one now. Just a few to get through today. That's all. I'd throw the rest away as soon as I got to the airport later. And that would be it.

Harry and I had always smoked together. In fact, he didn't even know I'd quit. Besides, no one here in Indiana had a clue about me.

The thought of Amy prompted warm shame. We had both quit smoking at the same time and she always commented when we passed certain milestones. *Today is the two-year mark*, I remember her saying. Two and a half years, three-years… she always said it. Sometimes we talked about it, how we used to smoke. What will I say when she remarks; *we hit our four-year mark*? I suppose I'll stand there and lie. Why not? No one will be the wiser.

I slipped through the glass doors and stopped at the front counter, almost as if I'd teleported there. A young woman, slightly overweight and chewing a piece of gum as if she were exercising her jaws for the gum-eating Olympics, stared at me. She didn't ask me what I wanted or even insinuated she cared.

"I need a pack of KOOL Superlongs, please." The words rolled off my tongue like an old pro.

The girl turned around and stared at the rows of cigarettes that covered the wall. I saw what I wanted in the small, green box and fought a brief urge to scream at her, *they're right freakin' there!*

"Are those 100s?" the girl asked.

"Yeah, 100s," I answered. "Bottom row, there."

She reached down, plucked the pack from its resting tray, and then faced me. She scanned them and told me, "seven-ninety-five."

Christ! I knew smokes had gone up, but that was two bucks more than I'd paid three-years ago. Still, I handed her a five-dollar bill and three ones willingly enough.

"You need matches?" She asked.

Smart girl. She saved me a trip back in here.

"Yes, please." I smiled, feeling like a dope. As she fished in a drawer for my matches, I tried to look calm and collected, trying not to show that I felt like a preacher buying a Penthouse Magazine.

She handed me my matches and I shot out the door quicker than shit through a goose. Back outside in the sunshine and gentle air, I felt much better. I smacked the pack against the heel of my hand a few times, tore the transparent cellophane off the top, flipped open the box top and pulled the thin foil from inside.

Was I really doing this?

I slid a cigarette out and popped it in my mouth, going through the motions like an old pro, the ramifications of right and wrong long gone – a one-way ticket, baby, and there ain't no stopping it. I flipped the match head across the narrow, rough strip and the flame sparked to life with a dull hiss. Carefully, so not to have the match go out (always a danger with the free, paper matches you get in gas stations), I stuck the end of the cigarette into the small flame and sucked on the filter.

Just before pulling the crisp and delicious smoke into my body, I wondered if I would cough like the first time I tried a cigarette fifteen-years ago on Del Mar beach in California, right out of boot camp. I cringed as I inhaled; prepared for the reaction my healed lungs would have to this filthy invasion.

No coughing. No gagging. No puking. The smoke entered me like a fresh burst of cool wind, soothing me like a shot of whiskey calms the shaking hand of the alcoholic. It felt natural, yet new, crisp and wonderful.

I blew the smoke out into the lazy air and it floated away like an apparition.

"Why did I want one of these so bad, Harry?" I said to myself, staring at the cigarette wedged comfortably between my fingers. The red, glowing end produced a thin stream of smoke that floated past my face. No matter, I guess. Amy would be pissed, or even worse, disappointed, but I saw no real reason why she needed to know.

Amy wasn't there with Harry and me in boot camp. She wasn't there when we'd gone to Twenty-nine Palms for three miserable months (where I'd gotten drunk and started a fight at the enlisted club and would have gone to jail if Harry hadn't hauled my stupid ass out of there), and she wasn't there when we'd gone to Iraq and believed we were the weapons of justice for our fallen World Trade Center.

She wasn't there that day I fired my weapon. *That* day.

That part of my life belonged to Harry and me – and now that Harry was dead, I supposed it belonged only to me. So, if I wanted to have a cigarette, by god, I didn't need anyone's permission to do it.

I gazed absently across the street, noticing two other cars parked fairly close to my rental. Two old people, slightly bent over and dressed nice, hobbled together toward the building.

"I probably ought to get over there," I said to no one. I checked for traffic and crossed the street, stuffing one hand into my pants pocket and holding the cigarette with the other.

After making my way over an ocean of mowed grass, my feet finally found the asphalt of the parking lot and I strode toward the door. I hated to admit it, but I *wanted* to see Harry's body. Not that I derived any satisfaction from it, but after talking to Bob this morning, I wanted to see it. I didn't believe a word of what 'ole Bob had said and still didn't, but it would ease my mind, nonetheless.

CHAPTER 5

Closed casket, of course. Both disappointment and relief swept over me, if that's possible. Sure, I wanted my curiosity satisfied, but I had no excitement at seeing my best friend's corpse nestled in a coffin.

I stepped through the double doors and into a large room where chairs lined both sides of the center aisle like faithful children listening to a story. They were all empty except for the first row.

Along the front wall, a tan casket rested like a boulder on a short pedestal. Colorful flowers decorated the sides and the back wall, many with little cards adhered to the stems that had private messages scrawled on them; all impossible to read from where I stood. The closed lid held half a dozen picture frames all perched along the smooth top. I'd never seen pictures lined up on top of a coffin before.

I recognized Harry's Marine Corps photo immediately, the one taken in boot camp with the iconic dress blues uniform. The others were mostly of Harry standing with people I didn't recognize. In one photo, he had his arm draped around a fellow Marine in uniform. I didn't know any of them and that bothered me. I'd been left out.

The largest photo, an 8X10 propped up in the middle of the casket's top, showed Harry smiling and hugging a frail sickly woman. I wondered who it was.

Disappointment stung my pride. Not that I had to be the focal point in Harry's life, but I must admit, I felt like I deserved a place on Harry's photo tribute. His father had called *me*, after all. Maybe I'd put myself higher in the pecking order of Harry's life than I belonged. *Don't think so highly of yourself, Mickey boy*. It certainly would not have been the first time I'd made such a mistake.

Harry's mom, along with four other people, sat in the front row. I gawked at the back of their heads, debating on whether or not to leave. Smoking another cigarette didn't sound bad. Maybe drive around town a little and pick up something to eat. *What do you think, Harry? Would you be okay if I snuck out of here and returned before the festivities begin?*

Festivities.

Harry would have laughed, but it felt empty in my own head. The two of us had always joked that we could have fun in a morgue. But here we were, for the first time in a morgue together, and this was no fun at all.

"Mick?" A female voice said from behind me.

I turned to see Harry's sister, Britney, with her hands clasped nervously in front of her, standing a few feet away. A tingle shot through me. I was seeing her for the first time outside of a photo. My God. She had her hair pulled back in a loose ponytail, revealing a face that encompassed a ravenous allure, momentarily erasing all thought in my feeble, male brain. A black dress clung to her body like a tight glove and her skin still radiated the youth and vitality I'd seen in the picture ten-years earlier. I wondered how old she was. She'd been a senior in high school when Harry and I were in Iraq, a couple of years younger than me.

"Britney?" I tried to sound as if I didn't recognize her immediately. Warmth crept into my ears.

"It's good to finally meet you." She held out her hand and I shook it. I hoped like hell my sweaty palms didn't feel disgusting.

"You too," I said. I struggled for something more, but came up empty. Her eyes were brimmed red and her voice sounded stuffy.

She glimpsed toward the casket and then back at me. "I wish it was under better circumstances."

I smiled thoughtfully and arched my eyebrows. *Me too.*

She crossed her arms over her chest. "Last time I spoke to him, he said they were doing well. I was in a hurry and didn't have much time to talk. I told him that we'd celebrate soon." Her voice trailed off, as if she were talking to someone else. I wondered who *they* were what they'd be celebrating, but figured it was none of my business.

"Shocked me too," I said, "definitely not something I expected."

She gave me an empathic smile and I suddenly felt stupid for what I'd said. *Always about you, huh Mick*?

"I'm glad you were able to come here for this. I know he'd be happy about that. He talked about you all the time."

So why ain't my picture up there on the coffin? "I wouldn't have missed this for anything."

She shook her head and pressed a hand to her mouth. Her face crumpled, but she pulled it together before it got awkward.

A slight pause crept between us.

"Do you live close?" I had to ask something.

"I live in Indy. Just moved there about six months ago. I stayed with Harry for quite a while after my divorce. That's how I know so much about you." She smiled at me again, but this time it appeared less grief-stricken, and contained a hint of sexy, though I'm not sure she meant it that way. My imagination outran reality sometimes.

"Hope you didn't believe everything Harry told you." I wondered if she knew Harry had planned to set me up with her when we got back from Iraq. I'd taken so many long looks at that picture he'd given me of her. And, I must admit, there were a few times I'd done a bit more than just look at it. I'd only been nineteen. Still, it didn't make me feel like less of a shithead.

"He had a way of embellishing things," she said, "and I knew him good enough to know when he was full of crap. Sounds like you guys had some fun times out there in California."

"Yeah, we did." *And Thailand, and the Philippines, and Australia*... Lord knows we had fun in Australia. I smiled as the list scrolled through my head.

She nodded and said, "I'd love to hear some of the stories."

No, you wouldn't, my mind shot. But from my mouth, the words, "I'd love to tell you some of them," spilled forth and hung between us like a motionless jump-rope. Our eyes met and she glanced away.

Oh sweet Jesus.

Cold sweat broke out under my arms and my balls shriveled.

I know what's happening here. At least I wanted to think I knew what was happening here. And it shouldn't be.

My cheeks tingled and my mouth filled with sticky spit. The girl from the photograph.

This is Harry's funeral and I'm married.

I wanted to reach out and touch her; place my hand gently on her shoulder, brush her tender skin with my fingertips, caress her slender neck. Breathe her warm breath.

The girl promised to me.

Her eyes found mine again. "Will you be around after the funeral?"

Wait, was she hitting on me at her brother's funeral? *No, dipshit, but you're acting like she is.* Still, it seemed odd. *She* seemed odd. As if none of this shocked her.

With God as my witness, I had not felt like this in years. Something primal was awakening inside me, and I liked it. I slipped my left hand into my pants pocket; the hand with my wedding ring on the finger.

"Yeah," I said, "I should be around for a little while."

"We're going over to the Golden Nugget afterwards and having a beer," Britney's lips moved flawlessly as they formed the words. "After that, we're all going over to Mom's. It's best to be with her right now. Having this funeral was a tough decision for her."

Why in the hell would having a funeral be a tough decision? Who cares. None of my business.

"We'll probably have a few drinks over there too and she usually goes to bed early; so we can all tell Harry-stories all night if we want."

My heart fluttered at the mention of beer. I smelled a distant, *liquory* aroma that I knew existed only in my head. *You have to stop*, Harry told me the last time we saw each other. *If you don't stop, you're going to either end up in jail or dead. And Mick*, he'd glared at me; his eyes met mine, *Amy's never coming back if you stay drunk.*

I didn't stay drunk. I quit drinking shortly after that visit. I didn't half-ass it either; I joined AA, participated in support groups, no more bars, no more liquor. I'd quit smoking a year later. Amy moved back from her parent's house in Colorado Springs, and my two daughters have never seen me drunk. At least, I don't think they have.

But had it been *that* bad? I drank a lot back then because I had always been a rowdy guy, always been a partier. Honestly, even though I'd gotten out of hand a few times, I controlled what I did, how much I drank. Typically, I'd have a few beers and stop. Just a few beers… and stop. It'd been that easy. When you got right down to it, I'd quit drinking for Amy; not for me.

And who was I trying to kid? Nothing about it came easy. Could I go through that again? Was I capable of only having a Coke while everyone else drank beer, laughed, and Britney hung out with me?

Stop focusing on that! I'm married! Think about Amy.

Talking to Britney in the same room where her brother's corpse lay rotting in a box at the front of the room, I pictured myself drinking a beer with her. Laughing, smoking a cigarette, and having a kick-ass time. I *saw* it! My hand folded around a cold can of Coors Lite, or vodka cranberry, kicked back in a chair telling stories about Harry and me.

And damn did we have some stories.

Everyone would laugh and ask for more. Britney would sit by me and I'd rave on about Harry and me stealing the HUM-VEE in Twenty-nine Palms, or the time we woke up drunk at this girl's house and her parent's chased us out of there, or the time we got into a fight with a bunch of Arabs in Bahrain over a game of pool or the best story of all, the one that always got people laughing and I had so much fun telling, was when Harry and I were in Malaysia and we got chased by monkeys through the streets for taking a bottle of whiskey and...

...and Britney would be there the whole time, next to me and laughing –

"So will you be here?" She asked.

I blinked. The world grew silent.

Say no, Mickey... just say no. "Yeah, I should be able to."

"Good. I'll find you after the funeral and tell you where to go." She sighed and her shoulders slumped. "I need to get up there with Mom and Arlene. We're supposed to be ready to greet people when they come in. Of course, Mom will have to stay seated, but Arlene and me will have to stand up there." Her voice faded a little as she trained her gaze back to the front of the large room, back to her brother's casket. "We have no idea if anyone from Mary's family will be here."

Mary? I opened my mouth to ask who Mary was and decided again that it was none of my business. I'm here to pay respects and leave. That's it.

"Let me know if anyone needs anything," I smiled, feeling far too giddy for a man attending a funeral. "I'd be happy to help out if you need it." I lied right then. I didn't want to help with anything. I wanted to smoke another cigarette, get this funeral over with, and get the hell out of here. My mind drifted to all the wrong places.

She smiled and said, "Thanks."

She shot forward and wrapped her arms around my neck. I don't mean one of those prissy little ass-out hugs either. She pressed her body right up against mine, her breasts smashed against my chest. Her hair brushed against my cheeks and I smelled the shampoo she'd used that morning. I placed my hand gently on the small of her back and held her. She might've been crying. I remembered how Harry had talked about her so much. Always my little sister this and my little sister that. A sudden urge to cry with her enveloped me; then she pulled away.

"I'll see you later, okay?" She stepped around me without waiting on my reply and strode toward the front of the room. Harry's dad wasn't here yet, or at least I didn't see him out here with everyone else, and I wondered how he was doing. He hadn't been at the house last night either when I met ole' Bob.

I stepped quietly out of the room and made my way to the front door of the building. Time for a smoke. Three-years without smoking and I craved one now more than ever. The fragrance of Britney's shampoo lingered in my nose along with the tautness of her lower back muscles under my hand.

Once outside, I pulled the smokes out of my pocket and lit one as if I'd been holding my breath. It tasted good. I'd call Amy and tell her that I had to stay another night and visit with Harry's family, that they'd invited me to stay for a get-together and that I felt obligated to attend.

What the hell are you doing, Mick?

I'll even say it in a way so it sounds like I don't want to, but that I must. *This'll be my last involvement with Harry's life,* I'll say and Amy will understand, or at the very least, she'll feel guilty if she objects to it. No lies. They really had invited me to stay.

You planning to tell her Harry's pretty little sister made the invitation?

I'd enjoy my smoke first. Enjoy it and relax for a moment. That's what I wanted. I thought about Harry as I stood there. I thought about Amy and the girls. I thought about Britney, I thought about the stories I could tell tonight. I thought about how a beer might taste and if I should have one, even though I knew for damn sure that I shouldn't, but I thought about it just the same.

And as I thought about these things, my eyes scanned the parking lot looking for any sign of Bob, and how he had said that Harry wasn't in there.

CHAPTER 6

I knew I was in trouble as soon as the beer flooded my mouth. The tingly flavor rushed across my tongue and engulfed my entire skull. I loved it. I would always love it, just like when I had the cigarette earlier. The recognition filled me with a sense of excitement and dread, mixed together like a deadly martini. Part of me wanted to guzzle the entire can in a single chug and then grab another. Another part of me, a deeper part, my soul perhaps, wanted to toss it into the trash and run like hell, screaming for forgiveness. The part that thought of Amy's face as she watched me, her eyes filling with tears as the old disappointment returned.

Don't ever try to control it, Mick, the words of Skip Jones, my AA counselor, echoed in my head. *If you're tempted, call me. Call ME!* And I had called him, many times in that first year. He'd remind me of exactly why I'd decided to quit drinking to start with. *This isn't about you, my friend,* Skip would say, *this is about your daughters and your wife.*

I brought the can to my lips and took another nice, healthy chug. I bullshitted my wife a little for the permission to stay here, but Jesus, this tasted good.

Only an asshole would do such a thing.

And only one person in Indiana knew I had quit drinking, or that I'd ever had a problem to start with, and that was Harry himself. No one here gave a shit about me. The babysitter's out, my friends, and 'ole Mick can be a man again. I'd control myself, because I knew that I could, and I would not overindulge because I knew that I couldn't.

And if Bob were here, that old fucking weirdo, I'd tell him to kiss my ass. I came here to celebrate Harry's life because we were brothers in the Corps. Because his dad had called me to come to the funeral. Because I would never have a friend like Harry again as long as I lived. Tears stung my eyes as that last thought materialized.

I took another drink and found myself wondering how much beer they had here.

■ ■ ■ ■ ■

"Funny isn't it," Britney said, "how you think of the things you'd do different after someone dies." She leaned against the kitchen counter with a beer in her hand, staring off into nothing. She'd changed out of the black dress and now wore blue-jeans and a white t-shirt that my eyes kept darting toward. "I meant to call him to see if he wanted to stay with me in Indy. Just for the weekend, you know, to hang out. I don't know why I didn't. I know he needed a break from Mary."

"Mary?" She'd mentioned that name earlier at the funeral.

"His wife. You didn't know her?"

Bob's words echoed, *him and that girlfriend of his.* "I didn't know anyone named Mary," I said and shrugged. I'd have to ask her about the cottage. I'd ask her about Bob too, for that matter.

Britney rolled her eyes. "She was something. He met her in the cancer ward at St. Methodist Hospital."

"Cancer ward?" The words crawled out of my mouth like a slimy worm.

"Yeah. He went up there twice a week for a little while after he got back from Minnesota." She must have detected the surprise on my face. Her eyebrows furrowed and she asked, "Didn't you know that Harry had cancer?"

The shock left me speechless. I'm pretty sure my mouth hung open. That large picture I'd seen propped on his coffin drifted into my head; the one where Harry had his arm around the sickly woman.

Goosebumps pebbled my arms.

Britney asked, "When was the last time you talked to him?"

My eyes trailed up at the ceiling and a lie popped into my head. I didn't want her to know it'd been so long. I felt foolish but decided not to slither out of it. I said, "Close to four years, I'd guess."

"Four years!" She seemed flabbergasted and I didn't blame her. "My goodness, a lot has happened since you talked to him. They diagnosed him with lung cancer last summer. It shocked all of us, but the doctors seemed hopeful. He did the chemo treatments and all that. It went away for a little while."

As Britney spoke, I drifted in and out of the conversation. The news that Harry had cancer hit me like a brick in the gut. Why hadn't he called me?

"…but they didn't know. So he had to go in once a month after the initial…"

Britney kept talking and I kept staring at her, watching her mouth move, but only getting bits and pieces. I felt betrayed. If the tables had been turned, if *I'd* had cancer, I would have called Harry, I know it.

"…before Mary started coming up to visit."

I gaped at Britney, my face probably looked like someone had soaked it in white paint, and said, "I'm sorry, what?"

She repeated it willingly enough, "He'd gone at least twice for his monthly checkups. Mary moved here with him about six months ago, I guess." She curled her lip on that last sentence.

"This is all so unbelievable." My mind floated a million miles away; only speaking to fill the space. "I didn't know any of it."

"You didn't know he got married or anything like that, did you?"

"No." I considered telling her about my conversation with Bob, but held off. I'd get to that.

"Yep. They got married in February… the twelfth, I'm pretty sure. They wanted to hurry because… well, you know. They didn't have much time." Britney looked away and took a quick sip of her beer.

I chugged too, then asked, "She had cancer too?"

"Oh yeah," she said, as if I should've known that already. "And way worse off than Harry. She had cancer in her brain and not supposed to live past the end of the year, but somehow she kept hanging on."

"And you didn't like her?"

Britney curled her lip. "It wasn't that I didn't like her, she was just always there, you know. She never looked well, always skinny, had to take about a hundred pills. I know it sounds selfish, but none of us knew what to do when she came around."

"I assume Harry's cancer came back?" I hoped I wasn't opening too many wounds here, but goddamn. She didn't seem to mind.

"About three-months ago, yeah. He went in for his normal check-up and they said they found a *hot spot*, whatever that means, and they needed to check it out."

"On his lungs?"

"Left lung. Creepy how it always comes back."

I nodded. It *was* creepy.

"They said they must not have killed it all with the chemo and that next they wanted to try radiation therapy. Harry said he'd seen enough people go through that and needed to think about it."

Tears welled up in her eyes right then and I felt uncomfortable. I didn't know if putting my arm around her crossed the line, but I had to do something. I couldn't stand there and let her cry. I shuffled next to her and put my arm around her thin shoulders. No big deal in that; comforting my best friend's little sister. What are best friends for, after all?

And Harry and I had been more than best friends, we'd been brothers. And brothers stuck together. As my hand brushed across the bare skin of her neck, I immediately thought of Amy and pushed the thought away, with considerable effort I might add. I didn't need that guilt trip right now.

"If you'd have seen him, Mick, it was so sad. He cried when he told me about it. He said he would lose his hair and that he'd lose weight." She leaned her head against my shoulder. "I remember the saddest thing he said was that he needed to decide if dying was better than dragging it out. He was so scared, Mick."

I swallowed hard. My heart sank and I fought to stifle an open sob. I'd seen Harry fire an M-249 SAW one handed, I'd seen him drink a full glass of Jack Daniel's without a breath, I'd seen him throw a guy across the hood of his car one night as we'd left a bar. No memory of Harry resembled a man defeated, but somehow, I envisioned him crumpled over, crying to his little sister. It was the fear I imagined in him, the fear of dying.

"I didn't know any of this," I said again. "When your dad called me, he told me about the car wreck… nothing about cancer or any of this stuff."

Britney stiffened and then pulled away. I searched her eyes, the slight down-curve of her mouth, and tried to determine if her face screamed anger or hate. What the hell did I say?

"Is that some kind of joke?" she asked and then seemed to consider what she'd said. "When did dad call you?"

"Friday morning, two days ago." *Jesus.* I had no idea what I'd said wrong, and no idea if I was still saying it.

"Dad?"

"Yeah."

She stared at me. Darkness swam over her eyes. An ugliness I didn't know she possessed.

"What's wrong?" I glanced around and then back at her.

"Dad died nearly five months ago, Mick. *That's* what's wrong." She clanked her beer down on the counter and glared at me. In that moment, she loathed me.

I stayed here for her. I drank a beer for her. I was enjoying myself because of her and I didn't want that to end. I wasn't trying to have an affair or anything, but hanging out with Harry's family didn't violate any laws. Can't a guy just have a good time?

Now this.

So who in the hell called me on Friday morning? That's what I wanted to ask her. *Did Bob know anything about it?*

Like she'd know.

"This is damned odd," I said. That weird conversation with Bob danced in my mind. Somehow, it seemed more pertinent now, but the pieces didn't click together. "Because whoever called me claimed to be Harry's dad. I had no idea your dad had passed away, Britney, please believe that." Damn it, I hoped she didn't think I'd lie about that.

"Who would do that?" Her expression softened and she grabbed her beer back up off the counter.

"I have no idea." My mind cast back to the phone call I'd received. *Harry died last night*, he had said, and *it was a car accident, most likely a drunk driver*. Why would someone pretend to be Harry's dad?

I tipped my beer up and drained it. I kept talking as I opened the refrigerator, pulled out another, and popped the top. "He said Harry died in a car accident and asked if I would come to the funeral."

"Car accident?" Britney asked. She put her hand on her hip and her eyes narrowed. "He didn't die in a car accident."

"Well then how did…" I clamped my mouth shut. I didn't know if I felt stupid or pissed. "Okay," I said, "time for a break. You want to step outside with me so I can smoke while we talk about this?"

"Hell yeah," she said and stormed toward the door, not waiting for me. "I'll have one too."

I grabbed another beer before heading outside so I wouldn't have to come back in.

To hell with it. I grabbed two.

CHAPTER 7

I shook out two cigarettes and handed one to Britney. She took it as we strolled to the end of a freshly stained wooden deck that overlooked the yard. The air, both refreshing and warm, bore the soft scent of something sweet… corn, maybe. I lit our cigarettes with the cheap, paper matches I'd gotten from the gas station and we both stood there leaning on the rail, gazing out across an ocean of green grass.

"I don't know who told you those things," Britney said, "but I'll tell you this," she turned to me, taking an angry puff from her cigarette, "this has been killing mom. Especially, being so soon after dad died."

"I can imagine," I said and finished off one of the beers I'd brought outside with me. An inkling to head home tugged at the back of my mind. "So, if you don't mind me asking, what happened to Harry?"

She took a calm drag on her cigarette, but I noticed a slight tremble in her fingers. "Harry and Mary have been missing for over two months. This'll sound freaky, but apparently, they decided to commit suicide together. He left a note and everything. Said *don't bother looking for us, you won't find us. This is what we have to do.* There was a lot more to it, but that's the long and short of it. I still have it if you'd like to read it." She looked at me.

I shook my head and felt like a bad actor. "No, that's okay." But was it? I *did* want to see it. My heart ached.

She continued talking. "The cops told mom about a month ago that we should consider having a memorial service for both of them to help the healing begin. You know, the grieving. So she decided last week to finally do it."

"Wow." Where would this end? Bob's words, *he's still out there* whispered through me. "That's got to be easier said than done."

"Mom refused to do it at first. Hell, she even thought he might've gone to Colorado to see you. But that didn't make sense either. His car was still here, all his stuff, even his damn wallet. Pretty obvious, he didn't go anywhere. You know how Harry always planned and prepared, never compulsive."

Yeah, I knew that. Everything had to happen in a particular order with Harry.

"The day they went missing, mom called and asked if I'd heard from him. When she hadn't heard anything by the next day, she called the police and asked for help." She paused and sipped her beer, then took a strong drag on her cigarette. I noticed how the sun reflected off her dark hair as she exhaled the smoke. "You have to understand, once we found out Harry had cancer, Mom freaked out. She always called to check up on him, making sure he took his medicine and went to his appointments. She'd know first if he was missing."

"What did the police do?" I popped the top on my own beer and I drank while she spoke.

"They searched his house here in town. That's where they found that suicide note. Then they went out to his place on the lake and didn't find anything there either. Except his wallet, they found that out there."

"Kate's Lake?" I asked, too quickly.

Her eyebrows furrowed. "How'd you know about that?"

"That's an even better story. I'll tell you in a minute." I wondered how she'd take it if I told her that 'ole Bob said Harry wasn't dead. It didn't seem as silly as it had at three o'clock this morning. "Go ahead and finish."

"Yeah," she said, "Kate's Lake. I hate that place. I don't know why he ever stayed out there. I rode with him once and he told me to wait in the truck. Funny, but I think that place scared him."

"The lake?"

"Something. That's how he acted anyway. The place is all weedy and gross. No one ever goes back there. You pretty much gotta have a four-wheel-drive to make it." She took another drag on her cigarette and squinted her eyes at me. "So how do you know about that place?"

I wanted to hear more about how Harry had gone missing and the circumstances that led to having this apparently *fake* funeral for both him and his wife, Mary. I wanted to compare it to what Bob had told me. Because as crazy as it sounds, I doubted Bob less and less, and the idea that Harry might be out at that lake sparked something inside me. Hope.

But I needed to tell Britney about what happened this morning. She knew I was holding back; that I had information I shouldn't know. If I didn't start to reveal, I'd lose her trust.

"I met this strange old guy yesterday." I glanced around and then I tipped up my beer and swallowed healthily. "Met him here, in this backyard." I pointed toward the open yard, as if she wouldn't understand if I didn't. "He asked if I knew about Harry and this place called Kate's Lake."

The first inklings of a buzz settled over me. After three beers! My muscles relaxed and I breathed easier. I chose words better and I knew Britney was more comfortable around me. Things finally started to click. I hadn't been this in-control of things in years.

She listened patiently while I told her about my 3 AM meeting. I left out the part about how frightened I'd been when Bob tried to open my motel door. I told her it scared the shit out of me and left it at that.

She shook her head, put a hand to her mouth, and then said she needed to use the bathroom and asked if I wanted another beer. "Sure," I answered and off she went.

I stood by myself, waiting and wondering. I played with my wedding ring, slipping it on and off and twisting it on my finger, though to be honest, my thoughts were less on Britney at the moment and more on Harry. A lot of information to process here.

Suicide. *Damn it, Harry.*

I stopped fidgeting and leaned back on the rail of the deck, placing both hands on either side of me, relishing the cool, rough texture of the wood. Footsteps clopped around the corner of the house, and within a few seconds, a young boy emerged, running gleefully to the door. He was five or six and had no concept of what was going on because he looked happier than a pig in shit. His parents, or a couple I assumed were his parents, followed closely behind with somber expressions, the kind you'd expect people to have following a funeral.

The guy, older and overweight, saw me standing there. He glanced down at something in his hand and then back up at me. *Did I know this guy?*

At the top of the steps, he said, "Mick Smith?"

"Uh-yeah." Damn, he knew my name.

"Guy in the driveway told me to give you this." He handed me a folded piece of paper with my name scribbled across the front - *Mickey*. "He said you were back here."

"Thanks." I wondered if he caught a whiff of beer on my breath. I tried not to exhale when facing him.

"No prob," he said and ambled inside.

I glanced down at the paper and before I opened it, I knew.

Fuckin' Bob.

I marched to the steps, hustled down and then slipped on the last step, nearly falling headfirst into the grass. I saved myself from an awkward and potentially embarrassing fall with a few lanky steps. I rounded the corner of the house and jogged out front where about a dozen parked cars jammed the driveway. I stopped and searched for any sign of an old man with gray, thinning hair.

Nothing.

And I knew the old bastard had planned it that way, otherwise, he'd have walked back there and handed me the note himself. I spotted a thick clump of bushes a short way down from where I stood.

But no Bob.

He's here somewhere, watching me. A chill raced through me because I knew that's exactly what he was doing. Hunkered down in that clump of bushes, spying on me.

I looked down at the note in my hand and opened it.

Mickey,

Come out to Kate's Lake, Harry asked me to find you. We have to kill Mary before she leaves the woods.

-Bob

My heart ka-thudded. *Okay, enough of this bullshit.*

Hopefully I wouldn't break his scrawny neck, but at this point, no promises. He crossed the line. *Kill Mary*? What the hell did that mean?

An old memory threatened to surface. One buried long ago with blood, alcohol, and tears. One only Harry knew because he'd been there when I'd done it. He'd been there when I'd fired. When the bullet…

No goddamn it! Not that!

I closed my eyes. I inhaled deeply. Settle the fuck down.

I'd find that old bastard.

My feet started to move when I heard Britney's voice behind me, "Mick?"

I stopped and turned.

"What are you doing out here?" She asked with a smile. She carried two cans of Coors Lite. One of them was mine and I was for goddamn sure ready for it.

"That old guy I told you about… he sent me a fucking note. Some guy handed it to me while you were in the house. That old motherfucker was right out here!" I pulled my cigarettes out of my pants pocket and lit one.

Britney's smile faded. She didn't know this side of me; a person she had yet to meet. The person Amy grew to hate years ago. The person who said words like *motherfucker* in front of women who deserved far better.

This was me getting drunk.

Get ahold of yourself there, buddy, my mind whispered, *you can control this. Settle down, have another beer, and try to relax.*

"I'm sorry." I ambled toward her. "I shouldn't have said it like that. It just freaked me out and with all the stuff we talked about…"

Her expression worried me. Distrust.

Likely, I'd blown any chance at –

At what, Mick 'ole buddy?

Nothing, goddamn it, I'm a married. Any chance at friendly conversation and coming up with an answer to all of this strange shit, that's what I'd blown.

Her face softened and her eyes opened wider. It occurred to me that I had no idea why Britney had divorced her husband. Perhaps he'd cheated on her and she gave him the boot. But maybe he was mean, or a drunk that knocked her around. What if I had opened an old wound? *What if? What if? What if?*

I took a healthy chug of my beer.

"Did you see where he went?" She asked. She glanced around the area like I'd done only a few moments before.

"Those bushes over there." I pointed. "He's probably gone now, though."

"That's Betty Crawford's place," Britney said, "she's lived there since I was born. Her place backs up to the park."

"The guy's crazy." I wanted to go after him, but didn't want to drag Britney into this; whatever *this* was.

"Let me see the note." She walked back to me, her hand held out, and stared at my fingers holding the piece of paper.

I wished I hadn't said anything at all. I didn't want to give it to her, but figured I didn't have a choice after the little shit-show I'd just pulled. I'd already told her about everything else and to hold back now would be mean.

I handed her the note and she read it. A trembling hand floated to her lips. "You should call the police on this guy." She used a *we're not putting up with this shit* tone. But her eyes said something entirely different. I couldn't tell if she was horrified or hopeful.

What if Harry *was* out there?

"Yeah," I said, "probably should call the police." I wondered if she thought the same thing I did… we should go to Kate's Lake.

Part of me said that to do so would be stupid and irresponsible, but a bigger part, a part forged in loyalty, told me that I should go out there, that I *needed* to go out there. Harry had asked for me.

I spoke as I contemplated. "It's weird, this morning the old guy didn't act like he knew Harry. Like he didn't want to be hunting me down. He acted more like he had to." I recalled the conversation early this morning at Denny's and how he'd leered out the windows as if expecting someone to be there.

Britney didn't respond. Finally, I asked, "How do I get out to this place? Kate's Lake?"

"No one ever goes out there, Mick." Her eyes crawled over me as if I'd made the most absurd comment ever. "I don't know why Harry was out there, I really don't. There's all kinds of stories about that place. Some say it's haunted or something." She met my eyes. "Unless you're from here, you'd never know it exists. I only know about it because of Harry. It's illegal to be back there… like government land or something."

"Yeah, but I gotta find out what this guy wants."

"You thought he was crazy."

"Yeah, but why's he trying to find me? Just me?"

She didn't have an answer and shook her head.

I asked, "Why doesn't anyone go out there? What's up with it?"

"First off, it's nearly impossible to get back in there, like I told you earlier, and it's trespassing on government land. I have no idea how Harry stayed back there. It's down in a place called the Bottoms. You need a four-wheel-drive."

"But people live back there, right? I mean, Bob does."

"People live in the Bottoms, but not back by Kate's Lake. I told you, there's all kinds of stories about that place. Supposed to be haunted and all that." Britney's eyes slipped back down at the note.

"I'm going tomorrow morning." I took a hard drag on my cigarette. "Can you tell me how to get out there?"

She hesitated, the silence stretching, then she said what I figured she'd say. "I'll go with you, if that's okay."

I feared this after watching her read Bob's note. I understood, of course. And I have to admit, I was okay with it. Not only because I loved being around her, God forgive me, but also because I didn't want to go by myself. I had no idea what to expect from the Bottoms or how to find Kate's Lake.

What would Harry say if he knew I needed his little sister to go with me? He'd never let me live that one down.

"Let's not say anything to anybody," I said, "We'll keep it between us for right now." I didn't want to get a bunch of shit stirred up before we knew what we were dealing with.

"I wonder why Bob didn't give it to you himself?" Britney asked. "He'd already talked to you this morning and he was here yesterday. Why give it to someone else?"

Funny she asked that because I'd thought the same thing myself. I'd also wondered why Harry didn't bring it himself. I mean, if he was back there. Which he wasn't.

I shrugged. "Probably thought I'd call the cops on him or something." Seemed reasonable to me.

"I guess."

"Let's go tomorrow morning. I'll pick you up early. Does that work?" I drained my fifth beer. I don't even remember opening it.

"That works." She folded her arms over her chest. "We'll need a different car though; yours won't make it back there." She seemed to think about it and then said, "unless we walked. Kate's Lake is about two miles past the edge of the Bottoms. Your car could make it through the Bottoms, if I remember right."

As we strolled back toward our spot on the back deck, my phone chirped in my pocket. I fished it out and read the screen. Amy.

"You need to get that?" Britney asked. I hadn't realized my pace had slowed.

"Nah." I stuffed the phone back into my pocket. "I'll call them back later."

Them, huh. Not her, just *them.*

Oh, stop it. No way was I talking to Amy right now. She'd know that I'd been drinking. She had an uncanny ability to sense that sort of thing. Better off waiting until tomorrow and taking the ass-chewing for not answering my phone versus trying to explain anything now. A can of worms that simply didn't need to be opened.

I followed Britney up the steps. My turn to go to the bathroom and get the beers.

"You need another one?" I asked pointing to her hand holding the Coors Lite.

"No," she said, "just started this one."

"Cool. I'll be right back." I slipped inside amongst the mourning family members and made my way quickly to the bathroom, did my business, then sauntered right up to the fridge. I snagged two cold beers and hurried back outside. I thought it would be best to have two, just in case Britney needed another one.

CHAPTER 8

I've heard you don't dream after passing out from a good drunk.

But I'll tell you right now, that's bullshit. I've had some of the strangest dreams of my life after passing out. Hell, I dreamt once of a place called Pizza-in-a-Cup that claimed to have the best pizza in the world, but to get to it; you had to climb a mountain. I climbed to the top, ordered my pizza, and it came stuffed in a Styrofoam cup. How weird is that?

I almost always have them, and this morning was no exception.

"What did I do to deserve this?" Harry asked.

We sat on the edge of a sand pile overlooking an ocean of tanned desert. Iraq.

"Where is everyone?" I spoke while staring at a red, dying sun. We were alone.

"They're all gone, Mick," Harry's voice waned, full of sadness. "They left a long time ago."

The sun's light turned the sky a dark crimson. The color of blood. The body of an Iraqi soldier lay a few feet in front of us. A hot breeze ruffled its clothing. Sand collected on the lifeless eyes and gaping mouth.

I tore my eyes away. I hated it.

"I didn't ask for any of this, you know," Harry said.

"Any of what?"

"This shit, Mick. I didn't ask for any of it. I joined the Corps to go to college; I didn't ask to get stuck in this shithole." Even while dreaming, I remembered how Harry used to say that same thing when we were in Iraq.

"None of us did, brother. None of us wants to be here." I rubbed my hand against my mouth to scrape away the dirt caked in the corners.

He turned to me and I knew something was wrong. His eyes looked different. I grew uneasy.

His head drooped forward like a child's might do when they're falling asleep.

Gritty air chafed my mouth. I spat and glanced at that body. It was closer to me. It began to stir.

Then Harry moaned. His head hung like a limp water-bag from his neck, lying on his chest. His eyes glared at me.

He was dead.

I tried to scramble away, but my heels dug into the soft sand. No traction.

Then the body lying in front of me sat up and I gaped at it. Sand rolled off its face in streams and spiders crawled from its mouth.

"I'm sorry!" I tried to yell, but it only came out in a muffled garble.

Then Harry spoke next to me. "We're in Hell, Mick." His lips worked as if someone had their hand stuck in the back of his skull making his jaw move.

I struggled for breath.

"He told me it would heal us," Harry said. The bones of his face protruded, as if his skin were a plastic bag sucked to his skull.

Something started to bang, like a hammer on an old piece of hollow wood... banging. From somewhere behind me, getting closer.

I was stuck... goddamn it, I was stuck...

...stuck in the covers of my bed. My feet were tangled and my head hung off the edge.

My eyes flew open. A ceiling light, a lamp next to me, a TV on a dresser. My motel room. The early morning light slammed everything into focus. I was yelling.

I clamped my jaw closed and glanced around, trying to sit up and found it shockingly difficult. My tongue stuck to the roof of my mouth like someone had stuffed it full of dusty cotton balls. My head throbbed and I imagined a large vice clamped at my temples, squeezing slowly, forcing my brains into my eye sockets.

Christ, I'd forgotten what this felt like. I'd had bad ones before, but this might rank up there as one of the worst ever. Each part of my body protested as I tried to move. The room rotated around me like one of those weird carnival rides, except this one didn't stop if you closed your eyes. With this came the sickening gurgle deep in my stomach and I held my breath, hoping it would pass.

A little voice whispered to get up and drink a beer or small shot of whiskey. A little hair of the dog. I needed to do something; I couldn't function like this.

A loud knock scared the hell out of me and I stared stupidly at the door. Who on earth would be here now? It better not be Bob again.

"Mick," the muffled voice of Britney from outside, "Mick, you okay in there?"

I placed my hand on my head and covered my eyes. *Jesus.* "Just a minute."

What the hell was she doing here so early? The clock read 6:37. Holy shit. I thought of Amy and the girls. I pictured them all standing here, gawking at me, and shaking their heads in disgust. A sob threatened to lurch from my throat, but I swallowed it back. I'd crossed a line that can't be uncrossed. Damn, I wished I didn't have to tell Amy.

I sat up and swung my legs over the edge of the bed. The spinning persisted and I knew from experience, you had to take your time at this stage; otherwise, you might end up puking your guts up before reaching the bathroom.

I debated whether to open the door right then or leave her out there until I got myself presentable. I didn't know. Leaving her out there sure as hell didn't feel right.

I thought back to last night. We'd been out on the deck for a great deal of the night. I'd smoked my whole pack of cigarettes. So much for smoking a few and tossing the rest in the trash. I'm supposed to leave today. *When in the hell is my flight anyway?*

Hell if I knew. I'd check my phone later.

Had I driven myself back here? *Dear god.* I pictured myself having to call Amy from jail and explain that I'd gotten a DUI. Then I wondered if I *had* called Amy last night. There is an unspoken rule about drunks – for some reason, they think it's necessary to call people at one o'clock in the morning and make fools of themselves. *Oh I hope to God I didn't call her.*

I heaved myself off the bed, swayed a bit, checked that I had shorts on, and stepped heavily to the door. As I trudged along, I remembered parts of my dream, the parts that hadn't faded yet. Harry's head dangling like a bag of water from his neck, but still talking to me. That body lying in front of us.

His words, *he told me it would heal us*, echoed in my head as I undid the bolt lock to let Britney in.

CHAPTER 9

"You were pretty toasted by the time we left last night," Britney said as I walked to the bathroom.

We? By the time *we* left? Oh shit.

"I'm feelin' it this morning," I pulled the door closed behind me, but left it open a crack to still hear her. "What time did we leave?"

I stared at myself in the mirror, hoping to God I didn't do anything stupid last night.

"Probably around midnight."

My mind swam with questions… Where did we go? Did you drive me home? Why in God's name are you here at 6:30 in the morning?

"Damn, I haven't drank that much in years." Start off with the excuse and then ask the questions, that's how to do it.

"Last night, you kept saying that you hadn't drank anything in like four years." Britney's words triggered an uneasy tingle.

"Well, it's not that I haven't drank anything, just not nearly that much," I lied. "That's why I've got this monster hangover this morning."

"You didn't act like you were *that* drunk," she said, "you must have been a little worse off than I thought."

You have no idea, baby. "So how did I get home?"

"You rode in my car. You don't remember?"

"Did you drop me off?"

"Yeah," she said, "And you kept saying *be here at 6:30*. You insisted on 6:30."

Yep, that sounded like me when I'm shitfaced. Amy always said that once I got stuck on a topic, I hammered it to death and kept repeating myself. Old habits die hard.

"Yeah," I tried to play it off, "I wanna get out there early so I can still catch my flight back to Colorado today."

"Ah." Then she asked, "I thought I heard you yelling in here this morning. Were you yelling?"

"Bad dream." I turned on the sink and said, "Nothing big, I have them every once in a while." Then started brushing my teeth so I didn't have to keep talking.

She didn't say anything else while I finished up. I splashed water on my face, slapped on some deodorant, and lumbered out.

She sat in a chair close to the door with her purse clasped in her lap. I had a strange intuition she was uncomfortable being here. The way her eyes kept darting around and the grip on her purse. We needed conversation so she'd relax.

To be honest, the prospect of going to Kate's Lake this morning didn't appeal to me as it had last night and I considered calling the whole thing off. Other than a weird phone call on Friday morning from a guy claiming to be Harry's father, a strange visit from a weirdo named Bob, and a creepy note, this was not my issue.

And who was I kidding?

I'd already committed to going out there and Britney was here, sitting in my room, waiting to go. Plus, I needed to get my mind off last night. I didn't want to dwell on what I might've done or said. What's done is done and can't be undone. I hadn't committed the unforgivable sin of infidelity. At least, I'm pretty sure I didn't.

"Did you have a tough time getting up this morning?" I unzipped my suitcase and pulled out a pair of jeans and an old blue Colorado Rockies T-Shirt.

"Not really. I didn't drink that much," she said.

"Well, that's good. At least one of us is capable of cognitive thought." I smiled and didn't look to see if she returned it.

"Mom asked where I was going." She tapped her foot as she spoke. "I told her I out to Kate's Lake with you. I feel so bad for her. I'm glad Arlene's there."

"Your mom knows about Kate's Lake?"

"Sort of. She knows it exists, but that's about it. She'd never heard of it before Harry."

"Hopefully we won't be gone long." I piled my clothes in my arms and said, "I'm gonna throw on some clothes and we can go."

"Are you nervous?" She asked.

"What, about going to that lake?"

"Yeah."

"I don't know if I'm nervous. I'm curious." I thought about telling her about my dream and decided not to.

"Seems weird," she said, "Us going out there. I mean, with that note you got yesterday and everything."

I shuffled into the bathroom to dress. My head still throbbed like something inside my skull kicking through my temples. "Yeah, I have no idea what we're looking for."

"Freaks me out." Her voice seemed distant, wary.

"Well, my guess is that we'll get out there and find a crazy old man named Bob and that's it."

I stepped out, fully dressed. Britney still sat in the chair, twisting her fingers together in her lap.

"All this shit is information overload for me." I stopped and squinted. "Suicide notes and all this shit."

She sat quiet and I said, "If you'd rather, I can go by myself and let you know what I find out." Not sure I meant that.

"No. I want to go. I'm a little scared is all. I did think we might want to call the police or something."

"Let's hold off," I said. If we called the cops, I'd be entangled more. Possibly keeping me here longer. And part of me still thought this was all a crock of shit. "I mean, we can call them if you want." I told her. "But I'd rather wait until there's something to worry about."

She considered this and then said, "I guess. If all we're gonna do is check it out."

I plopped down on the edge of the bed, happy to stop moving. "I gotta ask, what is it you're scared of?"

She looked at me. "I told you yesterday, it's supposed to be haunted. You believe in that sort of thing?"

I shrugged and gave a half-hearted nod. I didn't want to get into what I believed in.

"Well, there's all kinds of stories about the Bottoms." She fidgeted with her hands again, looking down at them as if she wondered how to work them. "It's just that someone died out there a few weeks ago."

"At the lake?"

She nodded. Even in the dim light of the room, her hair pulled back into a plastic clippie with a few stray strands hanging down made her wildly cute. The girl from the photograph. "Some guy out camping or something. Happened in the woods, about two miles from Kate's Lake."

"How?"

She didn't look up at me when she spoke. "He'd been missing for a while. It might've been an animal, like wild dogs or something." She paused and I thought, *Harry and his wife also went missing*, then she said. "There's No Trespassing signs up all over the place down there."

I didn't like the sounds of that. "Well, this all keeps getting better and better." Not only did we have all of this weird shit to contend with; it was also illegal. Great.

She nodded. "The Bottoms are like a bunch of these little cabins down in the woods, but I don't think the gravel road that goes down in there is private property or anything. The people that live there are a little different, kind of back-woodsy."

"Great," I said, still picturing wild dogs.

"The gravel road ends at Kate's Lake. But at the edge of the Bottoms, it gets rough, a lot of weeds and stuff." She settled her eyes on me. "Your car is at my mom's house still."

Nice. I didn't have my car. I'd gotten drunk and left it somewhere. Not the first time for that either. "Hmmm." Suddenly, making a trip to Kate's Lake sounded quite stupid.

But Harry had asked for *me*, according to Bob.

Would Harry make this trip if the tables were turned and I needed him to do something for me in the wake of my death? Absolutely, without question, he would.

Britney seemed to sense my unease. "That guy dying back in the woods has never happened before, that I know of. Kind of a freak thing. And like I said, there's a few people who live down in the Bottoms. Not sure how many."

"Like, log cabins?" This might be some Abraham Lincoln type shit.

She smiled, almost looking guilty. "No. We just call them cabins. They're more like shacks. There's a lot of little ponds and stuff down in there and the Wabash River runs pretty close to it. Harry said most of the people in the Bottoms do a lot of fishing. Believe me, there's nothing fancy down there."

Funny, when Britney told me about the Bottoms earlier and the cabins, I'd pictured these nice little cottages inhabited by retired people. But now that image transformed into something resembling a horror movie where the hillbillies exist like a different species, killing or raping strangers who go back in their territory.

But Harry would go out there for me. Damn right he would.

"Well," I got up slowly. "Let's drive out there and see. If we don't like it, we can always turn around and leave it alone."

"Yup, that we can." She lifted herself out of the chair.

We left the room, conversing as we walked out to her car about whether or not we should stop for coffee (I insisted that we should), and if we needed to get anything to eat.

In addition to all the other shit racing through my mind like Amy, the girls, my flight, Britney… I kept thinking of Bob. I wondered where he lived and what would happen if we found him. And Harry's words from my dream, *he told me it would heal us*. It was the only thing I remembered from that nightmare, but it persisted like an annoying song stuck in my head.

CHAPTER 10

First, we stopped at her mom's house and switched to my rental car; a yellow Chevy Malibu. As we climbed inside a fleeting thought about how much this damn thing would end up costing me popped into my mind. *Just one more day, shouldn't be too bad.*

From there, we stopped at a gas station outside of Gainesville along a stretch of lonely looking highway. I strolled inside and bought two cups of coffee. While standing at the counter, I spotted the cigarette packs behind the cashier. I'd smoked all of mine the night before and had the aching chest to prove it. I pondered the thought of not having any today and decided I didn't like that prospect. I'd get them, just in case I needed them. Hell, I already needed them. The webs we weave.

By the time I got back out to the car, the dashboard clock read 7:30. I thought of Amy back home. She'd be expecting me to call this morning, but last night's drunk still lingered and guilt shrouded me like a dark blanket. *Goddamn it, why'd I have to do that?*

I opened the passenger side and handed the two cups of coffee to Britney. She took them and shoved each into the respective cup-holder. I tossed the pack of KOOLs onto the dashboard. The sophomoric side of me debated on whether or not I should tell Britney that I needed to call my wife. *Quit acting like a fucking high school kid with a crush!* I was in my mid-thirties, for Christ's sake.

"I'm gonna call Amy real quick," I said, "You okay with waiting a few minutes?"

"Sure." She flipped the mirror down on her visor and studied her hair. Did she even know who Amy was?

Would it be so bad if she did?

"Be just a sec." I stepped out and sauntered a few yards away. I tapped Amy's name from my contacts and her picture splashed the screen – a recent one of her relaxed on our back deck smiling and gazing at me as I'd snapped the photo. One of my favorites.

It rang twice and she answered.

"Good morning," I said. Red shame engulfed me, like I'd been caught watching porn. *Be honest, you shit.*

"Hi." The bite in her word told me everything. *Hi* and then stopped.

"How's the morning goin'?" My words felt forced. Even the sound of my own voice betrayed me – hoarse and rough, like someone who'd gotten drunk and smoked a whole pack of cigarettes the night before.

"Well, the girls are up, getting ready for school. How's yours?"

"Not too bad. You remember that cabin I told you about yesterday morning that Harry apparently bought?" I recalled my last conversation with her. There'd been no lies between us at that time.

"Yeah, with the old guy at Denny's?" At least she'd heard me. She wasn't dwelling on my spending another day here, or worse yet, why I hadn't answered her call last night. Giving me the benefit of the doubt.

"Yep, that one. I'm going to help his family pick up some stuff he had out there."

"Hmm. How long will you be out there?"

"Shouldn't be long. My flight's at 4:15 this afternoon; so, can't be too long."

"I called last night," she said. *Shit.*

I already had my excuse planned out. "My phone died yesterday afternoon and I forgot my damn car-charger," I lied, very adequately I thought. "I plugged it in when I got back to the motel, but figured it was too late to call you back. I figured I'd call this morning rather than waking you up."

Silence. My conscience edged in. I should've known better.

This was not Amy's first rodeo.

Finally, she said, "You sound congested. Have you been smoking?"

If anyone had been standing there watching me, they'd have seen my cheeks flush red. *Goddamn it.* Can a man have no secrets?

"No," I chuckled. "I woke up this morning kind of stuffy. Might be allergies to the hay and stuff here." To hell with it, I lied about everything else.

"Maybe." Amy paused. Then she asked, "You want to say hi to the girls?"

"Yep." I was glad to be out of that fake conversation.

I talked to my daughters, asked the usual dad questions: did you eat breakfast, are you ready for school, are you looking forward to seeing your friends – and then Amy hopped back on the line.

"Well, call me today before you get to the airport." She didn't sound excited, like words spoken out of obligation.

"I'll call a little later, when we get back from Kate's Lake." I smiled as I said it.

I believed it then.

I rode in the passenger seat with my coffee cupped in my hands. We decided it made more sense for her to drive since she was more familiar with the area. Plus, I felt like shit. My head throbbed behind my left eye, but it had eased up. My stomach threw fits. That conversation with Amy bothered me. I fought a tremendous urge to call her back.

I've learned over the years that most things in life, where things come out wrong, you have every opportunity to prevent it. In hindsight, the warning signs were always there, and with a little age, you learn to recognize them. Toss in a little alcohol and a pretty girl, and you'd be surprised at how easy it is ignore them.

"The thing I've been wondering is who called you," Britney said while driving my rental car. She tapped her thumbs on the steering wheel, as if keeping time to a song, and kept biting at her lower lip.

"There's a lot of big mysteries," I said, "they seem to be popping up all over the place."

"Have you told anyone else about that call, besides me?" She asked.

I thought about it and said, "No. Except Amy, but I didn't tell her that your dad was d…", I caught myself, horrified I'd almost said *dead* so coldly, "that your dad had passed away. She still thinks your dad called me."

"Should we call the police, Mick, and show them that note? Sheriff Snider's a nice guy. He'd check it out."

"I'm starting to agree with you."

The closer we got to Kate's Lake, the more I concurred she had a damn good point about getting the police involved. This was getting too weird.

"We'll call when we get to the Bottoms." Relief touched her voice and I liked hearing it.

"That works."

I rode in silence as she turned onto a black-top road that led into a formidable forest. She said, "We're about fifteen minutes away, if I remember right."

When I'd thought of the Bottoms, I'd pictured thick weeds along the road with old, junked cars parked in front yards. Most likely a trail cut by two tire-ruts with waist-high weeds in the middle and the sides lined with groping tree branches.

I remembered what Britney had said about the phone call that I'd received on Friday morning to tell me Harry died. It wasn't her dad. Then who in God's name had called me? My mind shot to Bob, but he didn't know my phone number. No one here did.

No one, except for Harry.

CHAPTER 11

We turned onto a gravel road and she slowed as we neared a rusty, metal gate that stood open. "That's the gate to the Bottoms," she said.

I needed a cigarette.

"You mind if we stop and have a smoke first?" I asked.

The gravel road continued ahead and curved into a dark cluster of trees that shadowed everything beyond it. Around the gate, weeds grew, some taller than me, and I noticed an old wooden post with a decrepit piece of square plywood nailed to it with NO TRESPASSING painted in red across it.

I swallowed hard. An irrational nervousness swept over me.

The road disappeared into a tunnel of thick trees that gaped like an open mouth ready to devour whatever fool decided to wander inside.

The Bottoms.

"Sure." Britney eased the car over and stopped.

I stared ahead. "Looks spooky. Says no trespassing."

"Yeah," she didn't seem to pay much mind to the sign. "It's definitely off the beaten path."

I huffed a dry chuckle and heaved open my door. The humidity engulfed me. Sweat beaded my forehead. I stepped through the knee-high grass to the front of the car, then leaned against the hood and lit my cigarette. I didn't like this. It reminded me of every horror movie I'd ever seen where clueless teenagers wandered into cannibal infested forests. Those movies had always seemed stupid up until right then.

From behind me, I heard Britney get out of the car. Her footsteps crunched on the gravel like brittle bones as she walked up and joined me.

"I haven't been down here since last year when Harry took me back to his cabin," she said.

"Jesus. People live down in there?"

"Yeah. Not many, but some do."

"Great. Let's call the sheriff from right here."

She nodded, about to say something, when her phone rang. She dug it out of her purse and gawked at it. "Goddamn it," she said. I glanced over and noticed a hate-filled scowl etched on her face. A look I'd never dreamed her capable of.

"What's up?" I asked.

"Oh… I have to take this, okay?"

I shrugged. "Sure." I thoroughly enjoyed my cigarette and decided that I wasn't going another inch into that haunted forest without the police escorting me. I'd park my happy ass right here where the trees were thinner and a few rays of sunlight still splashed the ground. This was as good a place as any to suffer through a hangover.

"What?" Britney dawdled behind me and she sounded pissed. A brief pause, and then, "I told you I'd call you next week."

Another pause, then she said, "I don't need this bullshit from you, Jesse. Let me deal with Harry's funeral first. Can you at least let me do that?"

Pause.

"Goddamn it, Jesse."

Pause.

"He's a friend of Harry's."

I'd bet my ass that last statement was about *me*. Not sure I liked that.

Jesse must be her ex-husband or boyfriend or something. She didn't sound happy with him, whoever he was. What did I have to do with it? Either someone told him I rode out here with her or good 'ole Jesse had arrived right here in Gainesville, Indiana. I hoped it wasn't the latter.

Britney, still on the phone, said, "I'll call you later today and we can talk about it."

Pause.

"Okay." She pulled the phone from her ear, the pink case reflected a glint of sunlight, and stuffed it into her purse. She stood there on the gravel road, silent.

Then she bent her head down and covered her face with her hand. Her shoulders throbbed up and down and I heard her sniffle. That awkward moment sprang up again, just like last night while standing in her mom's kitchen, where the right thing to do was comfort her, but if I did, I'd feel like I was doing something wrong.

I hate shit like this.

I pushed myself away from the car and said, "Everything all right?"

She shook her head and stared down at the ground, then wiped her eyes with the backs of her hands. "My stupid ex. He won't accept we're divorced."

I nodded, no clue of what to say.

"He's here," she said, "Can you believe that? Here in Gainesville."

Well, wasn't that just fucking great. "Is he from here?"

"Yeah, well, he's from Waynetown, that's not far. He just needs to move on, ya know. Quit following me." She shook her head and wiped her eyes again.

"At least he doesn't know you're out here."

"He knows. My stupid sister told him."

Great. I took a deeper drag on my cigarette. I wanted to know everything about the man. How big? Seeking trouble? What did he know about me?

"Like an idiot, I told Arlene we were coming out here." She looked up at the sky. "God, why are things so complicated?"

I wondered if Arlene took a wee bit of pleasure in telling mister ex-hubbie about Britney hanging out with me. Fuckin' Arlene.

"Is he coming out here?"

"No. He said he'd wait at Mom's."

I felt better about that.

Britney glanced around as if searching for an escape route.

I asked, "You okay?"

"Yeah. I'll be fine."

"Wasn't he in the Marine Corps?"

"Yeah." She looked at me and chuckled a little. "Now he's sells vacuum sweepers. Can you believe that shit?"

"Nice." I considered saying something crude but didn't. The guy was a Marine vet and so was I. An unspoken loyalty existed there. "Hopefully he doesn't have a problem with me." Not sure why I tossed in that last part.

She laughed, but it was a timid laugh, the kind you might utter before the doctor puts you out to perform open heart surgery. "His problem's with me."

Suddenly, I deeply regretted getting drunk last night and having a cigarette (a pack of cigarettes) after years of getting things right. And now I had this ex-husband in the picture who most likely suspected me of trying to lay pipe with his ex-wife. That's what *I'd* think, if the tables were turned.

Fuck. I needed to get this over with, catch my flight, and leave this all behind.

"Well, that's good, I guess." I played it off like it didn't worry me.

"You won't have to talk to him. He won't come after us or anything." Her words prompted a foolish shame.

"I'm not worried about that," I lied, "I'm more concerned about you. But it sounds like you've got things under control."

"I'll be fine." She pulled her phone back out and started dialing numbers. "Gainesville's got one number for police, fire, and everything."

I shook out another cigarette.

She asked for Sheriff Snider, but must have gotten shifted to someone else. She looked at me, a tad annoyed, and mouthed, *Sheriff's not in yet.*

Then, "Hi Wayne!" Fake enthusiasm peppered her words.

She explained the situation and ended with where we were, parked outside the Bottoms, and then laid out the problem. I started to feel like I was the one who should've called.

She said *no* a couple of times and *yes* a couple of times. Pause. "What should we do until then?" Whatever *then* was. It's always weird standing there while someone else has a phone conversation. I leaned back against the car and peered at the Bottoms entrance while Summer bugs hummed in the weeds next to me.

Britney nodded. "Yeah. Okay." More nodding. Then, "Thanks Wayne, I'll have my phone. Call me when you get here." She ended the call and dropped the phone back into her purse.

"He wasn't that worried about it." She stepped over and leaned against the hood next to me, close enough to touch.

"Who's he?" I asked.

"Wayne Tillwood. We went to school together. Sheriff Snider's out, so I got stuck with Wayne." She curled her top lip.

"Ah. So what did Wayne say?"

"That Bob's a freak. Said he's always been strange." I wondered what she meant by strange, but kept my mouth shut. "He wants to see the note Bob gave you."

"Makes sense."

"He didn't sound that worried, though."

"Yeah, well he's not here."

"True."

I took the last drag of my cigarette and tossed it down onto the gravel. "So, is he coming out here?"

"In an hour or two. He has to wait until Sheriff Snider gets back."

I stared down that creepy road leading into the haunted forest. Two hours was a long time to wait. "All right, so what do you wanna do?" I asked. Her words about Jesse lingered; *he won't come after us or anything.* Did she think he scared me?

She shrugged.

I wanted a drink.

CHAPTER 12

"All right." I hardened my voice. I was still calling the shots on this thing and I didn't need anyone, least of all her, to swoop in and save me from people like Jesse. "Let's go on down. It's just a lake, right?"

"I guess," she said. "The Bottoms are confusing, though."

She folded her arms across her chest and I shot her a sideways glance. A few strands of dark hair had fallen from her clippie and fluttered by her face.

I asked, "Confusing, how?"

"It's like a maze down in there."

"It's starting to sound like that old movie *Deliverance*."

She shot me a strange look.

"Burt Reynolds, Ned Beatty. Going down the river…" I dropped it. She had no idea what I was talking about. Not everyone got the humor or the horror in that movie anyway. "Sounds like one of those places you might find in the backwoods."

She smiled. "I told you, it is." I loved that smile.

I could get her mind off of the dickhead ex-husband after all.

"We'll be good." I almost added *besides, I have a plane to catch*, but didn't.

"Wayne said it'd be best to wait."

I considered that. Thirty minutes wasn't so bad, but not two hours! I had shit going on today.

"You can wait," I said, though I didn't want her to. "But I'm going down there. I can still make my flight this afternoon if I hurry."

A short silence lingered filled by chirping crickets and the hum of cicadas.

She shrugged. "I guess, if you think it's fine."

"Only for a little bit." I glanced at her. The girl from the photograph.

"I'll be fine." She tucked stray hairs behind her ear. Her eyes caught mine.

I turned away and so did she. An awkward silence dangled between us. A well-placed joke or a bit of relatable sarcasm would have worked well and eased the tension. In my current state, dehydrated and head throbbing, I wasn't about to attempt either.

"Let's get this over with." I kept my eyes on the thick trees in front of us.

"Yep." She hurried around to her side of the car, the driver's side, and I went to mine.

As I got into the car, I pictured Amy and the girls standing in the field next to me. Just standing out there leering at me, watching me, accusing me. Strange how the mind works.

As Britney pulled my rental car back out onto the gravel road, she asked me, "Do you remember telling me last night about a picture of me that Harry gave you when you guys were in Iraq?"

Oh shit.

I tried to blow it off. "I'm starting to worry about what all I told you."

"It wasn't bad or anything. You said you saw my picture when you guys were in Iraq and that Harry was supposed to set us up."

"That much is true."

"Funny… Harry never said anything." She glanced over at me, then back at the road. "I was pretty serious with Jesse at that time, I guess."

Fuckin' Harry.

For the first time I wondered if, while we were in the litter-box and he showed me that picture and told me he would set me up with her, if he'd meant it or if he'd been blowing smoke up my ass.

Harry did that from time to time.

CHAPTER 13

Britney slowed down as we passed through the open gate. Trees canopied the road with branches dipping down like skeletal fingers. A never-ending shadow engulfed us.

"Is this a dead end?" I asked.

"Yeah."

"Where are the cabins?"

"Little ways down from here, closer to the river." Her hands clenched the steering wheel.

I imagined a damp, leafy smell outside. "You've only been back here once?"

"Yeah, with Harry."

"How far before we have to walk?" Maybe we should've waited for ole' Deputy Wayne after all.

"It's a little way. A few miles, probably."

That's a little farther than I'd thought. I imagined what Kate's Lake might look like. I hoped large and clear with plenty of open bank surrounding it. Why else would he have moved back here?

. . . . .

We passed by a few cabins nestled in the woods with muddy driveways spilling onto the road. *Shacks* described them better. I'd be shocked if they had running water inside. I'd seen a lot of shit in the military, places where people were so goddamn poor they had to shit in their own backyards. The Bottoms, right here in Taylor County, Indiana, rivaled those places closer than anything.

An older guy with a beard clinging to his face like dirty moss rocked in a chair in front of his shack wearing blue-jeans and a filthy T-shirt. He stared at us as we drove past. Not a curious stare, mind you, but one of those *who the fuck are you* type stares that made me wonder if he'd follow us. *That guy ain't the only one out here.* I was glad when that guy was well behind us and out of sight.

We came to a stop. We had no choice. The goddamn road ended. "We'll have to hoof it from here." Britney didn't shut the car off. She wanted me to agree before she abandoned any hope of turning around and driving out.

"Funny," I said, "I didn't picture it being quite like this." I chuckled. "It's like something out of a Vietnam movie or something."

"Told you."

"How far down that path before we get to Kate's Lake?" I nodded ahead.

"Couple of miles."

Would this ever end? "You bring your walkin' shoes?" I hoped she'd say *no, let's go back.*

"I'm up for it."

"Damn." I chuckled. Oh well. "It's a lot thicker woods than I thought." I considered telling her that we should wait for the cops, but of course I didn't. I remembered her on that phone with her asshole ex-husband, Jesse, and my heart hardened.

At my age, you'd think I'd be past this type of macho-adolescent bullshit. If it had been Amy sitting here instead of Britney, I would have said no damn way we're going back in there, and that would have been just fine, we'd have turned around and got the hell out of Dodge, laughing about how dumb we'd been.

But not today. Pride, baby. A simple photograph of a pretty girl I'd dreamt about in Iraq suddenly sprang to life and sat here next to me. "Let's do it." I opened my door.

No way this cowboy would admit he was scared.

CHAPTER 14

"At least it's not raining." I stretched and my head still throbbed, but not as bad. Thank God.

She traipsed around the front of the car to meet up with me. "Yeah."

The lazy chorus of cicadas filled every nook and cranny. Sweat beaded my forehead. Hot as fuck out here. I smelled water close by, sort of a coppery odor mixed with rotting fish.

We plodded down the path with grasshoppers popping out of the tall grass like popcorn kernels in a hot skillet. The car disappeared behind us in a wall of green foliage.

"Lions and Tigers and Bears, Oh my." I tried to lighten the mood.

Britney forced an unimpressed smile. "Any idea what he wants?"

"Who?"

"Bob, when he told you Harry asked for you?"

I suppose there was nothing left to do but talk about Harry. "God knows. I wish I would've asked more questions when we were at Denny's yesterday. I thought he was full of shit then." I didn't add that part of me still clung to that sentiment.

She didn't say anything at first, then she asked, "Did Harry ever meet your wife?"

I chuckled, a fake, nervous sound if I ever heard one, and said, "Oh yeah. He was with me when I met her. Amy and me have been out here a couple of times to visit."

"He was with you when you met her?" Her mouth opened in a wide smile.

"Yep. We were both drunk and saw Amy at a beach party in San Diego. Funny, he actually spoke to her first. I didn't talk to her until later that night when we were playing pool." All the sudden, I felt awkward talking about Amy. "Harry and me went everywhere playing pool. We won money in San Diego a few times."

"He told me about that! He *was* good at pool," she nodded as she spoke and kept her eyes on the path. "Were you guys together the whole time in the Marines?"

Ah, now *this* I could talk about. "Pretty much. He went to the Rock one time for a few months and I didn't. But that's about it."

"The Rock?"

"Yeah, Okinawa. Marines call it the Rock."

"He always talked about the things you guys did."

"We did a lot of crazy shit."

"He told me one about you and him puking over the side of a pier while other people held onto your belts to keep you from falling over the edge."

Ha! I remembered that night and holy shit was that funny. "Oh yeah. In Malaysia. We found a Karaoke bar that night and ended up drunk off our ass."

"That's the one."

"He told you about how he got drunk and wouldn't quit singing *Ring of Fire*?"

"And he can't sing worth a crap." Britney giggled when she said that. I noticed she said *can't* and not *couldn't*, but kept my mouth shut. I imagined Harry telling that story.

"Yeah, but it didn't matter that night. He was Johnny Cash."

We both laughed and then fell silent. The path narrowed and opened back up and we each had a tire lane to walk in. Even though the grass, weeds, and shrubs remained thick on either side of us, I noticed that the farther we walked, the trees thinned out. I hoped we were close to the lake; my sweat-soaked shirt clung to my skin like cling-wrap.

"I wish Bob would've told you a little more about where he lived," Britney said.

"No kidding. I assumed we'd see his cabin pretty easy. I'm starting to wonder if I'd see it three-feet in front of my face."

"Hopefully, it'll be close to the lake. I haven't been all the way back in there… he made me wait in the car."

"I can't believe that Harry drove back in here all the time."

"It didn't seem so long when we drove it." She swatted at a bug pestering her face. "I remember the weeds and stuff rubbing against the side of the truck, but it seemed shorter. Maybe because it was Spring. The leaves weren't so thick."

"Yeah." I kept my eyes trained in front of me as we walked, not wanting to plow straight into a big-ass spider web. She'd be impressed watching me beat myself to death to get a spider off me. I'd prefer to keep that little phobia to myself.

Britney folded her arms and rubbed her hands gently back and forth across her elbows. She shook her head occasionally as if shaking a bug out of her hair. I had a sudden urge to put my arm around her and then pushed the thought away.

An idea jumped into my head and it started to scare me. "I hope this guy doesn't have a bunch of dogs."

"You think he might?" Britney's eyes widened and her pace slowed.

I lit a cigarette and said, "I don't know. A lot of places out in the sticks like this would have dogs." I scanned the ground, searching for a healthy stick. I saw none.

"I don't remember any." She glanced down at the ground, then back up, hugging herself tighter.

"Look at that." Britney stopped and gazed off to her left.

Deep in the underbrush, the rusty remains of a chain-link fence, one that had been fairly tall back in its day, stuck out of the leaves like the ruins of some ancient Indian temple. The vines had all but destroyed it and left only the scarred metal remnants to prove that it had once stood strong. At some point in the past, it had stretched across the very spot in which we stood.

Staring at it, seeing it rotted and broken down, a weird sense of isolation swept over me, sort of like when you see those apocalyptic movies where all the people have died off.

"I don't remember seeing that," Britney said.

"It'd be easy to miss if you were driving." I wondered briefly if my rental car might have made it back here. The weeds would scratch it all to hell.

"Weird."

"I wonder how far it goes," I tiptoed to see beyond where we stood. "It looks like one of those tall ones with the barbed wire across the top."

"Why'd they put a big fence up out here?"

"Didn't you say this was government property? Whatever the reason, looks like it was a long time ago."

She shot me a dubious look, then shrugged and started walking again. I wondered if she felt the same way I did.

That we were doing something wrong.

CHAPTER 15

Bob found us a few minutes later.

We'd been discussing whether or not Bob had a cell phone. I'd concluded that if he did, he didn't know how to use the damn thing. Britney giggled and we both fell silent, retreating into our own thoughts.

That's when Bob spoke and scared the living shit out of me.

"Figured you wasn't comin'." His voice from somewhere off to our right.

Britney gasped.

He stood in the weeds and leered at us with those same piercing eyes I recognized from yesterday morning. He wore a pair of bib-overalls with a grimy white T-shirt underneath. His disheveled hair poked up in random clumps and I wondered if he'd just gotten out of bed.

"You scared the hell out of us." My heart hammered so hard my blood throbbed in my eyes.

"Didn't mean to." He shoved his hands deep into the pockets of his overalls.

"Got your damned note." I tried to sound commanding, like I was here to get this shit straight once and for all, but not sure I pulled it off.

"You alone?" he asked.

"Yeah. Just us."

"Call the cops?" Bob's eyes never left mine.

"No. No cops." I held his gaze. I hoped Britney stayed quiet.

"Who's she?" He glowered at her as if she were a virus.

"Harry's sister," I said.

His upper lip curled in disgust. I moved closer to her.

Bob's eyes narrowed reminding me of yesterday morning in the restaurant and how he'd kept glancing out the window, as if he expected someone to be standing there. He muttered something and then waded through the thick weeds out to the path.

We stepped back, giving him plenty of room. I wanted distance between him and us, just in case he did something stupid like pull a knife. Expect nothing, be ready for anything. Seeing him up close, though, in the daylight, I highly doubted he'd do anything dangerous. He looked frail, old, and tired.

Britney burst out, "Why did you say you talked to Harry?"

I shot her a *don't talk right now* glare, but her sights were on Bob.

He ignored her. I was grateful.

"Follow me back to my place." He leaned forward and spat.

She spoke through clenched teeth, "I asked you a question." She wasn't letting it go. This was the wrong time. She's the unexpected variable here. The piece that could make this all go bad.

"There's no time." Bob turned his back to us and started walking.

"Wait," I said. "What the fuck does this mean?" I held up the note, shaking it in the breeze.

"Goddamn it." Bob stopped, shook his head; then whirled on us. His eyes narrowed to slits and his lips peeled back to reveal blackened teeth. "You can either come with me or not. Don't much care, myself. This ain't my problem."

"What ain't your problem?"

He seemed to consider this. He glanced down at the ground, then back up at me. "Somethin' in the water. That's all I know."

I didn't move and neither did Britney. A bad feeling kissed my skin with cold breath, seeped through my muscles, and crept into my bones. Familiar words whispered in my ear, *he told us it would heal us*. Where had I heard that?

Bob shuffled toward us, his eyes wide. I side-stepped in front of Britney.

"It'd be better for me if you both leave," he hissed. "It's a goddamn abomination. But he asked for you." He nodded at me.

"Who?" Britney asked.

"Harry. Harry asked for him." Again, Bob nodded at me.

"Stop saying that. You're lying. Harry is dead." She sounded strained. Hope tainted her words and I hurt for her.

"I wish I was," Bob said. "I really do. But I ain't. And he ain't."

I searched his face for lies, for anything that indicated he was full of shit, and found nothing. True or not, Bob believed he had something at his house and he believed that Harry had asked for me.

"Let's go." I considered telling him we'd called the deputy and that he'd be out here within an hour or two. But I'd already lied about it and so I kept my mouth shut. I hoped I wouldn't regret it.

Bob turned and started walking again.

Britney's eyes grew wide and she mouthed the words *let's wait*. I flashed wide eyes at her and shrugged. I had no idea how to read her: if she was mad, if she was happy, or both. Now Amy, I could read like a book; I understood her. If this were Amy here with me, I'd be able to tell if she thought I was stepping in major shit.

We maintained a safe distance behind him. Our arms nearly touched and I could have easily grasped her hand, it was *right* there, and I thought I just might before we reached our destination. We were both a little freaked out here. My mind wandered and, in addition to all this other shit, I questioned whether hand-holding crossed the line.

Harry sure as hell would do it. In fact, if this were Harry walking down this path with Amy, he'd have his arm draped over her shoulders, holding her tight, comforting her. And on some level, I'm quite positive, Amy would want that. She'd expect it. Would Britney feel the same way or would she take it wrong and yank away, scowling at me with that *you piece of shit* gaze?

I swallowed hard. Our arms bumped and with practically no thought at all, I had her hand in mine. At first, she stiffened, but then she relaxed. I looked at her. She smiled back and then we both turned our gazes down at the path.

I fixed my eyes on Bob's frail frame, following him like a child might follow a grandparent into a church. The bones of his shoulders poked at his shirt. The bones. I wondered if Britney noticed.

I didn't remember him appearing this frail when we'd spoken at Denny's.

Holding her hand felt good and right. My mind burst with feelings I hadn't had in years. That initial spark. Amy and I had that once, years ago. Did we still? Lately, our days had become a series of tasks and our relationship was one of me being monitored versus accepted.

I wanted to know Britney better. After today, I'd never see her again… my girl from the photograph. What kind of work did she do? Why was she getting divorced? Who were her friends? Did she go to church? I didn't even know what kind of food she liked to eat.

For Harry's sake, I wished I knew her better.

The only thing I *did* know was that she tanned very well. Her skin glowed healthy and smooth. I knew that ten-years ago, when she posed for a picture where the hem of her shirt flirted with her navel, with one leg pushed out in front of her like a cheerleader posing for the camera, she was beautiful. As beautiful as she was now.

And knowing that was dangerous.

CHAPTER 16

We didn't talk much on our trek to Bob's cabin, which turned out to be a decent looking place. The shingled roof bestowed professional quality and the frame appeared to be made out of real logs. A shallow porch stretched across the front with a sliding glass door parked square in the middle.

I liked his place.

"Did you build this yourself?" I assumed he did since it was so far back in here.

"Yep."

It's funny how you visualize something in your head, but then when you see it, it's nothing like what you'd imagined. Like an actor on TV – you picture them as their rugged, I-can-do-anything, character, but in real life they're a foot shorter than you thought. I reacted to Kate's Lake like that.

The biggest surprise was how damn small it was; roughly the size of a basketball court. Not a perfect rectangle, of course, but it covered about that much ground. It was shaped more like a big D. We stood on the curve side. Bugs skimmed the top of the murky water. Tall, green grass lined most of the bank, along with a few clumps of short trees. After hearing Bob talk about it, I'd pictured something more ominous.

Hell, I would've called it a pond.

I stared across the lake and spotted another small cabin wedged into the trees, barely visible.

"I think that was Harry's." Britney pointed at it.

I shoved my hands into my pockets. It was strange staring at that place. "So this must be Kate's Lake?"

"Yep," Bob said over his shoulder again.

"Why's it called Kate's Lake?" I figured there must be a reason with a name as specific as Kate.

Bob stopped, lit a cigarette, and peered at the water. Beyond him, next to his cabin, I noticed the glimmer of a silver bumper fighting through leafy undergrowth.

"This here's my place." He shot a thumb at the cabin, then pointed at the lake. "That lake got its name from a little girl that drowned in it 'long time ago. It's just a story, far as I know, but that's what folks'll tell ya."

"Wow." I hadn't expected that. Britney's hand tightened around mine.

"Yep. She fell in and never come out." Bob's gaze across the water bothered me for some reason.

"Ah yeah." I remembered part of our conversation from the previous morning. "It's bottomless."

"That's what they say."

"I thought it'd be bigger."

"Nah. It ain't big."

"You ever been in it?" I asked. It looked like something easily walked across.

"Hell no, I ain't been in it. I just told ya the story." He spoke to me like I was an idiot.

I smirked. "Thought maybe you took a boat out or something, or fished in it." I guess a person wouldn't need a boat to fish in Kate's Lake, as small as it was.

I let go of Britney's hand and stepped closer to the bank. She stayed put. I lit a cigarette while staring across the glassy surface at Harry's cabin. I had trouble picturing him there. The place was so isolated and lonely. A small porch clung to the side and an empty rocking chair with peeling white paint sat idle like a lonely child. I pictured Harry sitting in that chair, staring out across the lake, smoking a cigarette.

My eyes crawled to a shape standing in the woods next to the porch.

My breath locked. A chill shot through me.

Someone *was* over there, staring back at me. I saw hair, got a quick glimpse of a pair of eyes, and a hand. My heart ka-thudded.

I whirled to Bob and Britney. "Did you guys see that?"

"See what?" Britney asked. Bob didn't say anything.

"Someone's over there by the lake." I pointed, but they were gone. "Looked like a woman. I only got a glance." *Mary,* my mind whispered.

Britney squinted. "I don't see anything."

Bob still didn't speak.

Britney said, "People live down in here." Her words didn't comfort me.

She was right, though. I don't know why I hadn't thought of that. It might have been anyone. A kid. Or some curious woman from the Bottoms who wanted to keep an eye on us. Maybe the man we'd passed in the rocking chair with the long hair and the beard.

"Well," Bob finally spoke, "Let's get inside."

I noticed his expression and how strange it was. His nose crinkled, and his eyes bore the look of a man about to do something he might regret, something he couldn't take back.

What's done can't be undone.

"Yep, let's see what you've got to show me." I dropped my half-smoked cigarette to the ground and stepped on it. I still tried to convince myself that I would make my afternoon flight back to Colorado.

■ ■ ■ ■ ■

We lingered back a few feet as Bob heaved open the sliding glass door. The horrid stench that wafted out was like sticking your head in a toilet full of shit. Britney's hand shot to her mouth. "Oh my God," she said.

I retched.

Bob glanced over his shoulder. "Smell's pretty bad. I ain't had no windows or doors open yet this mornin'."

"You got a sewer backing up or something?" I stepped inside thinking *how does he sleep in this*. Britney followed. My God, sewage smelled better than this. Like spoiled meat.

"It'll get better when I open some windows." Bob opened two windows above the sink. He crossed to the other side of the cabin, maneuvered around a coffee table, and opened another window. A little television sat perched on top of a flimsy looking TV stand; he stopped and rested his arm on it.

"Make sure the screen is closed on that door. Place will fill up with bugs." Bob shook a finger at the sliding door behind us.

I feared I might puke if I didn't get out of this place. Thank God, that rotting stink finally started to dissipate. It didn't go away, not by any means, but it became somewhat tolerable... either that, or we were getting used to it.

"What the hell is that smell?" I asked.

"I'll show ya." He looked at me, his eyes wider, and he breathed heavier, more rapid. "But she's gotta wait here for a bit." He flipped a hand at Britney. "I didn't know you was bringin' her."

I shot Britney a hesitate glance. "You mind waiting here for a bit?"

Anger flashed in her wonderful brown eyes, so deep and so alluring, and if she'd have said *fuck you* right then, it would have fit her perfectly.

"Sure." Her eyes softened.

I tried to smile and painted on a *thank you* expression. She patted my hand.

Bob shuffled to the back of the kitchen and waited for me. I stole a last glimpse at Britney. She clasped her hands between her breasts as if she were cold. I didn't like leaving her by herself. I didn't want her out of my sight. For the first time, I wished she had not come.

Bob said, "I ain't sure how long this'll take."

All of this was so weird. "What is it you need to show me?"

He led me to a back door beside the refrigerator. We stepped through, and just like that, we were back outside again. "You'll see." Bob didn't stop to look at me.

"Is it something Harry left in his cabin or something he told you before he died, something like that?" I wished he'd give me some idea of what I was about to walk into.

You know what it is, Mick 'ole buddy, a dark voice whispered, a voice I hadn't heard in over four years, a voice I thought had died. *It's about that guy you killed.*

Shut up! I came horrifyingly close to screaming it and my heart slammed a solid thump inside me. Not that shit, not now, not ever.

We waded through tall grass around the cabin. Bad thoughts kept trying to creep in on me. It was as if my mind were turning against me after years of healing. Bob stopped and I damn near ran into him. He stared at a set of weedy steps made out of railroad ties that descended down to a rickety basement door. His eyes darted back up at me. I thought his expression resembled what a doctor might look like before delivering terrible news.

"What?" I asked.

"You feelin' okay?" he asked. This may sound crazy, but for a second, I thought he'd read my mind.

Was I feeling okay? I don't know. What kind of question was that?

I'd gotten drunk and blown several years of sobriety, *I'm doing swell, Bob*. I planned to ask him about a lot of things once I learned his goddamn secret. Bob was being so cautious it made me a tad nervous.

Finally, I said, "I'm fine. You mind if I smoke?"

"Nah, you can smoke." He fished a bunch of keys out of his pocket and fumbled around with them until he came up with one. I lit a cigarette and got a couple of decent drags in by the time he finished. My stomach rumbled and I realized it was somewhere between 9:30 and 10 in the morning and I hadn't eaten yet.

Out here, that rotted stench wasn't so noticeable. Only the pungent odor of lake-water.

Bob gave me a final, weary look and then hobbled down the steps. Watching him sparked a childhood memory from my grandmother's house. Her old cellar out back. I remember following her down in there and how much I'd hated it. Going to that door had always scared the hell out of me. I had nightmares about it too. I'd dream that I was outside playing and then something would grab my feet, yanking me across the yard, and dragging me down to that cellar.

I shivered.

Bob's keys jingled and then he shoved the door open. From where I stood at the top of the steps, I saw only blackness. I took another long drag as I watched Bob disappear partway inside.

"He's out here." Bob spoke to someone in there. My chest fluttered and the hairs on my arms and neck stirred.

I listened. Dread sank into my belly like a rotting piece of meat, heavy and terrible. I thought I heard mumbling, but nothing more.

Run, Mick! Run your ass off. Get to the car, get to the airport, never look back.

I pictured Britney gaping out the cabin's window at the sight of me in an all-out sprint across this overgrown yard and down the lane.

To hell with her too. This is her business more than mine anyway.

That's right. What the hell was I even doing here?

He asked for you.

Danger, Will Robinson. The feather of a smiled touched my lips as I sought desperately to believe a reasonable explanation still existed. This would all end up being some stupid joke that wasn't funny.

"C'mon down," Bob called. He leaned half out of the doorway and his shadowed face peered up at me.

I create my own misery. I shouldn't have had that cigarette yesterday. I shouldn't have had a beer, for damn sure, I knew that. I shouldn't have gone with Britney to the get-together last night. I shouldn't have come out here this morning.

I shouldn't have come to Indiana in the first place.

But I did. And why?

For the same reason I plodded down those wooden steps to the basement door where Bob stared at me with wide and desperate eyes. I ignored every instinct that screamed this was wrong.

I stopped at the bottom. That rotted stench from upstairs thickened down here, like roiling smoke. I stifled a gag and took another drag from my cigarette.

"Step in here." Bob waved me in with one hand and held an old rag to his mouth with the other.

I flipped my cigarette behind me and stepped into the blackness. My shuffling feet echoed in the cramped space. A small window on the far wall, covered with thin paper, reminded me of a microwave oven door and a corner of the paper hung down like a lapping tongue. I thought, *that's gonna fall off.*

The putrid stink clung to the inside of my mouth and nose like dry dust. I retched again and shoved a fist to my mouth to keep from puking. My eyes watered.

As my vision adjusted, other things materialized like gray ghosts. The outline of a cabinet or large dresser loomed off to my right. I had a brief second to wonder how in the hell Bob got that thing down here.

That's when my breath caught and I stared at the silhouette of someone seated in a chair directly in front of me. The far window didn't let in much light, but enough seeped through to see a man sitting there - what looked like a bald-headed man.

And then it spoke.

"Mickey?"

CHAPTER 17

I squinted at the shape, trying to see more detail.

"What the fuck is this?"

Bob said, "We couldn't think of a better way to tell ya."

We?

"Tell me what?"

"That's Harry." He pointed at the dark figure seated in the middle of the room.

I faced the shape and peered into the blackness. "Harry?"

"Mickey." The words slurred, as if spoken through a mouth full of phlegm. "Don't leave."

I didn't move any closer. Something was wrong here, but by God, I *knew* it was him. He'd always called me Mickey. "What the hell, man?"

"I heard Brit upstairs." His words slurped and I pictured slobber dangling from his mouth. I cringed.

"She came with me." The ghost of a smile touched my lips, though I doubt he saw it. "I *finally* got to meet her." If this was truly Harry, he'd know exactly what I meant with that.

"She was getting married, you asshole." In any other circumstance, he'd have grinned as he said it, but I couldn't picture him grinning now. The last two words sounded labored, even painful.

But those words sealed the deal. I wanted to run to him. He needed help and we had to get him out of this nasty-ass basement. What the Christ was he doing down in here, anyway?

"You want me to go get her?" I asked.

"*No!*" Harry didn't yell, I don't think he could've yelled if he'd wanted to. "*Don't* bring her down here."

"Cool," I said. The wrongness thickened. The lights were off and I couldn't see him and I was fine with that. "What's wrong with you, man?"

"I'm all fucked up, Mickey." He wheezed and drew a labored breath.

I listened.

"Bob let me stay down here. He told me last week mom had my funeral. I told Bob to call you and say you were my dad to get you out here. It was shitty, I know."

I wanted to put my hands up and say *what in the fuck are you talking about*, but instead I said, "Yeah, that was shitty." I huffed a dry chuckle that was neither real nor funny. "But, I'm here now. You've gotta tell me what's wrong."

"I'm dead, Mick."

Cold daggers wedged into my chest. Goose bumps pebbled my arms. "Yeah, Britney told me about the cancer." I cleared my throat, not sure how to ask this next part. "How long you got?"

"No, you don't get it." Harry started rocking. I got the impression that he was crying, yet no sound escaped. "The water killed me over a month ago."

The first thing that popped into my head was, *so are you like a zombie or something*, and then we'd laugh. But to say those words felt inexplicably wrong. My mind kept overlapping itself, fumbling for words, and hoping somehow that this would all end up being something stupid.

"Harry, what the hell? We're both right here. Does this have something to do with the suicide note you left?" My best friend, the guy I'd gone to boot camp with, the guy I'd held one night after he'd gotten drunk and cried over a girl who'd stolen all of his DVD movies. Perhaps the cancer ate his brain and caused confusion.

Bob cleared his throat and asked, "Ya want me to leave?"

"No," I answered, a bit too quickly. I pointed at him. "Wait your ass right there. I'm still trying to figure this out."

The old man shoved his hands into his pockets and gazed at the floor.

I honestly didn't know what the hell I wanted anyone to do. Britney waited upstairs and Harry didn't want to see her for whatever reason. I should send Bob up there to talk to her; otherwise, she'd end up coming down here and I didn't need that shit. I didn't need her freaking out. I had that part covered for the both of us.

My heart raced and pulsed in my temples. I'd forgotten all about my hangover.

"I drank the water. So did Mary." Harry's slobbery voice startled me. It took me a few seconds to remember who Mary was.

"What water?"

"The fountain of youth, that's what it's supposed to be." His voice fell to a whisper, the regret bleeding through.

Fountain of youth? Perhaps going mad preceded death when death was imminent, but those words, *I'm dead* pounded in my head like an incessant drum. "What the fuck are you doing down in this shitty basement?"

He didn't say anything at first, and finally uttered, "I don't want to show you, but I will if I have to."

"Show me what?"

"What I look like."

Something about that scared me worse than anything. He needed doctors, not me. "Why'd you call me out here?"

"I need your help, Mickey."

"With what?" *The note,* my mind whispered, *this is about the note.*

"Mary," Harry said. "This is about Mary. I need you to do something for me."

"Your girlfriend?"

"My wife."

I remembered Britney had told me that. "Can't believe you tied the knot." I expected a chuckle, but nothing came. I wished I hadn't said it.

Harry sucked in a labored breath. "You'd be surprised what you'll do with only a few months left to live." A putrid stench wafted through space. I swallowed back a gag.

"Why didn't you call me when you found out?"

"It's not something you start calling people about." Harry's strained voice seeped through the dank air.

I stepped closer to him, unable to see anything more than his silhouette against what little light sifted through the window behind him.

"I guess." It seemed like the right thing to say. Fuck, I wanted of there.

"You *want* to tell people. I wanted to tell you." Harry's words still sounded slippery. "But I couldn't just call you up and say *hey bro', wanted to let you know I'm dying*. Goddamn, you've got Amy and the girls, I didn't want to burden you with my shit. Plus, you've got a good thing going by staying off the booze."

Hot shame flooded my cheeks. "Yeah, well, I fucked that up last night."

"In my honor?"

"Fuckin' A, it was. Why else would I get drunk here?"

I saw Harry's head shaking. "It wasn't because of what Bob told you, is it? He said he talked to you."

"No, it was at your mom's house last night." I sensed the old man listening.

Harry was quiet for a moment, then he said, "That's where you met Brit?"

"Yeah." I considered clarifying that I'd met her at his funeral, but that didn't seem pertinent.

"You're a dumbass, Mickey."

I know.

I turned to Bob who lingered in the cellar doorway. Time for him to leave. "Could you go up and talk to Britney. Keep her from coming down. Don't tell her he's down here." I flipped a thumb at Harry.

"I'll try." Bob shrugged and shook his head. "Not sure what I'm gonna tell her."

"I wish to fuck she hadn't come," Harry said. "I don't want her in this shit."

Guilt washed over me, but I still wasn't clear on what shit he didn't want her in.

CHAPTER 18

After Bob left, I dug out my cigarettes. Just before lighting one, it occurred to me that Harry had lung cancer. I stepped closer to the open door.

"Will it bother you if I smoke?" I asked.

"Mickey, you idiot."

"Skip the lecture."

Harry was quiet, then said, "Smoking won't bother me. Wish I could have one."

I lit my cigarette and stared at his dark shape, still rocking back and forth. I squinted into the darkness, trying to see some detail. My eyes had adjusted to the dim light and as I stared, faint lines on his chest started to appear. It could have been anything; a pattern on a shirt, something he was holding…

Maybe his ribcage.

I shivered. "Okay, so what the fuck's going on here? And don't give me anymore of this *I'm dead* shit."

Harry rocked in the chair. I glanced away and leaned back against the doorframe.

I shook my head. "Fucking suicide notes. Fake phone calls. Fake funerals," I thought a second, then added, "You sitting in a goddamn old man's basement. What the fuck?"

"Alright," Harry said, "here's what happened."

I took a good drag on my cigarette as Harry began to speak. I thought about Britney upstairs and hoped to God she wasn't able to hear us through the floor.

"I found out I had cancer about eight months ago. It started with pains in my chest, mostly when I was sleeping. The pain got worse and I couldn't sleep worth shit so I decided to get it checked out."

I listened in shocked silence as he told me about his treatments, about how he'd lost all of his hair and that it only grew back in patches. About how sick he'd gotten and that everything he drank or ate tasted like metal while he was on the chemo drugs. About how the cancer spread from his lungs to his throat and to his liver. About visiting a treatment facility in Minnesota called the Mayo Clinic. And about meeting a girl named Mary Prickett.

"It was love at first sight." As he spoke, I sensed a smile curling the corners of his mouth. "She was going through treatment. I spent about every free minute with her. After a few weeks there, my doctor told me that short of a miracle, they couldn't do anything else for me. He told me to go back home and be with my family. It tore Mary up. She had no family to go back to. Her parents had died and she'd been an only child. She'd die at that clinic, alone."

I cleared my throat and asked, "Where was she from?"

"Utah. Can you believe that?"

"Hmm. Never knew anyone from Utah."

"I loved her so much, Mickey. I couldn't leave her there to die alone. We got married. Mom about shit, but she was happy for me. We got back here to Indiana and started doing our treatments over in Lafayette."

I asked, "That when you got that cottage over there?" As the question hung in the air, a strong and sudden memory of the dream I'd had last night flooded my head and I saw Harry and me sitting in Iraq, right outside of Baghdad, just the two of us, gazing out across a desolate landscape while that body laid in front of us.

"No," Harry said, "the cottage came later. After we'd talked to a guy at the Home Hospital in Lafayette about Kate's Lake."

I took one last drag on my cigarette and dropped it to the dirty, concrete floor, then ground it into the cement with my foot. Did I really want to know about this? What's said can't be unsaid and something about that scared me. I shoved my hands into my jeans pocket.

He told me it would heal us.

"The guy's name was Lupis Rudolph," Harry said. "He said he lived out by a town called Black Rock."

Lupis. That's a fucked-up name. Like a disease. I asked, "Black Rock? Is that close to here?"

"Yeah, not too far away… twenty, thirty miles. It's pretty much a deserted ghost town now days. A lot of weird stories about that town. Lupis Rudolph said he was also receiving cancer treatments. Long story short, Lupis asked if we'd ever heard of Kate's Lake. I said *no* and of course Mary had never heard of it. Lupis acted like he was nervous as shit telling us about it."

Harry fell silent and that name rolled over in my head; *Lupis*. "That's it?"

"The rest of this will sound like bullshit, but it's true. Also keep in mind that when you're dying, you'll try about anything. If someone tells you that rubbing honey on your balls will cure cancer, you'll fuckin' try it. Keep that in mind, okay?"

I almost asked if he'd tried rubbing honey on his balls, but decided not to be a smartass. "Sure." I started digging in my pocket again for my smokes and remembered that I'd just smoked one, so I stood there, listening.

"He told us it would heal us."

The deepest chill I'd ever felt in my life settled into the base of my skull, below where my head was perched onto my neck. It crept down between my shoulder blades and then seeped low into my chest.

He told us it would heal us.

Suddenly, this was all too real. I had a plane to catch back to Colorado. If I left right now, I might make it to Indianapolis on time.

Would I go home and pretend like nothing happened? An image of Harry lumbering through the night, shuffling clumsily along deserted highways toward Colorado, scared me and I blinked the image away.

Harry kept going. "Lupis asked if I'd ever heard of the Bottoms and I told him that I'd heard of them, most everyone around here's heard of them, but few people have ever gone there. He told me how to get to Kate's Lake. He said there'd be a cabin back in there for rent and that he'd let us live in it."

I dug out another cigarette. My hands trembled. I asked, "So why didn't this Lupis guy drink the water himself if it heals people?"

"I asked him that too. He said he'd tried it but it didn't always work on everyone. He said it helped him, but didn't *heal* him." Harry tapped his hand on the rocking chair's arm. "I was desperate."

This Lupis fellow sounded toxic to me already. "You didn't purchase the cabin then?" I remembered Britney telling me about the cabin, but I'd heard about it from Bob first.

"Nope, we were just using it. Lupis knew he wouldn't get any money for it if we bought it, we didn't have a lot of time to make payments, ya know. Try getting a fucking loan when you've got cancer, Mickey; the banker has to fight back laughing his ass off in front of you."

"Everyone here thinks you bought the place and killed yourself," I said.

"Lupis said we could stay there for as long as we wanted. But, and here's the part that's gonna sound crazy, he said that Kate's Lake could heal our cancer." Harry stopped talking again and an uncomfortable pause lingered. Then he repeated, quieter this time, "he said it would heal us."

I stared at him. *He said it would heal us.* My arms pebbled as that icy chill bored into me. I said, "Heals everyone but him, I guess."

He chuckled, a hoarse and sickly sound, and then said, "I know. It sounds stupid, but we moved out here. And we drank the water and nothing happened. Mary even laughed about it in a sad sort of way. *We're so silly*, she'd said with a mixed sort of laugh and cry, *believing in this*.

"We ran into Lupis Rudolph again a few days later at the hospital. Mary didn't recognize him, she didn't recognize anyone at that time, sometimes not even me. Lupis asked if we'd drank some of the water and I told him we had. He looked confused and then said that he'd come out to the lake and show us where it's at. Sounds weird, I know. He showed up out here the next day. He took me down this path that's way the fuck back in there. I swear, we walked for miles, hours through the woods and shit. He had to help me with most of it; I wasn't doing so well at that time either." I pictured him stumbling through woods, perhaps wrapped in a blanket, pale and bald, coughing on occasion, and following this stranger. "We ended up at this cave like thing, stuck out in the middle of the woods.

"Lupis told me there were a few places where water got trapped and formed these little pockets that sat for millions of years. There's only a few of those pockets and one of them was right there in that cave. *If you drink this water*, Lupis said, *it'll heal you. Some people have even lived forever*."

I said, "The Fountain of Youth."

"Yeah, the Fountain of Youth, you got it."

I huffed a dark laugh, not because anything was funny, but needing to do something, and said, "Was there a time machine parked next to it? Sitting by a Unicorn?"

"I know, I thought he was full of shit too." Harry didn't laugh.

Knowing what the answer would be, I asked, "So… I guess you drank it?"

"Yep," Harry said. "We did." Harry's voice, that slobbery sounding voice that I'd gotten used to, grew quieter and I had to strain to hear him. I stepped closer. "I filled up two bottles of water," Harry said, "two empty bottles that Lupis Rudolph had with him. He stood there and smoked a cigarette while I filled them. When I got done, he looked at me like he was trying to decide if we should keep going. Then he flipped his cigarette away and took the two bottles I'd filled. *I'll take 'em*, he'd said, *you concentrate on getting back*. Man, I'm telling you Mickey, he seemed nervous as shit. So he carried the two water bottles and I followed, once again climbing over rocks and fallen trees as we made our way back through the woods towards Kate's Lake.

"When we got back to the cabin, he went inside with me. I noticed he was sweating like crazy. His hands had even started shaking. *Take a few chugs of this stuff*, that's what he said. *It'll take right care of ya*. And so we did, right there in that cabin, Mary and me drank our bottles of water. I had to help Mary with hers – she wasn't able to get out of bed anymore, but she drank it. I remember Lupis looking away when we were done, as if he was ashamed. At the time, I didn't think much of it, but looking back, I can see all of these things. And then he left. He just said his goodbyes and walked out."

I didn't let the pause linger this time. "So what happened?" I knew where this was going and I can't describe my emotions, sort of a jumble of fear, disbelief, and dread all mixed up together like some morbid cocktail.

"Nothing at first. But when I got up the next morning, Mary was up walking around. For the first time in over a month, she was walking around! But something was wrong with her, Mickey. She was pacing back and forth in front of the door. I asked her if she was okay and she didn't answer. Her skin was a bluish color and her hair looked stiff, like she'd slept on it for days. She paced back and forth as if she were late for something."

A small tingle stirred the back of my neck again. I pulled out another cigarette and lit it. I didn't care that I'd just had one; I wouldn't have cared if I'd had a hundred in a row. Harry stopped talking and sat there and I stared at his dark, motionless shape, squatted like a statue in the middle of the room, no longer rocking, no longer doing anything.

"What'd you need me for, Harry?" My hand shook. An ugly weight had formed in my stomach and made me queasy. Bob's note danced in my memory.

"She was dead, Mickey. At some point during the night, she died and then her corpse got up and started pacing in front of that door."

I hated this. I wanted to scream at Harry to stop, to shut the fuck up and stop this silly shit. *He said it would heal us.* "Harry, tell me what you needed me for."

"Maybe it was because she had brain cancer or something," Harry said. "That's why I didn't go crazy and she did. I went over to her and she looked at me, and…"

Stop, Harry. I don't want to hear any more of this.

"…her eyes weren't working right. It's like they'd turned gray or something. But she was staring at me…"

Shut the fuck up, Harry!

"…like I was a complete stranger. Like she hated me. She was insane, Mickey. She'd gone totally insane."

"Alright, that's it man." I wanted out of this basement, away from this place, away from the whole goddamned state. "I don't know what the hell's going on here, but this shit ain't funny."

"I never said it was funny."

"Why'd you want me out here?"

"To kill her, Mickey. I need you to kill her."

I stood there, dumbfounded.

"She's been out there in the woods for about two months," Harry said. "Sometimes she wanders up close to the cabin here. I've seen her looking in windows, it's almost like she remembers something, like she's looking for something, but then she always runs off when I try to approach."

"You're fuckin' crazy, dude." Nausea swept over me. "I don't know what this is all about, but it ain't funny." I don't know why I kept saying that.

Harry continued like he hadn't heard me. "Bob's too old to hunt her down. He shot at her a couple times when she was close to the cabin, but he's half blind. I still love her, but I know it's not her out there. I've heard what she's done and I know she'd never hurt anyone. It's whatever that damned water did to her."

"I'm gettin' the hell out of here." My stomach roiled. I flipped my cigarette to the floor, watched it impact with little flickers of sparks, and stomped it out.

"I also want you to bring me Lupis Rudolph."

I stopped for a moment, not sure why, and gazed at his dark shape. I knew that if I turned on a light, his skin would be a rotting gray with deep blue veins streaking the surface and dead eyes staring out at me, accusing me, begging me.

"And then I want you to kill me, Mickey. Before I end up like Mary. I don't want to go crazy, but I don't think I can stop it. I don't want to be like that. She killed someone last week, a camper not too far from here."

I faintly remembered Britney saying something about a camper who'd died a week or so ago. I couldn't recall everything she'd said about it.

"I'm sorry, Harry," I said and I truly was. "I gotta go."

"Mick!" His snot-filled words slurped out. "I need you. You're the only one I know who's killed someone."

I blinked. Shock settled over me. *How dare he... of all people, how dare he!*

"Goddamn you!" I hissed and pointed a rigid finger at him. "Go fuck yourself." I spat the words. He of all people knew better than to bring that up.

I headed for the stairs, half expecting to hear his wet voice calling after me, but it didn't. I clambered up the steps, bursting out of the darkness and into the lancing sunlight where the world spun. Blackness closed in on me; my vision shrank. Too much shit to deal with and I was dehydrated, I had a hang-over, I'd smoked too much.

I was passing out.

CHAPTER 19

I trembled next to the cellar steps, bent over and gasping as if having an asthma attack. *Don't pass out, goddamn it, don't you do it.* Harry's corpse was sitting down in that cellar and his dead wife was out here gallivanting around like some sort of zombie; according to Harry. I stayed put for a few minutes. The stagnate lake-water stunk stronger than ever and I wanted to gag. Kate's Lake smelled like something rotten.

Get it together. I sucked in a deep breath and steadied myself. He had no right, *no goddamn right*, to bring that shit up. He'd gotten me through the hell I'd endured after I'd killed that guy. I wanted to hate him for mentioning it.

The light-headedness finally passed and I stood up, felt okay, and then marched straight to Bob's back door. I had to get Britney. I had to keep it cool. So much I had to do. Did I really buy all of this shit?

I pushed through the door, harder than I meant to, and found Bob and Britney sitting at that small table in the kitchen. Britney's eyes narrowed when she saw me. What a mess I must have looked like to her. *Harry's right below you.* Sort of. It's part Harry. But also, part something else. Ghost? Zombie?

Fucking madness.

"We gotta go," I said.

She glanced at Bob, as if to confirm that it was alright to do what I said. He shrugged.

Get it together, Mick.

I moved around the table on legs full of concrete. "We need to get out of here." I reached out to touch her shoulder. My hand was shaking.

She looked at me. "What's wrong?"

"I'll tell you when we're out of here."

Bob stared at the floor and rapped his fingers against the table.

Britney got up and I grabbed her arm briskly enough so that she knew I wasn't playing around. We were leaving.

"What the hell?" She asked.

I led her out the door and we were stomping back down the path towards the car within a few seconds. I kept stealing glances over my shoulder. No one was following us.

Safely out of earshot, I said, "I'll tell you about it once we're in the car and driving away from here."

"What's wrong?" She sounded as frightened as I was, but who could blame her with me acting like I'd just seen a ghost. Shit, I guess I had.

Every little sound, the snapping of twigs or the rustle of leaves, nearly sent me into a screaming fit. Did I accept what Harry had told me? My God, I did.

Mary has been out here for two months. She killed a camper last week.

She might be watching us right now. Slinking through the weeds. Hiding.

"That was the freakiest shit I've ever seen," I said more to myself than to Britney. I rubbed my palms against the sides of my pants, as if I had bugs crawling on them. My heart slammed and I tried to calm down. A person's heart wasn't meant to beat that hard for very long. How long before it exploded and down I fell, deader than a hammer?

"Mick?" Britney's voice seemed distant, like an echo. She was trotting to keep up with me. I kept my eyes trained on the path ahead of us. We had to get to the car. How far was the damn car, anyway? All I saw were goddamn trees and bushes, and goddamn weeds. And I kept hearing weeds rustle, like something following us.

"Mick!" She grabbed my arm and planted her feet. "Stop!"

I whirled.

My expression must have been terrible, because she recoiled. "What did you see back there?"

I stared at her. I didn't want to tell her anything until we were safely in the car, and even then, I wasn't sure if I'd tell her the truth. "You don't wanna know."

"It was Harry, wasn't it?" Desperation clouded her face.

"Can we please talk about this when we're out of here?" I'm pretty sure I hissed those words more than spoke them.

"If it was Harry, I want to go back. I'll go back by myself if I have to." She folded her arms.

Is that the way it was now? She was tough, I had to give her that, and her marriage to an asshole had made her even tougher, but I didn't need this shit. I didn't want her out here by herself.

Not with Mary out here.

I said, "We need to go up and wait for that cop."

"Goddamn it, was Harry back there?" Her question was so simple, so pure, and it was hard not to spill everything to her. She had that way about her. She made you *want* to talk to her.

"Harry's dead." Even if she hated me after this, at least she'd be safe. For Harry.

Her face crumpled and I thought she might cry, but she didn't. "Then tell me what's wrong?"

"Something Bob showed me. The whole reason he'd been trying to find me."

"What was it?"

"I'll tell you on *the way* to the car. Is that cool?"

She stepped forward and said, "You'd better."

I stole a glance over my shoulder again. Still no one was following us. "He showed me something Harry left in his cabin," I needed to sound convincing if I was going to pull off this lie. "Something Harry said only I could see."

"Only *you* could see?" She sensed the bullshit in it. Her pace slowed.

"Yeah. It was something from our old Marine Corps days. Something he brought back from Iraq that he wanted me to have." *Good one, Mick.*

Britney said, "All this so he could give you something from Iraq? The note, the fake call from my dad, that old guy sneaking to your motel room at three in the morning... you're telling me it was all to give you something from Iraq?" She sounded as if I'd insulted her. And maybe I had. I dug out a cigarette and lit it as she spoke. "This doesn't make sense."

"I said I'd tell you in the car."

"Did you talk to Harry?"

Damn, she was persistent. "I'll tell you in the goddamn car."

I hated talking to her that way, but we had to keep moving, to get out of there, and if we didn't, we risked a lot more than being mad at each other. My headache slammed back full force, throbbing. I needed a damn drink. Come to think of it, I needed a lot of drinks.

Amy, where are you? I needed her so bad right now.

"You look pale," Britney said. "I wish you'd talk to me."

I almost said, *wish in one hand and shit in the other and see which one fills up first.* But I didn't. However, the fact that I even thought of saying it made me want to scream. It was more evidence of a person I once was, of a person I abandoned and swore never to resurrect.

She said in a sulking voice, "I have as much right to know what's going on as you."

Really? Did someone call you and fake to be your dad? Did an old man show up at your door acting like a loon? Did you *talk to a goddamn corpse?*

Nope, none of that happened to her.

He told us it would heal us. I want you to kill Mary.

"I know you do." I sucked a deep drag on my cigarette.

I want you to kill me, before I end up like Mary. And bring me Lupis Rudolph. That rotting stench that had infested the cramped space below Bob's cabin lingered in my nose like the nauseating memory of something puked up. Yellow paint glinted through the thick brush not far up ahead. A few hundred yards. My car! We were almost there.

Britney stopped and screamed at me. "What did you *see*?"

"Goddamn it, if you really wanna know... I saw Harry!"

We stood there, facing each other along that weed infested path as insects hummed a crazy background chorus.

"You saw him?" She choked the words. Her mouth fell open and I wished I hadn't said it. The car was *right* there.

"Britney," I had no idea how to tell her what I'd seen, or even if I should. "He was..."

Her phone chirped in her purse and at first, she didn't move and only stared at me. Finally, she dug it out and looked at the face. "It's Wayne." Wayne the deputy. She placed a hand to her forehead and I wondered if she might not throw the phone at me.

She shook her head, then tapped the face and slapped the phone to her ear.

Thank God. Get someone back here besides us, someone who has a big gun… big enough to blow a hole through concrete. I kept scanning the woods for any sign of a woman who might be lurking about, leering at us with wild eyes. *Gray eyes, remember?* Hunting us.

Either that, or I was going batshit crazy, which wasn't totally out of the question either. Would I know if I was?

"We're back here where the road ends to get to Kate's Lake," Britney spoke into the phone. "No, well, we decided to check the place out." She placed one of her hands on her hip. "Yeah, but you didn't know how long you'd be and we didn't feel like sitting along the road for hours. Mick has a plane to catch."

Sounded like Deputy Wayne was giving Britney the third degree for disobeying his orders. What kind of stupid name is Wayne, anyway? Fuckin' Wayne.

"We can't," Britney said. "You need to come back here. We found something."

I should've kept my mouth shut. The sense that I'd somehow betrayed Harry crept into my chest like a hairy spider. I was the only one on this God-forsaken earth that he trusted. He'd come to me for help. *Nice one, Mick.*

"Wayne, I…" Britney tapped her foot and her lips straightened to a thin line.

She listened for a moment, then said, "We'll come out, but I wanna talk to Sheriff Snider. Today!" She tapped the screen, shoved the phone in her purse, and then put a hand over her mouth. She stood rigid, like I'd seen Amy do when she was about to lose it.

"What'd he say?" I asked.

She stared at the road for a long second, then blurted, "He said to get out of here, that he'd meet us up at the gate." Her voice quivered.

"Is he up there now?"

"Yeah."

"Why won't he come down here?" I doubted she knew. I'd bet she wondered the same thing.

"I don't know. He said to meet him up on the road." She swiped a tear away.

I put my arm around her shoulders and pulled her close, pushing her along toward the car. She was stiffer than before. I thought she'd yank away, and even the words *get your hands off me* wouldn't have been misplaced.

"Where did you see him?" She asked.

A branch snapped in the bushes behind me and I whirled, gasping. Nothing but leaves and a wall of deep green. My eyes darted to every shadowed crevice, but I saw nothing.

I spoke without looking at her. "He was in Bob's cellar."

She looked at me and said, "What?"

"He wasn't right, Britney. He's sick." *Jesus,* why couldn't we keep walking?

He told us it would heal us, Mickey. I want you to kill Mary.

"I know he's sick," she said, "I've known it longer than you."

"Yeah, but I mean this is a different kind of sick. He was pissed that I'd brought you."

She didn't answer on that one, but she did start walking, thank Jesus!

"I swear to God, I'll tell you everything on the drive. We need to go."

"Why?"

How do I tell her a dead woman might come shrieking out of the woods? "You remember the note Bob gave me yesterday?"

"About the girl?"

"Yeah."

We reached the car and didn't waste any time climbing inside. I hopped back into the passenger seat, I suppose because that's where I'd ridden on the way out here, and she got in behind the wheel. I clicked the door-locks shut and instantly felt ten pounds lighter with that reassuring *clunk*. Silence inside with only my gasping. I licked my lips as she leered at me. "I'm okay," I said, not sure what else to say. *Calm the fuck down.* My head throbbed.

She started the car. That wonderful purr. We backed slowly down the narrow brick road. From the looks of things, we'd be backing up a while before we could turn around. *I should've drove.*

"Tell me about the note." Britney concentrated on navigating the car backwards down that shabby little road.

"Yeah. It was about Harry's wife."

I decided to give her the whole story and take my chances. "Harry found a place where he thought the water heals sicknesses and stuff. Don't ask me how or why, because I don't have a damn clue. I only know some guy named Lupis Rudolph showed him where it was at. It's way back behind Kate's Lake. He drank some of it and so did Mary. That's why he's alive and that's why his wife is alive." I wondered if my words sounded as ridiculous to Britney as they did to me.

"Mick, if he's back there and he's alive, I want to go…"

I wish she hadn't come, Harry had said.

Me too, bro.

"Wait, wait, wait… let me finish. The water didn't actually heal them. It made them worse."

Her eyebrows scrunched. "What? How can you get worse than cancer? You said you talked to him."

"I did, but he's worse than he was when he was sick." I licked my lips. Dangerous territory here. God, I wish I had a drink. This shit sounded so damned crazy. I thought of Harry sitting in that basement, stinking. Rotting.

"I don't know why you won't just tell me what happened." She was twisted around, one hand on the steering wheel, and gazing out the back window as she drove. I couldn't help noticing her shirt stretched tight against her breasts, her stomach flat. God, who thinks of shit like that at a time like this? I peeled my eyes away.

"I'm trying," I said and meant it. I was trying and admittedly feeling better the farther we got from that cabin. "The water made him sicker, it made both of them sicker, but in a different way." I fought for a way to explain it. *It's like they're zombies or something.* I didn't want her thinking I was crazy, though that moment may have passed long ago. "It's so goddamn hard to describe it. It's like making their bodies rot or something."

She reversed the car into a grassy swath along the side of the road and then leaned her head against the steering wheel. Her body trembled and her faint sobs made me feel terrible. I lifted my hand to pat her shoulder and tell her we'd get this figured out.

But my phone started ringing.

Perfect timing. I dug it out of my pants pocket and looked at the face. It was Amy. I considered answering, but couldn't do that with Britney sitting in here crying. I considered stepping outside and answering it, but a quick thought of Mary fixed that. I'd call her back later. I recalled the tone of our conversation this morning. *Have you been smoking*, she'd asked.

I sure as hell wasn't in the mood to get into that whole discussion. I stuffed the phone back into my pocket and waited awkwardly until it stopped ringing. I scanned the surrounding woods, keeping an eye out; wondering what might be out there watching us. Could Mary break a car window? Surely not. But what if she could?

I shivered. We needed to go.

"Look." I shook my head; then licked my lips. "I had no idea it was going to go this way. I swear to God. I wouldn't have done it like this on purpose."

"You're so full of shit!" The sudden anger hit me like a brick and I'm pretty sure my expression showed it.

"Who is?"

"You are." She turned to me, her eyes red and swollen, her cheeks soaked. "He's my brother and you tell me some f…friggin' (*the fortitude to drop the f-bomb wasn't in her*) story about water making them worse."

"I know how it sounds, but I swear it."

"So that's why I had to stay upstairs with Bob, like some little kid. You know how stupid I felt?"

It was Bob and Harry who didn't want her down in the cellar, not me. I turned back toward the windshield and glared out. "Let's just go up and tell that deputy what happened. Can we do that?" Anything to get her to put her foot on the gas and get us the hell out of here.

She slammed the car into gear and stomped on the gas, slinging gravel behind us. It clinked off the undercarriage. I scanned the woods as she drove. The car bumped and heaved on the old, brick road.

And then she hit the brakes, hard. We both yanked forward and stared straight ahead.

That man I'd seen earlier, one of the *Bottoms-dwellers*, stood in the road. Only now he looked taller. Larger. Meaner. His mossy beard drooped from his face like a clump of wasps. Stained overalls clung to his body, perhaps too tight, over a faded flannel shirt.

So much hair. Eyebrows, beard, mustache. Eyes, only black pits beneath all that mess, peered out at us. One of his hands curled into a fist. Goosebumps broke out across my arms and my heart fluttered. My best punch may only prompt a smile from this guy.

Britney said weakly, "Oh, that's just great." Her voice warbled.

"What the hell's he want?" I swallowed against a dry throat. The man towered in the middle of the road, like some ancient, horrible monument.

She shrugged and clamped the wheel. "He doesn't want us to leave."

I thought, *Harry never left.*

Then I noticed another person, not as big as the bearded guy, but just as ugly, lingering farther back behind this man, standing off to the side of the road, also staring at us. He wore a ball cap, filthy clothes, and had his hands stuffed into his pockets.

"I think you're right," I told Britney.

Neither of them moved. She gripped the wheel tighter and muttered, "It's like they're waiting for something."

I swore she was about to punch the gas pedal and plow that big bastard over. I clenched my teeth and braced my hand on the dashboard.

But she rolled down her window and yelled, "We called the police. They're up there at that front gate." I let out a breath I didn't know I was holding.

Her voice sounded small and I thought, *there's no way they heard that.* But to my surprise, the bearded monster in the road looked back at the skinny ball-cap wearing guy who nodded; then he turned back to us. At first, I thought he might charge us like some mutant, two-legged bull, but instead he stepped slowly off to the side of the brick road.

Britney rolled up her window and I noticed her hands were trembling. She said, "He's letting us pass."

She eased the car forward and as we passed that big sonofabitch, he stared at us. I never saw his shadowed eyes. Only those black holes under all that hair. I swore he could've reached out and flipped our car right over.

I told Britney, "I hope I never see that fucker again." I didn't care how sissy I sounded. I meant every word of it.

She sped up and I watched the skinny guy gawk at us. He wasn't so scary. At least, not at that time, he wasn't. As we left them behind us, I wondered if they knew Harry. Did they know what was happening back in there? I'll bet they did. Might explain why they were acting so damned weird. I wished my head wasn't throbbing so bad.

"Jesus Christ." I turned and faced ahead. "Remind me to never visit the Bottoms again."

She kept glancing in her rear-view mirror as if they might be chasing after us. I knew the feeling.

But they didn't. They stayed put.

Once they were out of sight, she asked. "So what'd Harry say?"

I took a deep breath, surprised she didn't want to talk more about those two weirdos. *This is her brother, remember?* Yeah, don't forget that. "He told me about how he'd found out about having cancer, about how he'd met Mary. About how their treatments had gone and how they'd gotten married. He told me about Kate's Lake and how he found out about it." I checked my mirror again, then looked over at her and said, "that's how I found out about Lupis Rudolph."

"I've never heard of him."

"Harry wasn't too happy with him."

"Weird," Britney said.

"He told me about how bad Mary had gotten. He also told me about how his chest had started to feel like a deflating plastic bag." I thought for a moment as we drove slowly over the rough road. "I didn't know any of this before now. I would have come out here, Britney. I swear I would have come out here to be with him."

Her stern expression softened, ever so slightly. "Why doesn't he want to see me?" Fair question.

"It's not that he doesn't want to see you." I clasped my hands together. "It's that he doesn't want you to see him."

She glanced over at me, her tear-flooded eyes finding mine. In that moment, she *did* believe me and in seeing that total trust in her face, the wounds between us started to heal.

CHAPTER 20

Wayne Tillwood his name was. About two inches shorter than me. Britney's eyes were still red from crying when we got out of the Bottoms and when Deputy Wayne saw that, the asshole had the audacity to glare at me while asking her if she was okay.

Wayne leaned against the trunk of his cruiser and we were leaned against the grill of my rental car. He faced us like a teacher scolding naughty children. I crossed my arms and felt relief at finally being out of those woods. I glanced back to make sure neither of those crazy looking guys were following us.

Wayne's eyes narrowed and he nodded toward me. "Did he hurt you?"

"No, Wayne," Britney shook her head and launched into explaining what happened. I debated on how I'd tell my part, on how I'd articulate what I'd seen in that cellar and what Harry had told me.

Don't get me wrong, I was damned happy to see a cop with a big gun on his hip. But the little bastard irritated me. I didn't see Deputy Wayne Tillwood believing a word I said. Of course, he'd believe Britney. He'd believe Britney if she told him that she'd farted and a goddamned genie popped out her ass.

Britney waved a hand at me and said, "Tell him, Mick. You're the one who saw him."

My mouth opened, but nothing came out. I wasn't ready for her to do that.

Wayne peered at me and asked, "Did you actually see Harry?"

I nodded. "I saw him. In the basement of that cottage. He's real sick. That guy, Bob, took us back there."

"Uh-huh," Wayne shifted his hands to his hips. "He's back there right now down in a cellar?"

"He's there," I said. Guilt washed over me. *I'm sorry, Harry.*

Wayne's mouth contorted and his eyebrows furrowed. "And there's a crazy woman in the woods who might be dangerous?"

More than crazy, I thought, but to keep the conversation from spiraling into something unbelievable, I said, "Yep."

Britney said, "You need to get Sheriff Snider out here, Wayne. It's dangerous. Two of those people that live in the Bottoms tried to keep us from leaving. They stood in the road!"

Wayne shrugged. "It's private property, Brit. Maybe they were wondering what you were doing."

"That brick road is private property?" I had no idea.

Wayne shook his head like I'd asked the dumbest question on earth. "You two had no business being down there. It's why that gate's there with the No Trespassing sign on it." He pointed at that rusty gate that probably hadn't been closed in over a decade. The placard with the red-painted NO TRESSPASSING hung crooked from a post next to it.

"Will you call the sheriff?" Britney was adamant. I assumed she must know the sheriff.

"He's over in Black Rock today." Wayne glanced at the two of us; then his eyes darted to the shadowed road leading into the Bottoms. "Tell you what, you two head back to Gainesville. I'll go down and check it out and let you know what I find. That work?"

She didn't answer and stood with her arms folded tapping her foot – a pissed off look if I'd ever seen one.

"I'll swing by your mom's and let you know what I found," Wayne said, speaking to Britney. I wasn't sure what I felt right then. I imagined Wayne going down those cellar steps, the rotting stench growing thicker, and finding Harry in that rocking chair.

A tense silence hung between them and finally she looked at me and said, "C'mon, Mick, let's get out of here." She turned back to Wayne and said, "You'd better tell me what you find. Call me."

He nodded. "I'll call as soon as I'm out of the Bottoms. I promise."

"You better."

She started to walk away and Wayne said to her, "Oh, one other thing."

"What?"

"Jesse might be over at your mom's house waiting on you. Someone told me he was in town looking for you." Wayne glanced away and added, "Didn't want you to get blind-sided. I can go with you, if you want."

She twisted away from him and marched back to the car. I did the same, but I shot Wayne a parting glance before I got in… the best *fuck you* look in my arsenal.

He glared at me, his eyes contemptuous and mean. 'Ole Wayne hated me.

Our drive back to Gainesville was filled with awkward silences and spurts of brief conversation. My mind drifted as I gazed out the window. How had things gotten so jacked up in the past 24 hours?

As we neared Gainesville, I blurted, "I'm gonna head to the airport after we drop you at your mom's."

She didn't seem surprised, but her words harbored an edge. "I figured. Doesn't your flight leave this afternoon?"

"Yeah. I'll have to bust ass to make it." The chances of making that flight were next to none. It departed in less than two hours. The drive alone was over an hour, if I remembered right. But at least I'd be there. Away from here.

Silence dangled between us.

To hell with Harry. This wasn't my business. I had a wife. Kids. How dare he bring me into this!

How dare he bring up the past the way he did! A past he helped me bury.

Britney and I made small talk on the last portion of the drive. *I hope you'll be okay, call me and let me know what happens*, shit like that. I apologized for leaving as we pulled into her mom's driveway. A beat-up Ford pickup truck, one I'd never seen before, was parked along the curb.

"It's Jesse's," she said flatly.

As we got out and stood in front of my car, another tear slipped down her cheek. God, I was leaving her in an awful mess. My girl from the photograph. The girl I was promised.

"Swear to me you won't go back there," I said. Her eyes darted around me.

"I won't."

"I mean it."

"Just go, Mick. This isn't your problem."

I wasn't sure if that was true or not, but I needed to go. Her ex-husband was in there and I didn't want to get involved in that shit. But leaving her here made me feel like I was doing something wrong.

My head hurt worse than ever. I needed to eat. My own guilt sprang to life and was eating away my insides.

So many things I could've said, but I said none of them. I turned and hurried to my car. I pulled out and left her standing there. I swiped my own tears away as she disappeared in my rearview mirror.

. . . . .

As I drove to the airport, I thought about her. I wondered what Deputy Wayne Tillwood had found. I said out loud, "Fuck that guy" because I didn't like him. Now I was talking to myself.

I'd also stopped and picked up a pack of smokes and a travel bottle of Jack Daniels, one of those tiny ones that didn't make that big of a difference. I needed something for my headache and to relax. I get that I shouldn't, but damn it, after what I'd been through today, I needed it to get my head straight. I drank the whiskey all in one chug.

You're messing up bad, Mickey, the voice of my AA Counselor thrummed in my skull.

"You don't know shit." I spoke out loud.

I needed to call Amy back. I had some explaining to do for staying an extra day. *You see,* I might tell her, *I got caught up in the whole funeral thing, I mean this is Harry we're talking about, darlin'. It was harder than I thought to show up and watch him get buried; then leave.*

That didn't sound bad. It was impenetrable, unarguable, rock-solid, and it was the God's honest truth - no woman alive could be pissed at a man with emotions that deep.

Except for Amy. She'd see through that lovey-dovey talk like rice-paper. I decided right then that this was an ass-chewing I didn't want. I'd text her from the airport – at least then she'd know I was on my way.

I thought about Harry. The image of him sitting in that dark room stuck in my head. That rancid odor, so thick I could chew it, baked into my brain forever.

Britney was probably home, or at least at her mom's house, arguing with her ex-husband. What would Harry have thought if I'd told him that his little sister's ex-husband was in town looking for her?

Or that I'd left her there, alone.

"I could always ask him," I said, referring to Harry, my words absorbing lifelessly into the cloth seats of the rental car. "He's sittin' down in the Bottoms right now." And for the life of me, God knows nothing was funny, I started laughing. I mean loud, screaming guffaws and as the sound echoed within the small space, it scared me. It was the sound of someone going mad.

I passed a blue sign with white letters that read: REST STOP 1 MILE. I had to get this car off the road. My screaming laughter morphed into a terrible, strangled sound, like someone who'd opened their closet door only to find that sometime during the night, they'd hung their children in there.

Harry wasn't the boogeyman. *But he's afraid of becoming one, that's why he wants you to kill him.* Because Mary is one already. Because they drank the water. The water makes you the boogeyman.

I wished he hadn't brought up what I did in Iraq, though. *That was unfair, Harry… bad form.* Anything but that. The faint odor of Iraq's dusty sand and burnt gunpowder swirled in the car and I clenched my teeth. *No, no, no!*

My hands trembled and I gripped the steering wheel. I felt fuzzy, disconnected, and my vision darkened around the edges, like I'd suddenly entered a tunnel. *Jesus*, I was passing out! I jammed my forefinger into my mouth and bit down, hard. Blessed pain. I had to get this car off the road right now.

I swung onto the rest-stop exit ramp. Picnic tables, trees, and a decent sized building stretched out across a well-maintained yard. Other than two semis parked in the parking lot, I was the only one here. Thank God for small favors.

I nosed the car into a parking slot and shut it off. The silence pressed into my temples and my thudding heart throbbed in my ears. I gazed out across the lawn and saw secluded picnic tables down in the trees. *This is a nice rest area.* I wanted to be down there, perched on one of the tables, drinking in the fresh air.

I opened the car door and stumbled out onto the pavement. At least I no longer felt that I was going to crash to the ground. I slammed the door shut and strolled across the grass to the furthest picnic table sitting out there.

I dug out the half-empty pack of cigarettes I'd bought earlier. *Did I already smoke half a pack?* My hands shook so badly that I was worried. I'd never shaken like this, not even in combat. Uncontrollable. Even the whiskey didn't help. I needed more. Those little airplane bottles don't hold a lot.

At least my fingers did what I wanted them to do, which was to light my cigarette. Amy's accusing glare haunted me, as if she were lurking in the weeds surrounding this place.

An image of one of my old drill instructors, now twelve years into my past, popped into my head. He stared at me, right up in my face, his lips snarled with that wide-brimmed hat pulled so low that I could barely see his eyes. Harry had hated him even more than I had.

Mickey Dickey, Sergeant Higgins growled into my face, the smell of coffee thick on his breath. *Do you want your mommy, Dickey?*

"Get out of my head, you piece of shit." I leaned against the picnic table holding the cigarette tucked between my fingers.

But he wouldn't leave. *You're pathetic, you know that Dickey? Mommy's not here, Dickey?*

"Kiss my ass!" I took a drag on my cigarette. I tried to get his ugly face out of my head.

The only thing I thought of was that goddamned morning prayer music that played every fucking day in Iraq.

Mickey Dickey, Sergeant Higgins was back like an old rubber boot that wouldn't get lost, *you ain't tough enough to handle me, so what the fuck are you gonna do now, boy? Crawl off into the woods and cry yourself to sleep, you little bitch?*

"Fuck you," I said. Thank God I was alone. At least, I'm pretty sure I was. I laid back on the surface of the table and stared straight up at a cloudless blue sky. Sergeant Higgins disappeared, his voice gone, his image in my head fading like that of a forgotten dream. Had he ever been here? Maybe, in the midst of my panic, I'd simply imagined it.

Or he'd saved me. Memories were weird like that.

I exhaled smoke into the air where it drifted above me like an apparition. It was shockingly comfortable lying on top of this picnic table. I could stay here for hours, days.

Harry. Holy Christ, Harry. My friend sitting in a cellar out in the woods next to Kate's Lake. That deputy likely shit himself when he found him in that cellar. I'm sure Harry hated me now. *I'm sorry, bro.*

My cigarette was almost finished. I'd call Amy as soon as I was done smoking it. I'd tell her everything, damn it all to hell if she didn't buy it, she didn't have to. I was the screw up here, not her. I deserved her wrath and whatever followed. Her words from before I'd left danced in my head, *I'm not doing this again, Mick.*

I'm sorry, baby.

And Britney, her pretty face etched forever in my memory. My girl from the photograph. A stranger, but yet, not a stranger. She probably hated me now too. I hoped she didn't. I should have stayed and helped her work things out. Best to call her right now, wasn't it?

Lying there, I couldn't recall one person who had a reason to like me. Not one.

My girls. Maybe.

An old voice popped into my head. One I hadn't heard in years. The voice of a man I loathed, but who also made a lot of goddamned sense sometimes. A man from my childhood, who my dad adored, and who was perpetually drunk with dirty hair and a scruffy beard. A man who scarred me.

A man named Chuck Verhey.

He whispered, *Amy hasn't scooted over next to you for years, little man, and when was the last time you laughed together, when was the last time she acted like she wanted to be with you versus just* obligated *to you? You're her pet, her project.*

"There's some truth in that," I said. Honestly, I was thinking of Britney when I said it. How shitty is that?

I wished I'd bought two of those small bottles of whiskey.

Amy was the good woman, the savior, the one who *stuck with me*. And what was I? I was the drunk, the loser, the one who would be lost if Amy had not *stuck with me*. As long as the little puppy doesn't keep shitting on the floor, we'll keep him.

Call Amy right now! *You know that ain't the way it is, you know it!*

That was when my phone rang.

I looked down at the face - 765 area code; that was here in Indiana. What if it was Bob again? Or Harry?

I tapped the green answer button, deciding to take my chances, and said, "Hello?"

"Mick? It's Britney."

I let out an anxious breath and said, "Hey Britney." I wanted to say something else, but nothing impressive came to mind. *I was thinking of you* seemed a bit pretentious.

"Did you leave?" she asked.

I hesitated, then said, "Yeah, I'm headed back."

She paused and gave me just enough time to feel like shit.

"I figured you would. I don't blame you." She sounded weak, defeated.

"What'd the deputy say?" I was curious as hell to hear what they'd found.

"He said he didn't find anything," Britney said. My eyebrows furrowed.

My hand crept to my chin. "Did he go back to Bob's cabin? Did he look in the cellar?" There's no damned way he could've missed it. The smell alone could gag a maggot.

"He said he did." Britney sniffled. "He even said he looked in the other cabin too. He said there was no evidence at all that Harry was back there."

I remembered the expression on the deputy's face when I'd told him that I'd seen Harry, how he'd put his hands on his hips, and looked at me in that *you're-full-of-shit* way.

I should hang up the phone right now, jump in my car, and keep driving to the airport. No harm, no foul. Sure, I'd given this number to Britney and told her to call if she needed anything, but she'd stop calling, eventually, if I never answered it.

Or, I could do what I wanted to do, what duty *compelled* me to do.

I sat up on the picnic table and let my feet dangle over the end. "Are you alright? I mean seriously, are you okay?"

"No, Mick, I'm not okay. My brother is out there. I believe you about that. My ex-husband was drunk when I got back here. He threatened to kill me. Can you believe that?"

A surge of red anger ripped through me and I stood up instantly, my adrenaline kicking in, my head clearing in a snap. "He what?"

"He threatened to kill me. He's never done that before. Never. He said he'd gut me if I kept screwing around. *Gut* me. Who says that to someone?"

"What a piece of shit." I paced. *That motherfucker.*

"My mom called the police and they took Jesse to jail and everything, but he's still here in town."

"At least he's in jail." My anger blossomed into white rage. I'm not sure I was helping her much. "How long will they keep him there?" I hoped she'd say forever.

"Wayne said overnight at the most, but more likely only a couple of hours since it's my word against his and he didn't actually do anything." Britney coughed, and then said, "I wish they'd haul his ass out of here, send him back over to Waynetown where he's from."

Waynetown's not that far away, I thought, but kept my mouth shut. I'd gone through there. Apparently to people in Indiana, Waynetown was far enough. 'Ole Wayne from Waynetown. Hard not to chuckle about that. If I hadn't been so mad, I would have. "Yeah. You good for tonight?"

"Oh, yeah. I'm gonna stay here at Mom's. I'd rather be here than in Indy by myself."

"Cool." A strange silence settled between us. Silence that said she'd called me for something else but didn't want to bring it up. "Something else wrong?"

After a short hesitation, she said, "I'm going out there to find him."

"Going where?"

"To Kate's Lake. I have to find him, Mick. I can't sit here knowing that he's out there."

"Please stay out of there." I gripped the phone. "Let the police handle it."

"They're not going to *handle* it." She spoke louder. "I doubt Wayne even drove all the way down in there. People here think he's dead. His funeral was yesterday!"

She had a point. No one was out looking for Harry anymore. But for her to go tromping off into the woods seemed absurd. By herself. With crazy people in the Bottoms. With Mary out there.

"We talked about this, goddamn it." I shifted the phone to the other ear. "Stay out of there; it isn't safe for you to go back there."

"I have to."

"Britney, c'mon." Desperation crept into my words and my heart wrenched because I had to admit I had feelings for her. I always have.

Ever since Harry handed me her picture in Iraq with unfulfilled promises.

"Thanks for everything, Mick." She paused and I fought frantically for something to say, something that would change her mind. "I'm glad I met you," she said and hung up.

She hung up.

And there I stood. I thought of hitting re-dial but only two things could come out of doing that: she'd either not answer, or she *would* answer and I'd be no closer to Indianapolis. For a second, I wanted to throw the phone; just throw it against one of these trees and watch it shatter to pieces.

My phone rang again and Amy's name and picture splashed the face. I stared at it, as if I'd never seen anything like it before.

Keep her safe, Mickey.

PART II
ALWAYS FAITHFUL

CHAPTER 21

When I was a kid, my dad hung around with this guy named Chuck Verhey. I hated that bastard and I hated my dad for liking him. At ten-years-old, I knew a dipshit when I saw one. Long hair, divorced, and 'ole Chuck got off on making fun of me. He'd drink beer with Dad and the two of them talked about women, talked about work, or whatever.

One time in particular, they'd been outside, sitting in two lawn chairs pulled up by the garage, drinking beer, smoking, and laughing (God knows about what). I walked past them to go get my basketball. No idea how it'd ended up over by them. "*Hey, little man,*" Chuck said. I glanced up at him and said "*Hey*" back, hoping it would end there. It didn't. His slurry words blasted into my ears, "*so are you gettin' any woodies yet, little man?*" Chuck Verhey laughed. Blood rushed into my face. My skin got hot. I knew what a *woody* was. My friends and I had talked about it. Some guys at school told me they'd had one, but for some reason, I had not gotten a *woody* yet. Never once. Herby Smith, who sat beside me at school, said that if you hadn't had a *woody* yet, it meant you were gay, because girls only liked *woodies.* Herby said the size of the *woody* mattered as well. Herby himself claimed to have a six-inch woody. I had no idea why girls would find that impressive, but a deep intuition whispered that Herby was right.

I gawked at Chuck Verhey and he burst out laughing. "*Nope,*" he said, "*you ain't havin' no woodies yet. Don't tell the girls or they'll think you're a faggot or somethin'.*" Goddamn, that's exactly what Herby had said! Herby with the six-inch woody.

The worst part of all, the one thing that sticks in my head like dog shit to a shoe, was my Dad's expression. I wished he'd hit Chuck Verhey right in the mouth. But he didn't. He laughed too. I stared at him, tears flooding my eyes, scared to death that my woody didn't work. My dad saw me; he saw my hurt. And rather than saying something like *okay, Chuck, that's enough*, he sat there. He looked down at the ground when he saw my tears. That's when I realized my Dad was a coward. He was scared of Chuck Verhey. That's part of becoming a man; learning that your old man is only human.

Twenty years later, I wondered what my little girls would think of me for what *I* was doing. I'd be home eventually and I'd apologize profusely for not taking their calls and ignoring their texts, for being gone longer than I said I would, all the usual shit you do when you've screwed someone over that you love. I knew they would still wrap their small arms around my neck, hugging me tight and loving me, happy I arrived home. I knew that because I knew them. But a lingering thought might materialize in their minds, especially in my ten-year-old, that something more important in the world replaced her. The part that realizes people can and will abandon you. The part that remembers when daddy used to drink a lot and when mommy hated him.

That was the devil in me, I'd told her once as she sat on my lap and had asked me why I had to go to the AA classes. *But he's gone now, sweetie. You helped him go away.*

. . . . .

I cried right then, driving down the interstate, heading in the opposite direction of my family and salvation, in the opposite direction of anything good. I cried because even though I tell my kids they are my whole life, even though we have cook-outs and go swimming, and sit at night and read books together, I've lied to them.

My life before them isn't just history… it's a demon lying dormant, waiting until I'm nice and comfy, before it rears its ugly head and says, *okay, Mick my boy, time to pay the piper for shooting that man.*

I thought these things as I drove toward Britney, toward Harry, and that sonofabitch Chuck Verhey was riding with me.

I dialed Britney's number when I was close to Gainesville. She answered on the third ring.

"Hello?"

"Britney." I lit a cigarette. "You got a minute?"

"Mick?"

"Yeah, I need to talk to you."

Pause, then, "Okay?"

"Wait until tomorrow to go out there, I'll go with you." I flicked ashes out the window.

"I thought you left?"

"I'm on my way back."

"Mick…" she remained quiet for a moment, a moment I didn't like, and then said, "there's so much stuff wrong here. You need to go home."

Go home. "I know, but no more bullshitting around. I can't abandon Harry."

Damn right, Harry, Semper Fi, brother. He owed me big time for this one.

She blurted, "I don't want you here." But the sternness didn't touch her words. I sensed relief in her voice.

"Let's talk when I get there," I said. "I'm a little screwed up right now. I don't know what the hell I should be doing, but I shouldn't be running away."

She didn't say anything and that bothered me.

I cleared my throat and said, "Give me about an hour to get there and I'll call you. Don't go out there by yourself."

Finally, she said, "I won't." It sounded like she was smiling when she said it. I pictured her sitting next to me and I smiled. "They also let Jesse out of jail, but he left town. Hopefully he'll stay gone."

Ah yeah, her ex-husband, Jesse. Goddamn, he got out of jail fast. "Jesus, they didn't keep him long."

"Yeah, Wayne was afraid of that. At least he left town. For now."

I said, "Yeah, that's good," then took a drag on my cigarette and added, "Guess I'll be talking to you in a bit."

"Thanks again, Mick."

Saying *no problem* was a stupid way to end the conversation, plus it was a lie. So I just said, "Talk to you in a bit," and hung up.

I was doing the right thing.

CHAPTER 22

Checking back into my motel turned out to be easy since I'd only left two hours earlier. They put me in the same room I'd had before. I dropped my bags on the floor and plopped down on the couch. The steady hum of the air conditioner soothed me and I thought fancifully, *what if I locked the door and shut off my phone? Hide from everyone.*

I needed to relax. I was wound up… another twist of the propeller and *snap*, the rubberband would break like a banjo string. I yawned and realized my buzz was fading, and my head no longer throbbed, thank goodness.

"What the hell did I get myself into here?" I spoke into the silence. My voice tumbled lifelessly into the shadows, absorbed like blood into a cloth.

A caught a glimpse of the shadows in the corner and for a sudden and horrible moment, I pictured Mary standing there, a wild grin spread across her rotting face, her hair matted in filthy clumps, and those eyes…

…she was insane, Mickey…

… peering at me, those murderous eyes.

I sucked in a breath and blinked, my heart hammered.

"Jesus, I need a smoke." I hoisted myself off the couch and rubbed my eyes.

I checked my back pocket, felt my wallet stuffed in there, and walked out the door. Time to hit the gas station and buy more KOOL Superlongs. I needed more smokes; a lot of them. I'd already smoked half a pack and had no intention of slowing down.

. . . . .

The clerk, a guy all of about nineteen-years-old, eyed me suspiciously as I sauntered down the aisle. His glasses reminded me of those old military spectacles with the thick, black frames.

I passed the coolers where cold drinks lined the glass fronts. I opened one of the doors and pulled out a frosty six pack of Coors Lite. *What are you doing, Mickey?* Harry might have said.

"Fuck you, Harry," I muttered as I plopped the six-pack of beer back in the cooler. Instead I grabbed the twelve-pack. If Britney should come over tonight, I wanted to make sure I had enough for the both of us. I sure as hell didn't want to run out. Even with all of the other shit going on, running out of beer could fuck everything up. I pictured it… sitting in my room later, talking with Britney, the conversation going well. Then I go to the little mini-fridge to get a beer and the fridge is empty! And the gas station next to the motel is closed. Nothing killed a party like running out of alcohol.

You're going over the edge, my AA counselor, Skip Jones's voice echoed in my head as I reached into the cooler and slid my fingers through the cardboard handle of another twelve-pack. I watched it happen as if watching a movie. I picked it up and headed toward the counter. *GO PUT IT BACK,* Skip yelled.

You're fine, little man. I hated Chuck Verhey, but just like my Dad, I needed him close.

Go call Skip, my mind screamed, *you can put this stuff back right now. Go call Skip! Better yet, call Amy. She won't leave you if you tell her the truth, if you let it all out.*

Oh Amy, I'm sorry, baby.

This ain't about gettin' woodies and shit anymore, Chuck Verhey's voice slithered into my brain like a bristly worm. My hands resonated with the weight of the beer I so desperately wanted. *You got some serious shit going on out here.*

"That's right." I clanked the two twelve-packs onto the counter. My mouth dried with anticipation. No one understood. *No one ever has, little man,* Chuck Verhey's shit-eating grin stretched across his face. *How many of them have been to war, Mick? Tell me, of all these people judging you for having a few beers, how many of them have been to war?*

Chuck had a damn good point. How many people *really* understood me? Amy, but lately I questioned that too.

I love Amy.

The kid rang up my order. "Throw in a pack of KOOL Superlongs too," I heard myself saying.

"Yep," he said and turned to get them.

Run, Mick. Run now, Skip said.

He said the water would heal us… I didn't want to hear Harry's voice right then. Not at all. But what choice did I have? Hell, everyone else was talking in my head. It was like a goddamn party in there. *I want you to kill her, Mickey. She's insane.*

"Anything else?" The clerk asked.

"Nope, that'll be it."

I watched my hands pay with a credit card. And then I strolled back outside carrying the two twelve packs in large, brown paper sacks. My new pack of smokes lay on top of one of them.

I don't remember the short walk back to my room, I just remember arriving, unlocking the door, kicking it open, setting the bags on the table and tearing into one of the boxes like a child on Christmas morning. My hand wrapped around the cool can, the fizzy pop filled my ears, and then the sparkly liquid spilled down my throat, and I was guzzling.

. . . . .

I'd taken down three before my mind leveled off and relaxed. I sat on the bed, a cigarette dangled from the corner of my mouth. The smoke drifted up into my face, making me squint with one eye. I had a fresh beer sitting on the nightstand and I scrolled through text messages. About a dozen from Amy. Christ.

Okay, control settled back in. That's what I do, goddamn it, I take control.

Call Britney first, Chuck Verhey said. *Let her know you're over here. You need to talk to her and she needs you right now.*

Chuck was right again, that piece of shit. Britney and I needed to get a plan together.

I'd call Britney; then I'd call Amy.

I wedged my cigarette into the ashtray on the nightstand and dialed Britney's number.

"Hello?" she said.

"Hey, Britney." I spoke smoothly, deliberately, ensuring no hint of slur touched my voice. "I made it back here. I'm back in my room."

"Oh, good." Awkwardness crept in.

"You didn't go out there, did you?"

"I said I'd wait for you."

That's cool, Chuck's voice echoed as I finished my fourth beer. I had a brief second to wonder if Britney heard me drinking it, then decided I didn't care.

"You wanna come over here so we can talk about this. I've got a few beers we can drink." My voice sounded odd to my own ears. *You're trying to sound like you haven't been drinking*, Skip Jones said. He knows his shit.

She hesitated and then said, "At your room?"

"Yeah." I wanted her in here, next to me. "Then at least we can talk in private."

Silence. She wasn't digging this. I added, "Or we could meet over at the Denny's or something, but I figured it'd be easier to talk here so no one can hear us."

Finally, she said, "I'll come over there. Give me about a half hour to get there. And Mick?"

"Yeah?"

"Don't try talking me out of going. I swear to God, I'll walk out of there. I've had too much shit happen today."

"I promise."

Lying was easier after a few beers.

CHAPTER 23

Amy's first voice-message was simple:

Just calling to see where you are. Is your phone off? The girls want to talk to you. I'm going to the store today and wanted to know if you need me to pick anything up. Give me a call when you get a minute.

On the second message her voice grew sterner, more incredulous:

You're probably on your way to the airport, but I haven't heard from you. Wanted to see how you're doing. She paused, then said, *Call me when you get a chance.*

On the third message, she'd had enough. I pictured her speaking through clenched teeth:

Where the hell are you? You're not responding to texts or answering your phone. The girls want to talk to you; I want to talk to you. Then she seemed to relax. *You know what, the hell with it. Do you what you want. But if you're drunk, do not come back here.*

I tried to remember when I'd received three calls and at what times. I'm pretty sure the third one happened when Britney and I left The Bottoms that afternoon. Damn it, if I called her now and told her I'd gone back to Gainesville, what then? I'm sure we'd laugh and joke about all this and then give each other little phone smooches.

Yeah right.

She'd be on my ass like a wolf on a sheep's throat. She'd never understand. She rarely understood anything that pertained to just me. Like

I had no life, I had no fears or problems that didn't somehow involve her. If she only knew.

I chugged the last of my fifth beer.

But goddamn it, I had to call her.

And tell her what? *What Mick? That you found Harry and he's a rotting corpse sitting in some old guy's basement.*

And the truth shall set you free. Whoever said that shit never had anything like this happen to them. I had to remember that this was Amy; not just some girl. In a marriage, at least in ours, there are unspoken understandings that each of us has of each other. On some level, she'd believe it, or at least, she'd believe that I believed it.

I'm not sure at what point I lit another cigarette and got my next beer, but I noticed that I'd done both. Oh well, that's why I got the damn twelve packs.

I need you to kill her, Mickey.

I thought of Harry in the darkness of that damp cellar, out in the woods. Alone. No idea how that stupid cop hadn't found him. Unless he didn't go down there; which is what I'd concluded.

Why in the hell had Bob let Harry go down into the cellar to start with? Why did Bob care? And why hadn't Bob run out of there screaming to the police? Something like that would drive most people nuts. But not 'ole Bob. In fact, looking back, he didn't treat it like anything out of the ordinary.

As if he *knew.*

Harry didn't show up on Bob's doorstep and ask *yo, you mind if I crash at your pad while I rot away*. Hell no. Something screwy was going on here. Bob played a bigger part in this game than he let on; somehow, someway.

And Lupis Rudolph. Who the hell was that guy? I'd bet my ass that Bob and Lupis knew each other. Harry said he met Lupis in the cancer ward in Indianapolis, which meant that Lupis most likely had cancer himself. So why didn't 'ole Lupis drink the water? And Bob behaved like he didn't want anybody around it and acted pissed that Lupis had taken anyone back to that fountain of youth.

Not a fountain of youth anymore; the water no longer worked. Had it ever? Had it ever been a place where people drank and lived forever?

I chuckled in the silence of my room and barely noticed the sun setting. Fountain of youth, my ass. And little fairies flew around the hundred-acre-woods where Pooh, Tigger, and the rest of the gang waited for Christopher Robin to come skipping down the path.

But the fountain *was* something. Harry *was* turning into something. Dimly, I remembered the rusty chain-link fence, aged and useless, that Britney and I had passed as we traipsed back to Kate's Lake. At some point in its life, that fence had been put there to keep people out.

She's insane, Mickey. She drank the water and went insane. She's out there in the woods right now. Sometimes I see her looking in the windows at night, but she always runs off before Bob can kill her. Why does Bob want to kill her? And why doesn't he kill Harry, if that's what Harry wants. Why *ME*? Goddamn it, why me!

Thank God I had the beer and the cigarettes. And, as shitty as this sounds, I decided *not* to call Amy. I didn't want to talk to her. I had to get this shit straightened out first.

Better to ask for forgiveness later than permission now, Chuck Verhey said and I toasted him for getting that one right.

Two things were at work here: first off, a hell of a good buzz had kicked in. Second, my best friend Harry Darnell was in deep shit, the deepest shit he'd ever been in.

"Hooo'ah, Marine Corps, Harry." I toasted to the empty room. "Brothers to the end." I drank.

I wished that I'd never joined the Corps, that I'd never met Harry, that he'd never shown me that picture of Britney that branded itself into my memory forever.

Wish in one hand and shit in the other, see which one fills up first, Chuck Verhey said and laughed. Either Chuck or my dad had said that.

Harry was asking me to do the unthinkable, but damn it, what choice did I have? Good 'ole Harry, my best friend, my brother, Harry Darnell who'd kept me from going crazy in the Marine Corps.

Who'd been there the last time I killed someone.

CHAPTER 24

The sand is cool and I wish the smoke would clear so I could see. Days and nights are no longer separate. It's all blackness.

"Stay locked and loaded," Sergeant Davis yells. "They're out there."

Sweat drips into my eyes. I wipe my sleeve across my slick forehead. I might die here in this sand.

Harry lies next to me, his rifle aimed into the darkness, the stock wedged tight against his shoulder. "What did I do to deserve this, Mick?" He keeps his voice low.

Sergeant Davis marches back and forth behind us, barking orders.

There's twenty-seven of us lined up, ready to annihilate anything that moves; hearts pumping, eyes wide, scared shitless. I check the safety on my rifle. It's off, I'm ready. Terrified, but ready. I wait.

"You think they'll try to come through here?" I whisper to Harry.

"Fucked if I know," he hisses back.

I jam the stock of my rifle deeper into my shoulder and place my finger on the trigger.

Part of me wants *the Iraqis to come through here. Part of me wants to see their stupid faces come charging out of the darkness.* I want *to pull this trigger. "Show your ugly faces," I mutter, unsure of whether Harry heard me or not.*

And then I see it, out there in the darkness, lurking in the wall of black smoke, their approaching faces...

Knocking. A thousand miles away. I forced my eyes open; then blinked away the fog. I was on the floor. The room swirled and I closed my eyes.

Bam! Bam! Bam!

Definitely a knock at the door. And loud.

Damn it. "I don't fuckin' know," I yelled and stumbled to my feet. No idea why I said *that*.

Bam! Bam! Bam!

Jesus Christ, Harry. Harry's here and for one crazy moment, I wanted to scream. But it couldn't be Harry. "It's not Harry, you goddamn idiot," I said. Britney. Britney was on her way over. We'd talked earlier. I thought about the picture of her that Harry gave me, with her hands on her hips and her tanned leg thrust forward. Was this fate? Perhaps. Fate brought us together, Britney and me. Fate.

Before Amy.

Finally, I staggered to my feet and nearly tumbled into a small nightstand perched next to the bed. I caught myself, barely, and then stood there. "Goddamn," I said, "I'm fucked up." How much did I drink? I'd only bought two twelve-packs. *But you ain't drank like this for four years, little man,* Chuck Verhey said. I forgot about that bastard. At least I still had Chuck. I waited for Skip to answer, but he said nothing. Apparently, he'd given up on me. "I'm no fuckin' good, Skip," I said into the darkening room.

I glanced at the bed and my heart sank as if it suddenly turned to lead. My phone laid there. I'd been using it. *Oh fuck.* "Who'd I call?" I hoped to God I hadn't called Amy. Please, don't tell me I called her. I don't remember it.

Black out. Been awhile since I had one of those.

I knew Britney was waiting, but I had to check the phone, I *had* to know. The room slanted to the left, letting me know my buzz still held strong. I must've only been out a few minutes. I half walked, half stumbled to the bed and plucked up my iPhone.

My thumb fumbled for RECENT CALLS. *Oh Jesus.* Right there, her name, AMY, clear as a bell. I'd called my wife. I'd called Amy and passed out while talking to her. In the back of my mind, I hoped she'd hung up on me before I fell. I hoped to God we hadn't been talking and the last thing she heard was me hitting the floor.

"Ah, God." I sobbed and shoved a fist to my mouth. I hated myself. "You're so stupid, you fuckin' idiot." I started to cry and I slammed the phone against my forehead. "You're so stupid, Mick." No one deserved to be like me; no one should ever turn out like me. I hoped my girls... my sweet little girls, didn't turn out like their loser old man.

I staggered to the door, shoulders slumped, and no longer cared what Britney thought. I needed to see her. I needed her close, I needed her smell, her presence, her admiration. Someone to save me. Someone to wrap their arms around me and say that everything's going to be okay. And she would, I'm sure of it, because she knew what we were going through out here.

I opened the door with tears drying on my cheeks. I had a second to register that I'd been hit square in the mouth and I was falling backward, my arms flailing, reaching for something to grab onto. I collided with the floor, the back of my head cracking the thin carpet. One of my empty beer cans crunched under my back.

A voice, distant and strange, almost as if from a dream, yelled, "You wanna fuck my wife, you sonofabitch?"

The world swam away, the blackness creeping in from the sides, the voice still yelling, "Did you fuck her, you bastard? You ain't never gonna touch her again, I'm makin' sure of that."

And the dark descended.

CHAPTER 25

...the faces loom in the blackness like an army of walking dead.

This is war.

Fear rips through me and I brace my rifle against my shoulder. My finger dances on the trigger.

"Oh Jesus. Oh Jesus Christ," Harry mutters.

"Are we supposed to shoot?" I ask. Sergeant Davis said to shoot anything that moves. Why wasn't anyone else shooting?

I watch the faces drift closer; close enough now to see the silhouettes of their bodies.

"Are we supposed to shoot them?" I hiss.

"I don't fuckin' know," Harry says.

Seven goddamn miserable months; that's how long we'd been here. Talking about home, talking about women, talking about booze, talking about being human again and getting out of this shit-smelling litterbox. Seven motherfucking months!

Goddamn it, why isn't anyone firing?

"This is fucked, dude," I say to Harry. "I could hit the bastards from here." And I could, by God, I had one in my sights right now. Center mass.

"He said to shoot," Harry says. "So why ain't anyone shooting, Mickey?"

"That's what I'm saying."

Now there are more of them. Dozens. They're everywhere and they just keep coming.

And they're carrying something. I hadn't noticed it before, the smoky haze hid it, but now I can see it. They're carrying rifles and it looks like they're in the ready position.

They don't know we're here. They don't know. But as soon as they do, they're going to fire. If they fire, some of us will die here. Maybe all of us! They might start lobbing grenades.

We've got the element of surprise. Adrenaline pumps so hard my hands shake, shake so bad in fact, I'm not sure I can hit anything.

They're carrying rifles!

From behind us, Sergeant Davis yells, but I don't understand.

I fire.

I pull the trigger once, twice, three times and I watch the Iraqi in my sights collapse like a heap of old sheets. I expect to hear the entire line of Marines open up, M-16s firing like mad, ripping and tearing and destroying.

But I hear nothing except Sergeant Davis behind me screaming, "Cease fire! Cease fire, goddamn it! They're surrendering!"

My breath catches as I notice that what the Iraqi's are carrying aren't rifles. They look *like rifles, but what they have are short sticks with white flags tied to the end. And now, since I shot one of them, they're all on their knees, thrusting the sticks in the air.*

"Goddamn, Mick," Harry says.

"I thought it was a rifle." I swallow hard. Coldness seeps into me.

"What the fuck's wrong with you, Smith?" Sergeant Davis hollers. "You didn't hear me yell?"

"I didn't hear a damn thing," I yell back.

"Nobody else shoot anything," Sergeant Davis paces back and forth behind the line. "Looks like the bastards are surrendering. We'll wait on the MPs."

I lie there, staring out at the man lying still on the ground, the dead one, the one I shot. I can't stop looking at it and I'm suddenly woozy and this all starts to feel like a dream, like a weird dream where only stupid things happen, mistakes like this happen.

I wipe sweat from my eyes. It seems like forever before the MPs get there. And when they do, everyone stands up. My fellow Marines, my comrades, are looking at me and I don't know exactly how to interpret their stares.

I trudge to where the dead man lay motionless. I spot the two bullet holes: one in the guy's chest and the other in his face, I hit the guy right above the upper lip. The nose and top of the mouth are gone and thick liquid oozes out, a black liquid, what would have been red if it weren't so dark outside.

Seared forever into my memory, a sight never to be unseen again except when drowned in alcohol.

I reach down and take what looks like a wallet sticking out of the guy's front shirt pocket. It suddenly all seems so pointless. All this shit, this war, this country. Burnt gunpowder infests my mouth and I retch. My throat tastes like blood.

I open the dead man's wallet and the first thing I see is a picture of two smiling children, a girl and a boy. Children. I glance down at the dead man again, at the jagged hole in his face, and then back at the picture.

"Oh Jesus Christ." My hands start to shake.

I fall to my knees in front of the dead man and pull frantically for a first aid pouch from my pack. Stop the bleeding and start the breathing. I find it and yank out a large pressure bandage. I'm crying. I place one of the bandages on the man's chest and another on the grotesque hole in his face.

My cries become wails and I dig for another bandage. "Corpsman!" I scream and look up. My platoon gathers around me, staring at me.

"I need a corpsman!" I scream again, but nobody moves. They all stare.

I push the bandage against the jagged face-wound and something gives under my hand with a sickening crunch, teeth or shattered bone, and I jerk my hand away.

And then a hand is on my shoulder and I turn to see Harry. Harry wraps his arms around me.

"He's gone, Mickey," Harry says. "It was an accident. You didn't know."

A gust of wind whips the picture of the two children away, carrying it somewhere into the darkness, somewhere far… away….

…someone leaned over me. Opening my eyes took the will of God, like trying to force open an old window stuck from rust and age.

My mouth felt puffy and I wanted to put my finger to my lips, but I didn't dare. Not yet. I didn't want to move anything. I wanted to find out where the hell I was.

Someone said, "Dude." *Dude?* Like hearing a voice from the far end of a narrow tunnel. "Yo, you okay?"

"Haaphnnnd?" Holy shit, I couldn't talk! I heard my voice making noise.

"Keep still, bro," the voice of whoever was bent over me said, "cops and shit are on their way."

Cops? Gainesville. Deputy Wayne Tillwood. My swirling thoughts started locking together, very slowly, like a massive jigsaw puzzle with pieces floating in space.

Waiting on Britney. That's what I'd been doing. And I'd called Amy. Oh Christ, that's right, I'd called Amy. I'd been drunk.

Hell, I was still drunk.

"That dude messed you up a little," the voice said.

I squinted at the blurry face looming over me – a young guy, late teens or early twenties, with long hair and I noticed his earring, glimmering silver.

Someone else stood behind him, hanging back by the door. It looked like a girl. Britney? That's when I noticed the other thing, the thing I didn't like – it was dark outside. For some reason, *that* scared the shit out of me and I'm not sure why.

Someone had hit me when I opened the door.

A guy with a shaved head, a big guy, wearing a t-shirt with cut-off sleeves.

"Fucker hit me." My words still slurred, like talking with a sock stuffed in my mouth. They came out sounding more like, *ucka 'it me.*

"More than once, dude. He beat the hell outta you," the young guy said. "I called the cops, me and my old lady. But it takes 'em a few minutes to get out here."

I scraped my tongue against my lips. My upper lip felt like a balloon and my nose ached like someone had rammed a hot poker up in there. This sucked. This sucked bad. I needed to know how long I'd been out.

I squinted at the girl standing by the door. Skinny. Scraggly hair. Not Britney.

I placed my hand on the floor and pushed up, and then slipped and flopped back down onto my back, gasping, sucking in with a hiss, as pain, piercing and horrible, shot up my left side.

"Whoa, dude, don't try to move," the kid said, "you're pretty banged up."

"Help me up, kid," I said. The searing pain in my lip hurt like hell and my words still weren't clear, but they were better than they were. I grabbed his arm.

"You shouldn't move, man."

I gripped his shirt. "Help me off this goddamned floor."

He hesitated, glanced over at his *old lady* who shrugged; then turned back to me and started pulling me up as I lumbered to my feet. The pain in my side flared, like something stuck in there. It hurt! But I kept going, I had to get to my feet. Had to.

I made it up. Then I limped my way over to the bed and plopped down on the edge. I wished I'd gone to the couch so I could lean back, but too late for that; I wasn't moving again.

I saw my smokes sitting on the nightstand next to the bed. I wanted one, oh dear God, how I wanted one.

"You mind grabbin' me one of my smokes?" I flipped a finger at them.

The kid snatched them off the nightstand and shook one out for me. "You gonna be okay, man?" he asked as I fished a cigarette out of the pack.

I tried to smile, but gave up in a hurry. "Yeah, I'll be fine. Ain't the first time I've had my ass kicked." And that part was true, but this was the most damage I'd ever received from a single ass beating.

The kid handed me my lighter and I lit my smoke.

"What's your name?" I asked noticing the litter of beer cans around my motel room. *Way to go, Mick.*

"Uh," the kid seemed confused, as if he'd never been asked that before. "I'm Ronnie." He turned and pointed at the girl behind him. "This here's Loretta."

Ronnie and Loretta, I thought. Something about it seemed funny and I wanted to laugh. Him and his *old lady*. I suppose I shouldn't be too ungrateful; sounds like Ronnie and Loretta saved my ass.

"Did you see who got me?" I asked.

"Yeah. I didn't know him or nothin'. But I seen him. So'd Loretta. Big bald guy." Ronnie stepped back and stood by his *old lady*. Whoever thought of that term, *old lady*, and did they know how utterly stupid it sounded?

Big bald guy. Well, at least I remembered that part correctly. "What time is it?"

"About nine or so. That dude ran off. You been layin' up here a half-hour, at least," Ronnie said.

"Cops on their way?" I remembered Ronnie saying it earlier, but I asked anyway.

"Yep. I called 'em as soon as I seen that guy hit you."

Jesus H. Christ, I thought, *thirty minutes ago I got my ass kicked and the cops still weren't here?*

Ronnie, as if reading my mind, said, "Deputy stopped by here already and told me to keep an eye on ya 'till Sheriff Snider showed up. Said he was lookin' for that guy that hit ya, but don't remember his name either."

"Jesse. His name's Jesse." I took a long drag on my cigarette.

"Yeah, dude!" Ronnie snapped his fingers and pointed at me. "That was it. Jesse."

Sonofabitch caught up with me. Guess I should've seen that coming.

"Was there a woman here?" I asked Ronnie and Loretta. "She would've been looking for me. Brown hair. Pretty."

Ronnie thought a moment and then said, "Nah, ain't nobody else been here. Just that deputy."

So, the deputy had already been here and he'd gone to find Britney's ex-husband; ostensibly for beating the shit out of me, but more likely so he could play Britney's hero. Honestly, I hoped Jesse would meet Wayne's 9 MM. I touched my tongue to my swollen lip again and winced.

I'd called Amy during my drunken black out. My chest fluttered and my insides coiled, like a snake stirring in my guts and eating its way out. I don't know what I'd told her, nor do I know what she'd heard last. I closed my eyes wishing I'd wake up from this horrible dream.

I needed my phone. There might be messages on it. Maybe Britney had called. Or Amy had called me back or sent me a text. I needed to know these things.

My aching side felt a little better. Not much, but a little, which eased my mind. For a bit, I'd worried that something may be seriously wrong down in there.

"Ronnie," I said, my eyes darting around the room. "You see a cell phone laying around here anyplace?"

"Yeah, dude." Ronnie plucked it off the floor and handed it to me, then stepped back to Loretta who still had not said a word. She shot me sparse glances as if I bore some awful disease. Perhaps she'd never seen someone beat up before. Maybe this was the first time she'd seen anything.

"Thanks." I glanced at the screen. Seven missed calls and two texts. One new voice message. All that shit in a half an hour!

As I started to scroll through the missed calls, I asked Ronnie, "Hey, you mind grabbing me a beer? They're on the counter." I didn't care that they were warm.

"Sure, man." Ronnie got to it, stepping around me, his long hair swaying back and forth.

"Grab yourself one too, if you want. If you're old enough." I read the texts. Both from Amy. Damn it. One of them said, *I hate you for this.* A tear stung my eye and I swiped it away. The world sucks and a cruel god somewhere was laughing his ass off.

Ronnie handed me a beer. I opened it and drank. The liquid stung my swollen lip, but I relished the pain and drank some more.

Two of the voicemails were from Amy and I could only imagine what they were, and five were from Britney. I tapped the latest voicemail from Britney and waited.

Then her sweet voice spoke into my ear and my heart crawled down into my guts:

Hey Mick, I've left you a ton of voicemails. Things are all screwed up here. They let Jesse out of jail…

… No screaming eagle shit…

… and he's called me about ten times. He's drunk, but he said he was going home. So hopefully he does. My mom's pissed at me for going out to Harry's place with you. I was gonna come straight over to your motel, but figured since you weren't answering you decided to head back to Colorado. I don't know. I hope you did. She paused and took a breath.

I'm going back there, Mick. I'm on my way there now. I've got to see Harry. I know he's in that guy's cellar. I know you talked to him down there. Call me if you get this. If you want to call me, that is. I understand if you don't.

And then it ended. That was it.

I let the phone fall into my lap and pressed my palm to my forehead. "No, no, *no!*" I said. "Goddamn it, Britney!"

Harry's words, *don't bring her down here*, echoed in my head.

I rubbed the heels of my hands against my eyes. A dull ache rolled slowly through my left temple.

"Goddamn it, Britney," I muttered again. *I'm sorry, Harry.*

"Everything cool, dude?" Ronnie asked.

"No. Everything is not cool." I pictured Britney driving through the Bottoms in the dark, by herself. She'd be scared. I hoped she'd be too frightened to do it. But she wanted to see Harry.

And then, I pictured Mary, *it*, tearing out of the trees and foliage, her hands curled into murderous claws…

…she killed a camper last week…

…and those eyes, those murky gray eyes, full of madness, locking onto Britney and attacking her. Britney's painful screams would drift hauntingly through the dark woods as Mary's fingers bore into her soft flesh, ripping, pulling, tearing.

My God, what do I do here?

Piss on 'em, Chuck Verhey's voice flared in my head. *This ain't your mess, little man.*

I thought of Amy, my girls, I thought of Harry, and of Britney. All these people counting on *me* to do something, all having different expectations of what that something should be. What in God's name had I gotten involved in out here? I wondered what Kate's Lake *really* was. I recalled those old fences around it and Britney said the government owned it. What the hell? Abandoned government experiments or something? A place where you drank healing water would not have remained a secret this long.

Unless it didn't work.

I stood up and felt wobbly, but that could be the alcohol, some of it anyway. I stuffed my pack of smokes into my shirt pocket and grabbed my keys.

I looked at the kid, Ronnie, and then at his *old lady*, and said "Listen, when the sheriff gets here, you tell him I split, okay."

Ronnie nodded.

"Tell him I'm headed for the airport, cause that's where I'm going. Tell him he can come *there* and talk to me if he wants, but I'm gettin' the hell outta Dodge."

Ronnie's eyebrows furrowed like he wanted to ask me a question, but instead he said, "Right on, man."

"You got that? I'm getting out of here and going back to Colorado." I pointed my finger at Ronnie when I said that last part.

Ronnie nodded and said, "Yo, man, I'll tell him."

As I passed by him and Loretta, a pain shot up my left leg and I nearly stumbled; Jesse's big bald-headed ass must have kicked me in the leg or something. "Thanks for calling the cops and helping me out."

That seemed to help because Ronnie relaxed and smiled, "No problem, man. Didn't want him messin' ya up too bad."

I started my car, hoping like hell the sheriff wouldn't pull in just as I pulled out. No way I'd pass a sobriety test. Once on the highway, I lit a cigarette, wincing against the pain of moving my arm, the pain of breathing, even the pain of the soft paper of the cigarette filter against my swollen lip.

I had forty miles of road to cover before reaching Kate's Lake. Even if I had something that would travel the speed of sound, I couldn't get there fast enough. Britney was there. I pulled out my phone to dial her number.

"I'm coming, Harry," I spoke inside the space of my empty car. "Semper Fi, brother."

CHAPTER 26

By the third ring, I knew she wouldn't answer. Either she knew it was me and didn't want to talk, which didn't seem likely, or she was in the Bottoms where reception sucked.

Or Mary had gotten her.

I slammed the heel of my hand against the steering wheel.

Finally, it went to voicemail. I damn near hung up, but decided that just in case she got a signal out there somewhere, she should know that I was on my way. I wished I could talk to Harry.

"Hey, it's Mick." I hate leaving messages. "I got your voicemail; sorry I missed your calls. I met Jesse," I laughed a little, then said, "If you get this, call me. And don't go out to Kate's Lake by yourself. Wait for me at the gate, I'm on my way there. You hear me… I'm on my way. I'll go back there with you."

I hung up the phone. The sound of the engine working overtime filled the space, along with the flowery smell of whatever fragrance the rental car company put in these things. I flipped my cigarette out the window. I approached the gas station where Britney and I stopped earlier that morning and pulled in.

"This won't take but a second," I said to myself.

You're doing the right thing, Chuck Verhey said, *hurry your ass up*.

I slammed the shifter into park and climbed out. I couldn't run, it hurt way too bad to run, so I shuffled. My heart raced and my palms sweat. I needed something else, something I knew I had to have and it wasn't alcohol or cigarettes. The thought of it sparked dread and my hands shook.

Something I hadn't touched since the desert of Iraq. And once I held the cold, dead weight of it, there'd be no turning back.

This'll help, Chuck said.

"Damn right, it will." I slid open a glass door and pulled out a twelve-pack of beer. This would help everything.

I plopped it onto the counter. The clerk gawked at me as if Ted Bundy had walked into his store. This surely wasn't the same guy from this morning.

"And a pack of KOOL 100's," I said.

"You alright?" He was an older guy and wore a blue Indianapolis Colts T-shirt.

"I'm good," I said. Then added with a wry smile, "Stay away from ex-husbands."

"I could'a told ya that." He didn't smile. He must not have thought that shit was funny.

I wanted to ask him, I *had* to ask him, but fear paralyzed me. That other thing I needed. As he started ringing up my stuff, I licked my lips and closed my eyes. *You've got to, Mick.* I realized right then, I hadn't even called it by name yet, I still referred to it as *it*. Surely, this guy would know where I could get a… *it*.

"Hey, uh," I hesitated. Behind him, glass bottles of whiskey reflected the ceiling lights. He stopped and waited for me to finish.

"Do you know where I can get a gun?" I asked.

Say it Mick, Chuck Verhey said. *And if you need one of those bottles behind the counter, you go on and get one of those too.*

A gun.

Gun.

The old guy leered at me, then asked, "You from around here?"

"No. From Colorado. Out here for my best friend's funeral."

"Ah," he said, "you must'a been a friend of Harry Darnell then."

"Yep, that's it."

He finished ringing me up and then said, "That'll be $21."

I reached for my wallet, and while I did, he started speaking again. "So, you come out here for Harry's funeral, got yourself beat up..." he shook his head as he took my card. "And now you want a gun?"

After hearing it like that, I wished I hadn't asked for anything. I wished I hadn't even of come into this place.

"Harry and I were in the Corps together," I said, "I was gonna go target shooting, you know." Jesus Christ, that sounded stupid. A beat-up guy asking for a gun because he wanted to go target shooting in the middle of the night… way to go, Mick.

"Ah." He handed me back my card. "Other'n Walmart or someplace like that, I don't know where a guy might get a gun now. Hell, even Wal-mart wouldn't just hand it to ya. You gotta wait a week or somethin' like that. I don't know."

I forced another fake smile and said, "Thanks for your help," then grabbed my stuff.

"Sure." He'd call the sheriff as soon as I stepped out the door; I'd bet my ass on it.

I hustled back into my car and decided to backtrack toward Gainesville rather than turning right to go to Kate's Lake, it pissed me off to have to go the wrong way, but just in case that clerk watched me leave, which he probably did, he'd send the sheriff the wrong way.

Good thinking Mick, Chuck said and called to me from the cardboard box riding in the passenger seat. I ripped it open and pulled out a beer. I chugged; then glanced into my rearview mirror. The lights of the gas station were barely visible and I didn't see another car in sight.

"Time to run around." I slowed, flipped a U-turn right there on the highway, and slammed on the accelerator. That clerk might see me drive back past and recognize the car (remind me to never get a yellow fucking car again), but I doubted it. Who cared anyway? Chaos had me in its grasp, I was listening to Chuck Verhey, and 'ole Mick, father of two, husband to one, teetered dangerously close to the edge of madness. The razor's edge.

I considered calling the cops right then, but they'd have questions I wasn't ready to answer. They'd ask me about Jesse, about my wounds. They'd notice I'd been drinking. They'd talk to that clerk and question why I asked for a gun. Piss on all that.

If I did what Harry was asking me to do, I was going out to Kate's Lake to kill someone. God help me, but I was. And whether or not I could do it remained to be seen.

You've done it before, Chuck said and I swear I heard that sonofabitch laughing.

CHAPTER 27

There were three empty beer cans scattered on the passenger floorboard and a full one wedged between my legs when I reached the Bottoms. I lit a cigarette and rolled to a stop. In the dark, the woods looked much worse, sinister, like a black abyss leading into another world where devils roamed and horrible creatures lurked behind dead trees.

No sign of Britney's car.

I needed to call Amy and tell her that I loved her and that I was sorry for failing her and the girls. Guilt gnawed at me like a filthy rat. And she wouldn't understand, not in a million years.

How had things gotten so out of control so quickly?

I'm such a fool.

"You've got a right to question me, baby," I said aloud in that idling car. "You've got a right to question everything."

I lit another cigarette and stared into the blackness. I did not want to go in there.

Hold up, little man, Chuck said, *maybe Britney didn't go down there. She might've chickened out; she might be sitting at her mom's house right now.*

I thought about that; then said, "Yeah, but she'd have called me back if she wasn't down there." That's what I hoped, anyway.

I stared at my phone's soft light and scrolled to Amy's number and dialed. I squeezed my eyes shut and waited. It only rang once and then went straight to voicemail. Damn it.

"Hey baby," I said. "Guess I screwed this one up." *You're drunk talking now*, I thought, *get to the point*. "Look… I've got one more thing I gotta do, it's about Harry. There were some things I didn't know, some weird things." Goddamn it, I slurred to beat hell, I heard it in my own words. "I'll call you in a little while. Tell the girls I love them and I miss them. And I love you."

I pulled the phone away and hung up. Fucking voicemail.

I sat in my rental car, a KOOL cigarette burning between my fingers. Tears rolled down my face and dripped onto my bloodstained shirt.

I sobbed, "I love you!" into the silence. My baby girls. I pictured them in bed right now, going to bed so they could get up for school tomorrow. Each of them sleeping, eyes closed, dreaming about something special.

I chugged the last of my beer and tossed the empty can down onto the floorboard to join the others. Getting out another one was easy and I had the tab popped and was drinking before you could snap your fingers.

Don't go, little man, Chuck Verhey said. *Just wait here. She ain't down there. Look how scary that road is.* He wasn't kidding about the road looking scary. *You think she'd keep going?*

"So what the hell?" I said. I thought about Chuck's comment and deep down, I knew he was wrong. Britney *did* go in there. She did it because she loved her brother. That girl didn't have a chickenshit bone in her body.

She didn't, Chuck said. *You should at least make sure she didn't go back home. You should at least check.*

"Shut up!" I yelled into the car. "Shut the hell up!"

I drank my beer and stared into the woods.

Strange, being parked out here along this old road, alone.

"She's down there." I took a good long drag on my cigarette. "I know she is."

Even the people inhabiting the little shacks along the way were scary, let alone Harry's zombie wife wandering through the woods. Hell, Harry himself terrified me. And Britney didn't know about any of that.

A shiver raced up my spine and I was glad I had my cigarette as I shook.

"Too many things to lose, bro," I said. I spoke to Harry now. Harry would know what that meant. Harry would understand.

Mick the dick, the voice slammed in my head like a hammer. *You gettin' scared again, Dickey*?

I smiled. My lip stretched like a tight balloon, but I smiled anyway.

You know the secret, Dickey? Sergeant Higgins growled into my ear, just like he did in boot camp all those years ago.

"Fuckin A, I do." I chugged my beer and shifted the car into Drive.

You remember what I told you, right Dickey? It's how you stay sane, Sergeant Higgins didn't yell, he didn't scream; he simply spoke.

The car rolled forward and my smile broadened.

"Hell yes, I remember," I spoke to that sonofabitch Sergeant Higgins, the one who had pushed me beyond what I ever thought possible. The one who had shown me how to face fear, how to overcome it, and how to stay sane. Staying sane, that was the tricky part. Because to do it Sergeant Higgin's way, staying sane was the tightrope you had to walk.

You've got to go crazy, Dickey.

"I know."

No, you don't. This time, you're gonna have to go nuts.

"I know." And I did know. I knew what he was talking about. And it was happening. Abandon the fear of death. Focus on nothing except the task ahead and not care whether you lived or died accomplishing it. It's not something that happens naturally; it comes with training and experience. It's that essential element that makes up the most dangerous animal alive – the Marine.

The car's headlights cut the blackness like sharp steel through flesh. I passed by the old rusty gate and under the canopy of trees, shrouding me in darkness. I took another swig of beer and placed it carefully between my legs, having nothing but the dashboard lights for company.

I drove into the Bottoms and there was no turning back.

CHAPTER 28

My headlights caught the flicker of a car bumper shadowed by weeds and my heart sank. I'd still hoped Chuck was right and that she'd chickened out and gone home. But Chuck Verhey was always wrong – you'd think I'd have figured that shit out by now.

Her car sat dark and silent, like an abandoned coffin. Skeletal shadows stretched and twisted as the lights of my car splashed across leafy branches. My eyes played tricks on me and more than once, I thought I caught the shape of a person standing out there, one of those bearded freaks.

Or Mary.

I parked behind her car and got out, a cigarette hanging from the corner of my mouth and carrying a beer. The open-door warning of my rental car dinged shockingly loud in the silent woods, so I slammed my door shut, killing the noise. I left it running for the lights. I'd use my phone's flashlight to walk the trail, but honestly, I had no idea how much battery I had left. As I stood there, the darkness pressed in on me, devouring the light, the blackness so thick I could drag my fingers through it.

I ambled straight to the driver's side window of Britney's car and peered inside, hoping to see her sitting there. No such luck. *Damn it, Britney.* I leaned back against her car and smoked. I felt reasonably sure I was being watched, but the thought no longer terrified me.

Fuck 'em.

If one of those hicks from the bottoms decided to get in my way, I'd kill them. Simple as that. I had no weapon except my fists, feet, and teeth, but if anyone decided to fuck with me, they'd better be ready to step into a whirlwind.

I whispered, "Go nuts, Dickey, just go nuts." Fear lurked all around me. I couldn't let it in; I couldn't let it touch me. Wasn't it Roosevelt who said there was nothing to fear but fear itself? Or was that Kennedy? I'd bet neither one of them had been down in the Bottoms.

I stepped back to my car, grabbed my smokes, another beer, and then shut off the idling engine. A few seconds later, the lights died and darkness shrouded me.

There were two things that I found completely unbelievable. One, that a place this dark existed in the world. Two, that Britney had parked back here and walked that path; a path barely visible.

She'd gotten out and walked it alone, so compelled that waiting until daylight wasn't an option, as if she'd already waited far too long. The thought of her walking timidly through the weeds and tall grass, her beautiful eyes wide and terrified, most likely her hands clasped together in front of her (unless she had a flashlight – she'd have held that with both hands), brought another tear to my eye. I wanted nothing more than to get her out of here. That's what I owed Harry because I'm the one who got her into this shit.

Shut up, little man, you're drunk, Chuck Verhey said. *Quit talking and start walking.*

I lumbered forward, one foot in front of the other. On my way.

▪ ▪ ▪ ▪ ▪

Insects chirped, buzzed, flew: a cacophony of shit I didn't want to see. I kept feeling something crawling on me. I swatted at things close to my head or on my neck. The deep stench of stagnate lake water grew stronger and I caught a whiff of decay. I wondered if Mary would stink like that. Would I smell death in the air as her corpse lurked in the darkness?

I shivered.

I'd smelled Harry, hadn't I? His vile stench filled Bob's entire basement.

I turned and glanced behind me, no longer able to see the cars. No surprise there; they could be fifty feet away and I wouldn't see them. No turning back now. God knew what I'd find when I arrived.

A full moon was my only saving grace and my eyes finally adjusted to its gloomy light. If not for that, I'd have to use my phone's flashlight, which would totally screw my night-vision. At least it made the path visible. Which meant if anything was out here, like one of those crazy Bottoms-dwellers, or a dead woman named Mary, they could see me too.

I was in the middle of thinking that, when a twig snapped in front me and I heard shuffling through the weeds. I stopped breathing, and thank God for that, otherwise I would've screamed.

CHAPTER 29

And then my phone buzzed in my pocket.

I froze. Everything stopped. Someone stood in front of me, I sensed it. No more than twenty or thirty feet. The moon's light cast shadows, deep and patchy. The darkness, especially darkness this intense, can throw off your sense of distance; everything sounded close enough to touch.

I might have to use the flashlight after all.

My phone buzzed again and I kept my eyes trained straight ahead, watching for movement. I reached into my pocket, never taking my eyes off the path. I had to see who it was. It might be Britney. As soon as I got the phone out, it lit up. I closed my right eye (my shooting eye).

Amy.

Good grief. I had other shit to worry about right now.

She'd leave me a message and when she did, the phone would chime, louder than a motherfucker. I quickly pushed the button for SILENT, and then shoved it back into my pocket. I did all of this while holding onto my beer. I also wanted another cigarette.

I opened my right eye and peered into the darkness, looking for any sign of movement. I listened. Shadows everywhere. Nothing moved.

Get the hell outta here, little man, Chuck Verhey whispered. He must have been scared too. *You don't know who that is out there.*

"Shut up," I hissed. I tipped my beer up to my lips and drained it.

If whoever skulked out there had a gun and intended to shoot me, they would've done it by now. I'd given them a target clearer than a Texaco sign when I looked at that phone.

I pulled out my smokes and lit one, breaking every tactical rule in the book.

Do you know what the bead on a cigarette is, Dickey, Sergeant Higgins asked.

Goddamn right, I knew.

One inch above or one inch below. My hands shook as I smoked. Maybe I'd startled them. Maybe they hadn't had their gun ready, but now they did. And they were sighting in, getting the bead on the little red cherry as I inhaled, an inch below my cigarette, which would put a bullet directly through my chin and throat. Let 'em try. If they hit me, it was all over, but if they missed, I'd know exactly where they were.

"Mickey?" The wet, slobbery voice drifted out of the dark and amazingly, relief washed over me.

"Harry? That you?" I asked.

"Yeah." I heard the shuffle of feet again through the grass, moving closer.

Within a few seconds, I saw his silhouette lurching in short, staggered movements. The darkness hid his features (which I was okay with), but I still had to look away. The moon's glow made him unnatural and ghostlike.

"Scared the shit out of me, bro," I said.

Harry didn't answer and I remembered what he'd said to me earlier about Mary going insane.

"Sorry," Harry said. He stopped about ten feet away. He didn't make a sound, not even the faintest breath.

"What are you doing out here?" I asked him. Of all things, I hadn't expected to run into Harry while walking down this path.

"Looking for Mary," he said.

"You just decided to go look for her? Tonight?"

"I look for her every night," he said, "It's the only time I can get out. And I can't move well anymore, Mickey. My arms and legs don't work right."

"What if someone sees you? You might get your ass shot."

"I have to find her." He still had the same vernacular as Harry, but the soggy sound of his voice nauseated me. *Rotten*, Chuck Verhey said, *you're thinking it sounds rotten*. I came shockingly close to yelling at Chuck to shut up, but clamped my mouth shut. Harry would think I'd gone nuts.

"Lupis Rudolph was here tonight," Harry said. "If he finds her, I don't know what he'll do."

"Lupis Rudolph? The guy that showed you the fountain?"

"That's the guy."

"He just showed up?" That seemed damned odd to me. I smoked my cigarette.

"Yeah. I saw him over at my cabin. I don't have a clue why he's here tonight, but he is. I don't want him to find Mary." Harry shuffled closer to me, then stopped.

He's here because Britney's here, my mind whispered. Blood drained from my hands and pooled in my legs. I don't know why Lupis Rudolph would have anything at all to do with Britney, or how he'd even know she existed, but in my world of gummed-up logic, I knew somehow that I was right.

"Something's fucked up here, bro," I said as I smoked. *Bro*. That's a word I used to say a lot when I was drunk, or getting drunk. Smoking out here was stupid, but at least I'd stopped shaking. Mostly I had. "Why'd he just show up?"

I wondered if Harry knew Britney had come out here. I should've told him right then, but he'd be pissed at me for not keeping her safe. Still, he *needed* to know, and I had to tell him.

"He's looking for Mary." Harry slurped on the word *Mary* and my skin crawled. "I don't know why he came out here tonight, but I'm sure that's what he wants."

"He may want something else." I dropped my cigarette and smashed it into the ground with my foot. "Britney's out here. Her car's parked a ways back and she ain't in it."

"Britney?" He fell silent, as if the darkness had swallowed him.

"Yeah. She knew you were back here, she knew something was up."

Harry didn't say anything.

"Her ex-husband beat my ass in my motel room." I felt stupid telling him that. "When I got myself back together, it was nearly dark. I listened to my phone messages and she was on there saying she was coming down here. I came as fast as I could, but she beat me to it. She's out here somewhere."

At first, I thought Harry would never speak again, then he said, "Goddamn it, Mickey."

I lit another cigarette. Good for the nerves. "Look, you know me," I said to Harry's shadowy silhouette. "I've got Amy and the girls to get back to, but I don't want Britney getting hurt. I mean that."

"I know," Harry said. "And I don't think Lupis Rudolph is just some guy. There's something fucking majorly strange about him. Almost inhuman."

I thought, *everything about all this is majorly strange and inhuman*, but simply said, "Let's get moving then."

But Harry didn't move. He stood there. "I have to give you something. I'll lay it on the ground here and then step away. You can come over…"

"Come hand it to me." I held my hand out as if wanting someone to shake it. He didn't want me to see him up close. Though I didn't have a clue what he wanted to give me, I knew it bothered him. "Just walk over and hand it to me."

He stood like a black statue.

"Bring me whatever it is you've got." My heart pounded again, but I loved him, God help me, I did. I would not slink away in fear of facing my brother. A sudden flash of the dream I'd had the night before slammed into my head. *Don't bite me, Harry!*

He took a lumbering step forward and then another. My night-vision had adjusted enough to pick out a few more details. He was bald and his skin was so pale, and it appeared to sag off him, like rotting meat detached from the bone. His eyes were black pits in the dark; holes in his skull. His mouth wasn't open, and I was glad for that, I don't know why. His clothes hung off him and I guessed they were from Bob's wonderful wardrobe of bib overalls. And finally, there was the stench. The rancid odor of decay.

Then my dead friend stood directly in front of me and for a terrible moment, my mind split. Part of me wanted to scream and fall to my knees… *please don't bite me, Harry!* Another part wanted to run, but I knew for the time being anyway, I'd be okay.

"It's okay if you can't look at me," Harry said.

Harry had always stood about four inches taller than me, but death had crippled his body and he was no longer the taller guy. He hunched over, favoring his right side, and his eyes were barely above mine.

"Let's just get this done." My voice warbled, but I maintained my bearing. "What do you have for me?"

He extended his hand and I shrank back, as if he were handing me a spiny sea urchin. "I wouldn't do this if I didn't have to."

My heart beat harder, slamming in my chest like a fist pounding against my ribcage. "Harry," my words died in mid-air and I stared at what he held.

Chuck Verhey screamed at me to *run, you goddamn little coward*. And I saw the dead and bloodied face of an Iraqi soldier, his eyes glaring up at a dark sky; the photo of two children fluttering away across a desert.

I saw these things as I stared in horror at the 9MM weapon Harry held out to me.

. . . . .

"I'm sorry," Harry's slobbery voice drifted from his shadowed face, "but I can't work it anymore. My fingers don't feel anything."

I have no idea how long I stood there, staring at the dark shape protruding from Harry's hand, a nefarious shape of a thing that brought nothing but pain to those who used it. *I'll never touch another weapon again*, I remembered saying when we got back to the states. I'd said that to Harry and he'd clapped a hand on my shoulder and said, *If you ever have to, things are out of control.*

"Guess things are out of control," I said. I didn't know if he heard me or not. A short while ago I asked a gas-station clerk where to get one. Now it was right in front of me like a scaly snake poised to strike.

I thought about asking him if he minded holding onto it; I'd grab it if we needed it, but that seemed like a stupid thing to say. I killed an innocent man ten-years ago, but that was over with and done, put it to rest already. I could do this. I *had* to do this. Because that's what good men do; they adapt and they overcome.

"Harry..." I reached out and wrapped my fingers around the plastic palm guard with my index finger resting against the cool metal of the receiver. My hand immediately started to shake as Harry let go and I took the weight of the gun.

"One in the chamber?" I asked.

"Yeah."

"Thought you said you couldn't work it?"

"Bob loaded it for me."

I shifted my gaze to him. "Where's Bob?"

"He's back at the cabin."

I thought about asking more questions, Lord knew I had them, but decided to pursue it later. I nodded. I pushed the magazine release button with my right thumb and it slid easily out into my left hand. Fully loaded. I slapped it back in. Sixteen shots.

"I'm sorry." Harry shifted his gaze to the ground and the moonlight reflected dully off his bald head.

"You got anymore clips?"

"Two more in my pocket." Harry dug clumsily in the pocket of his overalls and withdrew two fully loaded magazines. He almost dropped one before I grabbed them. One of my fingertips brushed against his hand; his skin cold and solid, like touching a gravestone on a winter day.

"If we see Mary, I want you to kill her, Mickey." Though his voice sickened me, I heard the pain behind it. The sadness.

I didn't answer. What would it be like to come across Mary? Would she jump on us? Did she move like Harry, all decrepit and clumsy looking? I wondered if Mary lurked more in the shadows out by Kate's Lake rather than this far out, but then remembered hearing about that camper who'd been killed in these woods. I also wondered what Bob was doing right now. Perhaps sitting in his cabin, his feet propped up on the little coffee table? That didn't make any sense. At least he'd be there if Britney showed up and I thought that was a good thing. And then another question hit me, one that sparked dread and pebbled my arms with goose bumps…

Why hadn't Harry seen Britney on his trek down here?

It would have taken her a while to walk the two miles. And Harry certainly wasn't breaking any speed records.

"Did you take the path down here?" The weight of the gun grew more comfortable in my hand. I liked it.

"Yeah."

A pause hung between us and he knew something weighed on me. He asked, "Why?"

I glanced around us. More and more dark shapes of trees and bushes materialized as my vision adjusted. "You should've passed her. She would've taken the path too. You should've passed her on your way out here."

Harry didn't say anything at first. He knew I was right. Then he said, without much conviction, "She might'a hid when she saw me."

A new panic stirred inside me, roiling below the surface. *She's in trouble, little man,* Chuck Verhey whispered, *and you will be too if you don't beat-feet out of here.*

"Fuck you," I said. Harry didn't say anything, he knew I talked to myself. He'd seen it before.

I looked at him, into his pale face sagging in the moonlight, into his black pearl eyes, and once again my mind slipped closer to an abyss I might never climb out of. A shot of understanding passed between us. Our worst fears drifted through the air like telepathy… *Britney was dead.* Mary had killed her. Or worse, and I don't why I thought this, *Lupis Rudolph had found her.* I'm sure Harry thought that too.

"All right, here's what we're gonna do." I forced my eyes to stay on Harry's face, as hard as it was to do that, I did it. "I'm heading to the lake, to Bob's cabin. We need to get there."

Harry stood motionless; listening and understanding.

"I can't wait on you," I said, "Unless you can walk fast."

"I can't. Go without me."

"I want you to go to your old cabin," I said. "Make sure she's not there. I'll go to Bob's. If we don't find anything, we'll meet by the lake and go from there. Sound good?"

He nodded and said, "See you on the flip side."

I remembered the last time Harry had said that to me; about two hours before I shot that guy in Iraq. "You know it. Ain't no turning back this time. If anything gets in my way, I'll kill it."

I caught the slight nod he shot me. He knew I wasn't bullshitting around.

CHAPTER 30

I limped through the tall grass, wishing like hell I could run. That sonofabitch, Jesse. Pain in my side flared with each punishing step. I hoped I didn't have any broken ribs, or worse.

I'd been able to hear Harry shuffling behind me for a little while, but now he was too far back. I headed to Bob's place, hobbling and wincing, determined to get there. *Please be there, Britney*. I fought an impulse to yell out to her, but doing that would alert Lupis Rudolph. Maybe he knew I was there or maybe he didn't, but damned if I planned to give him a warning. I don't know why that guy scared me so much, but he did, and I hadn't even met him.

The stench of stagnate water thickened; getting close.

I wished I hadn't drunk all those beers, yet I wanted another one right now. I wanted a smoke too. I could make a list of shit I wanted and wished for. Like how I wished I hadn't come out to this bullshit place to start with.

Goddamn, I missed Amy right now. I wondered if she'd fallen asleep yet. It would be an hour earlier there, so she was most likely up and watching TV still. The girls probably were too, but they'd be going to bed soon since they had school tomorrow. I usually put them to bed. What was Amy telling them about me? She had to tell them something. And if Amy knew what I'd been doing (which surely she suspected since I'd drunk-dialed her earlier), what would she tell my girls then?

And Britney.

My God, what had we gotten into out here?

I'm surprised Chuck Verhey didn't have a smart-ass response to that question. I was sobering up. Chuck only became obnoxious when I got drunk. When I was sober, he'd always been reasonable. Sometimes, I barely thought of him at all.

Weeds brushed against my legs and occasionally, a thin branch would swipe across my face. The clear sky helped some. The full moon helped a lot. I glanced up a couple of times, amazed at how many stars splattered the sky out here; it was crystal clear. Iraq had been like that, parts of it anyway. Stars peppered the sky like twinkles on glistening water. Iraq had been so many things.

That's when I caught the dark shape of a man standing in the weeds along the path. A dark silhouette, huge and still. My breath stopped and my heart thumped a heavy ka-thud. Terror shot through me and I nearly cried out. Details swam into focus. The outline of long hair. Thick beard. Massive body.

That long-haired bastard who'd blocked the road earlier today.

I gripped the gun tighter.

"Yo?" My voice drifted lifelessly into the dark. The man didn't move. I wondered how far behind me Harry was and if he heard me.

My sweaty palms made the gun slippery in my hands. "I'll tell you right now," I tried to sound threatening and I think I pulled it off reasonably well. "If you decide to…"

Behind me, something large scuttled through the brush and crashed through weeds, moving goddamned fast. I stumbled back and raised the gun, but couldn't see a damned thing. The large, bearded man suddenly darted off into the weeds, moving with unusual grace for a man of that size, almost animal-like.

My harsh breathing cut the darkness and I tried to quiet down, but it only got worse. Uncontrollable. Gasping. Sweating. Gun shaking in my trembling hand. My throbbing heart pulsed heavily in my neck.

A shadow burst from a line of darkened trees, charging straight at me, like a massive dog. A slow moan escaped my throat. Instinct kicked in. I raised the weapon.

I fired. Center-mass. The weapon's crack ripped the thick darkness. The recoil jarred my wrist and arm.

The creature tumbled, as if it stepped into a deep hole. It bellowed and that sound chilled me to the bone. A human sound. I gawked stupidly at it thrashing in the weeds. A dying animal. A screaming man. I had no idea what it was, but it flailed, kicked, and flopped about like a dying bear.

Run, Mick!

I kept the gun aimed in its direction. *And where in the hell is Harry?*

The thing's movements slowed to intermittent jerks and twitches, until finally it remained still. I wanted to know what the hell I'd just shot, but no damned way I was stomping out into those weeds to inspect it. What if it wasn't dead?

And what about the other one?

I whirled and kept the gun raised; aiming into the darkness. My trained eyes scanned for movement. Searching. *Knowing* it was out there. Somewhere. The big-bearded man who'd darted away like a panther lurked out there, possibly watching me right now.

My breathing settled into rhythmic ins and outs. My heart thrummed. Sweat trickled down my cheeks in cold drips and I heard everything around me, like spiders scuttling over dead leaves. But my hands didn't shake. My knees didn't wobble.

I was in control. In my element. Even the dull pain in my side had melted away. If that fuck-head Jesse popped his head up right now, I'd blow it off.

I scraped my tongue across my dry lips, brushing over the puffy flesh with a pleasurable sting. Nothing moved out there. Nothing at all.

"Listen, fucker," I spoke evenly into the night. "If I see you, I'll kill you. That's your only warning." I meant every goddamned word of it.

I scanned the path behind me. Still no sign of Harry.

He might've gone another way. Which would explain why he never encountered Britney on her way down. *But he said he took the path.* But he didn't say he took *this* path. How many ways were there?

And most troubling… had Britney encountered any of these things I'd shot? Or Mary had found her. Jesus Christ, I had to get moving. I had to get down there. Now.

I lowered the gun, but maintained a healthy grip. I scanned the area where the other creature had died (where I assume it died), my eyes peering at the shadowed weeds and tried to detect any sign of movement. I stared hard and listened. Nothing. Not so much as a slithering snake.

Don't go over there. I didn't want to, God knows I didn't, yet I needed to know what lay in those weeds. What was I up against? So much confusion right now. Was Mary lying over there? But the creature I shot had moved like an animal, not like a person.

Britney. *Get to her, now.*

I checked behind me one last time to make sure Harry wasn't there. He wasn't. Nothing but a gaping black hole within the trees. I kept a tight hold on the gun, my forefinger rested comfortably against the receiver ready to squeeze the trigger.

I'm coming, Britney. God, I hoped she was okay.

. . . . .

I reached Bob's cabin a few minutes later and surveyed it from where I'd stopped along the path. The lights were on, but no one appeared home. I slipped into the taller weeds and watched for any sign of movement. A soft, rumbling noise came from inside the place, which at first had me stumped, but then I realized it was a portable generator running from down in the cellar.

If anyone was here, they were hiding. And why would they do that if they didn't know I was coming? My side ached again, so I lowered down to one knee to relieve some pressure. It helped a little.

That's when I caught a glimpse of something moving inside the cabin. Just a quick roll of a shadow across the ceiling, but I saw it, clear as day, through the side window. Someone *was* in there. But this felt wrong. All wrong. I stared and waited. A hopeful part of me yearned to see Britney look out the window.

And wouldn't you know it, that's when my cell phone vibrated in my pocket? Goddamn, it scared the living hell out of me. It buzzed four times and went to voicemail. *What if it was Britney?* Whipping the damned thing out while I hid in these weeds seemed stupid. I might as well be carrying a lightbulb over my head.

Off to my left, Kate's Lake spread out like a shiny black blanket. I edged closer to the bank, shuffling down a short, but steep incline where I could move easier and undetected along a thin swath of muddy bank. Fewer weeds.

I half slipped, half stumbled down to the water's edge. My feet plopped into the wet mud, but I didn't fall on my ass; thank God for small miracles. I lingered on the bank and gagged on the putrid smell of rot and decay wafting from the water.

Or what I'd assumed to be coming off the water.

I turned toward Bob's cabin and froze. Hairs on my neck and arms stirred and my balls shriveled as if trying to climb up inside of me. About twenty feet ahead, someone crouched by the water's edge, squatted as if taking a shit. The moon's glow illuminated them as if God himself were pointing out this abomination.

Oh Jesus. Oh, Jesus Christ.

Mary.

She either hadn't seen me or didn't care because she never looked up. I forgot about any pain in my side or my lip. I completely forgot everything. A weird floating sensation engulfed me, like a bizarre vertigo where I might topple over and go headfirst into the lake.

She rummaged through some sort of bag; her head, sparsely dotted with clumps of stringy hair, leaned over it as if she'd never seen anything like it before. I had a second to think of how easy this shot would be. But I couldn't move. I gawked and wondered if I might puke.

Mary was naked. Large spots on her skin were either smears of dried mud, or open sores. I couldn't tell which, but the horrid stench stirred another wave of nausea. I wanted to look away, but my eyes remained fixed. Her lips pulled back in a sickening grimace, revealing ugly teeth that looked far too large. Maybe that's what dead people look like. Either that or her lips had rotted away. I swallowed back a rising gorge.

She yanked something out of the bag, held it in front of her and studied it curiously, as a gorilla might examine a watch tossed into its cage. Something short and round, about two inches long. She dropped the bag in front of her and held the short, round thing. Part of me wanted to see her better; part of me was glad I couldn't.

What she did next horrified me. She took the thing in her hand and rubbed it awkwardly against her lips, or what was left of her lips. Staying in that crouched position, she rubbed it like a toddler using crayons for the first time.

It's lipstick, I thought. *She's trying to put on lipstick.* Fear fluttered in my stomach. Recognition. She'd found lipstick in that bag.

I'm not sure what I'd expected Mary to be or what she would look like, but finding her along the bank of Kate's Lake trying to put on lipstick was about as far from what I'd pictured as you could get.

I stepped toward her and raised the gun, aiming directly at Mary's head. It wasn't Mary that terrified me as much as the discarded bag lying on the ground, the contents spread out like garbage. The pink face of Britney's cell phone half buried in the mud.

CHAPTER 31

Shoot her.

What if she doesn't die? What if it doesn't die?

And maybe it wouldn't. Maybe it would be like in those zombie movies where the walking corpses take bullets but keep right on coming. My breath wheezed in jerky hitches, but Mary still never turned and looked at me.

"Mary?" My voice sounded distant and dreamy.

Mary stopped and swiveled her head like an owl. It made me want to scream. Her eyes were black pits, and her mouth was a grotesque grin full of teeth.

"Where's Britney?" My dream voice drifted out and I kept the gun aimed directly at her face.

"'Ah 'itney," the thing said back to me. Similar to Harry, her voice was slobbery, as if speaking through thick vomit. "'Ah 'itney," she said again.

At first, I didn't have a clue, but then it dawned on me. She was repeating what I said.

"Where's Britney, yes, where's Britney?"

"'Ah 'itney." She held up the small tube of lipstick in front of her decayed face, showing me, as if this were something to be proud of.

Terrible thoughts streamed through my head, thoughts of Britney lying somewhere in these weeds, torn open, and Mary feeding on her soft insides. Or she was in Kate's Lake, floating face down in the black water, or worse yet, her hair drifting lifelessly in the water as she sank for an eternity in a bottomless lake.

Stop it!

Mary stood and faced me. Weak breath escaped me as I gaped at the impossible. She wasn't tall or necessarily threatening – she didn't growl or anything, but I stutter-stepped back. She still held the lipstick. I barely made out the sagging breasts, the protruding ribcage. Something dripped from between her legs and after a few seconds, it became evident as I watched the tiny things fall, sometimes in clumps, and land on the ground in squirming piles.

Maggots. Maggots were falling out of Mary's vagina. *Holy God.*

This time, the hot roiling in my gut heaved upward and I puked on the muddy bank of Kate's Lake. I hadn't eaten much, so it was mostly liquid, but once you got it started, it could be a bitch to get it stopped. I heaved, swallowed back the burning bile and stomach acid in my mouth, and heaved again.

Get your shit together, Marine! Sergeant Higgins screamed into my ear, coming to my rescue. And he was right; I had to get my shit together. I'm pretty goddamn sure I lost my mind, but I still had to do something, even if that something meant running like hell, screaming like a banshee back down the path to my car.

Mary lurched toward me and I stumbled back, a small moan escaping my throat.

Just then, the lights of Harry's cabin flicked on from across the lake. The lights caught both mine and Mary's attention.

Her head cocked and twisted to face the cabin. "Arry."

She slobbered the word again and it hit me, she was saying *Harry*. I hoped like hell it was Harry in there.

"Mary," I said again, my voice shaky, "Where's Britney?"

"'Ahs Itney," she looked back at me, *it* looked back at me, the horrid pits of her eyes gaping like yawning mouths. "Itney."

"Yeah, Britney."

"Itney."

Holy shit, was I really having this conversation? "I need to know where Britney is."

Mary flipped a hand up toward Bob's cabin. It was a subtle gesture, not much more than a flip of the wrist, but it told the whole story. If Mary wasn't full of shit, or confused, she was telling me Britney was in Bob's cabin. "Itney." Drool bubbled out of her mouth and hit the mud in wet smacks.

Movement in Harry's cabin caught my eye again. "Harry!" I yelled. "Harry!" Please God, let that be him in that cabin.

Kill her. I knew I had to; I had to pull the trigger. My grip tightened on the gun, my finger rested on the trigger. *Pull it!*

"Harry!"

Pull it, goddamn it. Pull it.

"Harry!"

She'd spoken, she'd known who Harry was. She'd known who Britney was. She'd *known*. What if she were still alive, somehow?

Pull the damn trigger, you chickenshit, Sergeant Higgins screamed into my ear.

"Harry! Goddamn it, get down *HERE*!"

She didn't choose to drink the water. Harry did that for her. She didn't choose to get brain cancer. This thing, this rotting thing standing before me, was a woman in her late thirties and nothing good had happened for her. Nothing. She didn't choose anything in her whole miserable life. She held the tube of lipstick up in front of her as if she were surrendering, as if she were telling me that she didn't want any of this, that she wanted to go back home.

The door to Harry's cabin banged open and I saw him lumbering across the small porch, heading toward me.

He tried to yell, but it was garbled.

I kept the gun aimed at Mary who stood with her head tilted awkwardly. She glanced at Harry and for a second, I thought she'd yell back. She dropped the lipstick into the wet mud and crouched back down.

"Hold on," I said. Not sure why I said that.

"Shoot her, Mickey," Harry was close now, stumbling through the weeds, trying to get to me. "Shoot her!"

My hand trembled. My finger found the trigger. I didn't want to do this.

Mary twitched, then flipped her attention back to me and clenched her filthy teeth. She sprang. Powerful. Animal-like. Too late to fire. She collided into me. I reeled and smacked ass-first into the soft mud. I held onto the gun though, by God, at least I did that.

She loomed over me. Her rotted mouth opened wide. Her black eyes reduced to mere slits and her hand curled into a claw.

"Shoot her, Mickey!" Harry was on the bank, staggering toward us.

Mary faced him and hissed. I tried to scramble backward, to get out of reach, but my feet struggled to catch traction in the wet mud. I raised the gun. Mary sensed it, because she looked back at me and gnashed her teeth, like a crazed dog about to bite, and then she scampered away into the weeds.

I rolled onto my belly with the gun outstretched, but saw nothing. She was gone.

Harry shuffled up behind me. I cried out and flipped over and pointed the gun at him. He stared at me from that sagging face, from those shadowed eyes.

"What the fuck was that?" I nearly screamed the words. "What in the *fuck* was that?"

Harry remained stoic as I struggled to my feet. I kept the gun aimed at him.

"That's what she's turning into." He spoke quietly.

"Why didn't you tell me?"

"I tried." His face was so pale and distorted; it reminded me of one of those rubber Halloween masks.

"You didn't tell me she could do that," I said, "You said she was insane, you didn't say she could move like *that*." I lowered the gun; I wasn't going to shoot Harry, not yet.

"I didn't know she could do that either." Harry touched his face. "I haven't seen her in weeks."

Not sure why, but I was getting pissed off. "That's fuckin' bullshit, man. This is all bullshit. Can you do that, move like she does?" I gripped the gun tight at my side.

"Not yet." Harry's hand still covered his face. "I told you, that's what I'm trying not to become. I don't know if I can stop it, though, because I keep having weirder and weirder thoughts sometimes. Terrible thoughts." He spoke so quietly on those last words, I barely heard him. I wondered what he meant by *terrible thoughts*.

But I stayed silent. Because fuck Harry, fuck Britney, fuck all this shit. It was out of control. I wanted to find Britney, I really did, and it hurt like hell that I didn't know where she was, but goddamn it, I had my own family to consider. I didn't need this crazy shit. This was beyond crazy… this was lunacy!

I told Harry, "*Fuck* you for bringing me out here."

"There was no one else I could call."

"I'm leaving right now!" I spat the words. "Mary said Britney was up there in Bob's cabin. Go check it out." I glanced over at the contents of the spilled purse, just dark shapes in the mud, but the cell phone caught the reflection of Bob's cabin lights. My chest ached.

Harry didn't know what to say.

"I'm not going up there." I flipped a hand at Bob's cabin. "I'm walking my happy ass back to my car." I thought of the woods and how goddamn dark it was, and of Mary.

"Can you at least try to get Brit out for me?" He shuffled back. "Please get her out of here."

"I don't even know if she's alive." I pointed to her spilled purse on the ground. Sadness gripped me, but I held my ground. I was leaving. "Mary was digging through her shit when I walked up."

"*You* brought her down here." Harry's slobbery voice growled and I saw the grimace cross his darkened face. "*You* brought her down here and got her into this shit. I didn't ask you to do that."

"Go to hell, Harry." No way he was laying this guilt trip on me. "You should've told me what was going on. I wouldn't have brought her if I'd known."

"Like you would've believed me. And look at you," Harry inched toward me, his head cocked and his voice low and mean. "You piece of shit. What the hell were you doing with her to start with? Huh, answer that, you drunk fuck!"

My words fluttered away like frightened crows.

"It's the same old shit with you, Mickey. Only this time I'm not there to save your stupid ass." His lips pulled back and revealed dark teeth. I smelled the rot leaking out of his insides.

I glared at him, pissed and terrified. "I didn't ask for this shit."

"You think I did?"

"You know what I'm talking about." Goddamn right he did.

"I know. I was there, remember?"

I looked at him and I saw Harry. *My* Harry. "Yeah, I guess you were."

"It wasn't your fault."

I glanced down at the gun and chuckled, a dry, humorless sound. "Sure it was, Harry. And everything since then has been my fault too. You said it, I'm a drunk, I like your sister… guess I never forgot about that picture. I'm fresh out of excuses."

Harry listened. I don't know if this was the right time or the place, but I kept talking, more to myself than to him. "You know what I've wanted to do for the past ten or so years?" I didn't wait for an answer, I ran my finger down the short smooth barrel of the gun. "I've wanted to die. I've wanted to go over there to Iraq and apologize to that guy's kids, then disappear. Cease to exist. How's that for being jacked up?"

"Mickey…" Harry's words were weak, so I cut him off.

"It's all bullshit, man!" I said. "We flew home, Harry, and people lined the goddamned streets, cheering for us, giving us high-fives and shit."

"Mickey…"

"We weren't heroes, Harry! Who the hell were we to come home acting all bad and shit, like we'd done something great." I wiped away snot with my dirty hand.

Harry wheezed, "We were just trying to survive. No one wanted a war."

I screamed at him, "*I did*!" I pointed the muzzle of the gun at my chest. "*I did*!"

Harry shuffled closer, not speaking this time, but stepping close enough to touch me, if he'd wanted to. Maybe he never understood since we'd never talked like this, not about the war anyway. Maybe, and this might be the bubble gum at the center of a blow-pop, I didn't know any of this shit either. It poured out of me. Maybe it was the alcohol, maybe it was my dead friend standing here talking to me, maybe it was so many things, like not being able to pull the goddamn trigger a few minutes ago when I had Mary in my sights. *Maybe, maybe, maybe*… there was a lot of that going around.

"Don't you get that?" A sob lurched out of me and I swallowed hard. I leaned over and placed my hands on my knees. "I could justify what I'd done if they'd have just fought, Harry. If they'd takin' one motherfucking shot at us. Just one!"

I fell down onto my knees, then plopped backward onto my ass, and sat there. Kate's Lake stayed silent, not caring. No one cared. No one ever cared.

Wasn't this the damndest thing? All the shit going on, Britney missing, God knew what else, and here I was, sitting in the fucking mud.

Then Harry plopped down next to me, all awkward looking, like sitting here was the most painful thing he'd ever done. *Can he feel stuff?* But still, he was doing it. Despite the fact that his sister was out here, somewhere. That Mary lurked in these shadows. He sat here with me.

I laughed, even with everything else going on, I laughed. "I went nuts a long time ago, Harry."

"Nah, you didn't. You started drinking."

We stared at the lake, and then Harry said, "You wanna have a smoke?"

Goddamn it, I loved him and for the first time since this whole mess started, I realized I was going to lose him, and I couldn't imagine a world where he didn't exist.

"You serious?" I chuckled.

"Yeah. You got any?"

"Is a frog's ass water tight?"

And then we'd both laughed, or at least, Harry tried to.

CHAPTER 32

Within a few minutes, we concocted a half-ass plan. It would've worked, too, if Lupis Rudolph hadn't screwed everything up.

After my emotional melt-down, a strange calm washed over me. My sense of urgency ramped back up and our top priority was finding Britney.

I smoked and Harry watched... I know he wanted one, but he told me it would be useless to try since he couldn't breathe. We both smiled, despite the sadness of it all. Thoughts of Mary lurked under the surface like a dangerous snake.

"There's something more to this place than just a lake and a weird pool of water," Harry said, leaning sideways, half on his elbow.

"Let's stand up," I said. I couldn't stand seeing him so uncomfortable anymore.

I hoisted myself up and he reached out to me. I grasped his hand and that familiar revulsion crept up from my belly as I squeezed his cold and solid flesh, pulling him up to his feet. But I didn't let go.

"I'm thinking you're right." I took a drag on my cigarette. Weird how I hardly noticed Harry's decayed stench anymore. "About the lake."

"It draws people, or something." Harry stumbled, but kept his footing. "Lupis Rudolph is one of those people. It's like he needs to bring people here."

"Like he brought you and Mary here?"

"Yeah. He acted nervous, like he didn't want to stay any longer than he had to."

"But he's here now?"

"Yeah." He shrugged which made me think he wasn't completely sure about that.

I asked him, "Is he supposed to keep the place a secret or something."

Harry paused, as if considering this, then said something even more unsettling, yet felt more right. "No… it's like he *owes* it something."

Like he owes it. I wondered how old Lupis Rudolph was. Perhaps the water kept him alive, living forever, and there was a price for using the water that way. Maybe it needed to consume life to give life and that's why Lupis hung out in cancer wards and lured people out here. A chill raced down my spine.

Time to get moving. We'd already wasted enough time with my little outburst.

"I don't like the sound of that," I told Harry, "let's work the plan… I'll go through the basement, try to sneak up to the door. If Britney's in there, I'll hear her from down there. You stay out here and watch, make sure no one comes out. If they do, watch where they go. I don't plan on being in there for long." In and out, that was the plan.

We nodded and it was done. The great battle plan. What a couple of dumbasses we were. Had I known how bad things were going to get, trust me, we'd have called the National Guard.

I led the way, climbing the short incline back up to the path, keeping a tight grip on the gun. I heard Harry behind me, slipping and flopping, making every effort to be stealthy, but failing miserably. Hopefully no one in Bob's cabin heard him. I had no idea if the old bastard was on our side. My gut told me he *was* on our side since Harry brought him in on this shit when he'd had Bob call me, but I wasn't taking chances. I wished I'd asked Harry more about that guy.

I reached the path and kept a steady pace through the thin trees. I didn't look back to check on Harry. I listened for anything that might come scrambling out of the darkness… my biggest concern was Mary, of course, and that big guy who'd darted off into the woods. It dawned on me that I forgot to tell Harry I'd shot something a ways back on the path.

By the time all of these thoughts had processed, I'd made it to the back of Bob's cabin. I couldn't see anything in detail, but the lights from inside provided enough illumination to identify what I needed. The outline of the back deck loomed in the dark like a ghost ship and I knew that under that, were the steps and the little door to Bob's cellar, where I'd first seen Harry.

That's where I needed to go first, in case she was down in there. *What if there's no door to get into the cabin from down there? I'd be trapped in a basement.*

I stopped and leaned against a tree. I looked up through the shadowed leaves and saw the stars sparkling against a crystal-clear sky. Going through the cellar was too much of a risk, and if one of them caught me down there, I'd be cornered like an animal in a cave.

I tried to picture Britney, hopefully sitting in Bob's cabin having a cup of coffee with him, just shootin' the shit. But then I thought of Mary and the lipstick. The scenarios of how Mary might've gotten it started playing in my head; uninvited scenarios, I might add, and I squeezed my eyes shut, forcing those thoughts away. I had to, because in all of them, Britney was dead. *Ah, little man, payback's a bitch*, Chuck Verhey's voice tried edging its way back in, but the alcohol was wearing off and he wasn't making much sense.

"Fuck off," I hissed. Time to go.

I left the cover of the tree and snuck to the edge of the deck. I stooped down and listened. At first, there were only the sounds of the darkness; bugs, frogs around the lake, shit like that, and, of course, that goddamn generator running from down in Bob's basement. If there was anything going on inside that cabin, I couldn't hear it. I wished I could shut off that generator.

If the lights were off, it might give me a split-second advantage. Of course, it would also leave me just as blind as anyone inside. So piss on shutting off the generator.

That's when I heard a voice, very low and barely audible. Someone inside there was talking. A man. Just mumbles. I pictured Britney inside and Lupis Rudolph, whom I'd never seen but only imagined as an enormous, brooding individual, running a knife blade up and down her body, preparing for the thrust.

I climbed up on the deck and slinked to the door. I stayed crouched; the weapon gripped in my hand, held out in front of me, my right forefinger resting against the trigger guard, ready to act. *Please God,* I thought as I approached the door, *let me pull the trigger if I have to.*

Remember Iraq, little man, Chuck Verhey whispered into my ear. *You shot an unarmed man.*

Shut up, I wanted to yell at him. I needed that asshole to shut up right now.

You know, the dead Iraqi that you're convinced is standing out in your living room every night.

Shut up! In my mind, I yelled it. The door loomed only a few inches away. Flimsy. Breakable.

The dead man, Mick m'boy, that you shot, that you know stands outside your house in the dark, sometimes looking at your daughters through their bedroom windows. He's out here, little man. He's out here.

He's dead! I lifted my foot and I thrust it forward, connecting with the small door in a solid hit. It caved to the sound of breaking plastic and clanging metal, I burst through, holding the gun at eye level. The door slammed against a counter and glass shattered.

My eyes swept the kitchen and I saw nothing except for one person I didn't know sitting at the small table. I leveled the gun. *Center-mass.*

"Who the hell are you?" I said and moved closer, the sites trained on his chest.

The man smiled. He was balding, slightly overweight, and looked to be in his fifties. *Lupis Rudolph?*

"I asked, who the hell are you?" I yelled this time. I was sweaty, splattered in mud from the bank of Kate's Lake, and my face was bruised. I'd already shot one thing tonight and feeling confident I could make it two.

The man's smile never faltered and he gawked at me, like someone insane.

"I'm only going to ask you one more time, motherfucker, or…"

"Or what?" the man's voice boomed inside the small space and it shocked the hell out of me.

"I'll kill you," my voice warbled.

No you won't, Chuck Verhey said.

And dear God, I'm afraid Chuck was right.

CHAPTER 33

"I don't think you will." The man tapped his fingers on the table. "But far be it from me to assume, so, allow me to introduce myself." He stuck out his hand. "My name is Mr. Rudolph. Most people call me Lupis. You can do the same."

I blinked, dumbfounded. My heart slammed. "I swear to God," I growled. I cocked the gun, yanking back the receiver and letting it go, chambering a round. Not impressive. It ejected the bullet that was already in the chamber which fell to the floor with a lifeless clunk.

Get it together, little man.

Fuck you, Chuck.

Lupis Rudolph put his hands in the air. Like a father playing cops and robbers with his toddler, he didn't look scared at all. The smirk never left his face. "I give up," he said. "Let's just chat for a bit. Does that work?"

I wished my damn hands would stop shaking.

"Listen, Mick, I'm not the bad guy here." Lupis still held his hands up in that stupid *please don't shoot me* gesture. "There really are no bad guys. Even that guy you shot on the path down here, he didn't know any better."

Wait, what? "That was an animal."

Lupis's eyebrows raised and he glanced to one side. "Yeah, well… whatever."

I swallowed against a ridiculously dry mouth. "Why are you here?" I faintly remembered my conversation with Harry. He owes it something. He *owes* it.

"I might ask you the same thing," Lupis said.

"You know why I'm here." The gun shook horribly in my hands. I tried to make it stop, to *will* it to stop, but it wouldn't.

"I know why you were here this morning." Lupis chuckled and shook his head. "But for the life of me, I don't know why you're here now." His brow furrowed.

I glared at him. Something was wrong here, way wrong, and I couldn't pinpoint it. It was like peering through glass with a slight imperfection; something only visible from the corner of your eye.

A voice inside me whispered, *he's faking it.*

That wasn't Chuck Verhey, or Seargent Higgins, or not even Skip Jones that said that. It was me. All me.

He's faking it.

I thought of Mary, rotting and putrid, squatted on the bank of Kate's Lake with the contents of Britney's purse spread around her. Of this whole mess. Of Amy and my girls sleeping at home.

Run, Mick!

"How 'bout a drink, Mick?" Lupis's words broke my reverie and I gawked at him.

"We'd have to check the fridge." Lupis lowered his hands to his lap. "But we've got some beer. And I'd bet my ass that 'ole Bob's got some whiskey stashed around here somewhere." He nodded and grew still like a snake coiled before the strike.

Speaking of Bob, where was he? Where was anyone?

"Where is she?" I asked. I still hadn't lowered the gun.

"Who? Mary?"

"Britney. Where is she?"

Lupis's eyebrows furrowed again and he seemed to consider this. "I don't know any Britney. I know Mary."

"Where's Bob?" I was running out of things to ask.

"Well, he's not here, I can tell you that. He wasn't here when I got here." Lupis stared at me and the thought I read on his face was, *how long are we going to play this stupid game.* "Maybe he went into town for something." Lupis yawned.

He actually yawned.

He knows you ain't gonna shoot him, Chuck's voice taunted me. *Have a drink with him. You'll learn more and you're hands'll stop shaking.*

I glanced around the cabin. Nothing looked out of place, but yet this was all so wrong.

"How 'bout that beer, Mick?" Lupis asked. "You can catch me up on what you're doing here. I can help you."

Lupis Rudolph reminded me of something, I'm not sure what, but it wasn't anything good, I can tell you that much. I thought of one of those ventriloquist dummies with those large, beady eyes and glossy hair.

Don't be distracted, little man. Britney was missing, my best friend stood guard outside, Bob was nowhere to be found, and I had a gun pointed at this guy.

At the guy who showed Harry the fountain.

The fountain of youth.

At the guy who, in a round-about way, created Mary.

Lupis's smile widened as I thought these things. He seemed to know. That smile wasn't right, not quite grotesque, but broken all the same. It was too wide. Teeth gleamed through the thin slit of his parted lips and for a horrible moment, I thought some of them were pointed.

I blinked hard. *I'm imagining things now*. Had to be.

"Look." Lupis slapped his hand on the table and startled the shit out of me. "I tried to play it nice, tried to make things easy, but you obviously want to be a dickhead about this whole thing."

Lupis's voice melted into a deep, fuzzy drawl, like someone might sound on an old-fashioned tape player with dying batteries. He shook his head as if disgusted.

"I'd have been perfectly content with letting you go, but I reckon it's best that I don't. You're getting too many people meddling around down here. You checked your voice messages lately?"

The whites of his eyes darkened yellow, like the milky tint of dehydrated piss. He was changing, right in front of me, transforming. There's no other way to describe it.

"I guess you haven't." His jaw jutted, distorting his words. "But you should. You'd know what I'm talking about. And that pretty girl you're looking for…"

My chest tightened. *Shoot him…*

"Mary got her. I'm not positive on that, but I heard someone scream a little while before you showed up and Mary was out there."

"Who are you?"

Mary got her.

"I told you already, my name is Lupis Rudolph. Guess you could say I'm like the caretaker in these parts."

Shoot him, little man!

Coffee with Bob yesterday morning jumped into my mind. Him glancing around, like he expected someone might be watching him. He'd seemed scared and I'd chalked it up to him being crazy. But now, in the presence of Lupis Rudolph, I had an idea of who Bob might have been looking out for.

Someone who frightened him.

CHAPTER 34

Silence hung between us. Whether it was thirty seconds or thirty minutes, I have no clue and Lupis didn't seem the least bit concerned. He just sat at the table, staring at me. His eyes reminded me of a blind man, with the milky irises and ghostly pupils. But Lupis Rudolph wasn't blind, not one bit. That sonofabitch saw everything.

"Okay," Lupis said in that bizarre voice, "I guess you're gonna pass on that drink. I'm telling you though, we could make a lot more progress if we did this like men."

Should I yell out to Harry?

If he didn't know where Britney was, why was I still talking to him?

But, he'd shown Harry the fountain. I needed to know more about that. I could still help Harry.

He *owes* it something.

"Here's what I'll do." Lupis placed his meaty arms on the table and leaned forward. "You're obviously a smart guy, Mick, and you're not going to be dissuaded here, I can see that now, and I like that in a man."

Shoot him, Mick!

But my finger wouldn't squeeze. He wasn't armed and that meant everything.

"If you sit down here." Lupis lightly tapped a spot on the kitchen table. "I'll tell you everything. Damn it, you're right, I do know what happened to your pretty little girlfriend, and what happened to Harry, and what's about to happen to everyone else. Just have a beer with me. Could you extend me that courtesy for the information you need to know?"

What choice did I have?

"All right." I tried to use my *don't-fuck-with-me* tone. "But this better not take long. You understand me?"

"Read ya loud and clear." Lupis smiled and that smile bothered me, as if I'd made a deal with the devil himself.

I backed up to the fridge, opened it, and grabbed two cans of Coors Lite. Weird that Bob had the beer I liked. I expected he'd have something cheaper, like Pabst Blue Ribbon, Hamms, or just BEER. But no, it was the good stuff (or what I called the good stuff).

I stepped back to the table and plopped them down. Lupis reached over and grasped his, popped the top, and took a long swig. "Ahhhhhhh," he growled. "That's good."

I eased into the chair, feeling like everything I did was a mistake. I popped the tab and sipped. It was good, I had to admit that. It helped me calm down. I took a longer, deeper drink. Oh yes, this definitely helped.

"You can set the gun down, Mick," Lupis said. "I promise I won't bite."

"I'll hang onto it." I drank again.

He shrugged. "Go ahead and have a smoke." He gestured to a small, plastic ashtray parked in the middle of the table. "I'm sure Bob won't mind."

I shook out a cigarette and lit one. "Where's Britney?" The KOOL 100 dangled from the corner of my mouth.

Lupis drank his beer and sat it down, then cupped both hands around it, as if it might fly away if he didn't hold onto it. "I won't lie to you, Mick, she had a run in with Mary. I wasn't bullshitting about that. But she might've gotten away, lost in the woods right now or something. Scared shitless, but okay."

I had no idea whether to trust him or not, but the thought of her hiding out there lost tightened my chest. "Why didn't Mary kill her?"

"See, this is why I wanted to talk about this with ya." His grisly eyes found mine and the bastard tried to be sincere, but everything about him screamed danger.

My, Grandma, what BIG teeth you have.

Lupis twisted the beer can in his hands as he spoke. "Mary isn't evil. She isn't good, but she's not some vampire, or anything like that. She'll kill if threatened, but so will Harry eventually, when the sickness gets him."

"The sickness?"

"Yeah." Lupis shifted his gaze to the table's surface. "That's what I call it. It's death, Mick. The sickness is death. It'll make him crazy, eventually."

I remembered Harry saying he'd fight it as long as possible. *The sickness*. "What is Mary? When I saw her down by the lake a little bit ago, she moved like a cat or something."

"It's not what she is," Lupis said, "It's what she's becoming. She and Harry both. All of them do eventually"

That statement made me shiver and I took a long drink of my beer, draining it. I thought of those people along the path, the big man who moved like an animal. The thing I'd shot.

"Need another?" Lupis pointed at my empty can and I nodded reluctantly. I needed to hear what he had to say.

He got up and walked gracefully to the fridge, only taking out one can of beer, the one for me. "You see." He slid the cold can across the table to me and settled back into his chair. "The fountain is not the fountain of youth anymore. It may have been at one time, back in its day, but not anymore. Not since I started watching over it."

I popped the tab on my beer and listened, a thousand thoughts danced in the back of my head, a thousand voices screamed at me to do something, but they were all screaming different things.

"So what's Harry becoming?" I asked, more relaxed. Less jumpy.

"Good question." Lupis nodded. "I'm not sure there's a fancy name for it."

I thought about when Mary had jumped at me. How she'd sprang ten feet through the air.

Lupis rapped his fingers on the top of the table, as if he were thinking about something, perhaps how to explain what I'd asked. What I noticed most was how long his fingers were. They seemed to have grown at least an inch or more since I arrived. Looking at him, another memory danced just out of reach, something that Harry had said.

"The only way I know to describe it is like this." Lupis stopped tapping his fingers and took a drink of his beer. "Let's say at one time, the fountain was a place you could go and drink and be healed. Like I said, I'm assuming that at one point it was like that, I personally never saw it. I wasn't given the fountain until recently, like the past hundred years or so."

Questions popped into my head, but I listened.

"The fountain of youth is what it *was*, not what it is now. Even this little lake out here, Kate's Lake, is fed by some of the same water that feeds the fountain, but it's much less powerful, less concentrated. But enough so that if you drank it, you might get a touch of the sickness. That's why it has that name, you know. The little girl who drank out of it lost her mind. I remember that day."

I lit another cigarette and cocked an eye in Lupis's direction. "What day?"

He gazed past me, *through* me, off into space, into a place only he could see. "The day that little Katie Summers drown in that lake. That's where it got its name, you know. Kate's Lake."

"When?" My dream-like feeling swelled.

"Oh damn," Lupis looked up at the ceiling. "That would have been a hundred years ago, I guess. I'm not sure exactly, but it was something like that."

Get ready, Mick, my mind screamed. *Things are about to go bad.*

I didn't know if that was my voice or someone else's, and I didn't care. What mattered is that I knew it was right.

Lupis kept talking, almost as if he were enjoying the discussion, like a forgotten old man in a nursing home who finally had someone to listen to him. "Poor little thing had pneumonia and back in those days, it was pretty common to die from that, especially out in the sticks like this. I took her to the lake here and had her drink from it. I figured it'd heal her, but it didn't. So I took her to the fountain and that did it! She seemed to get better. But a few days later, she went bad."

Lupis suddenly seemed distraught. Genuinely sad. The expression passed as quickly as it had come. "Her daddy ended up drowning her in the lake. There wasn't anything else he could do for her, you know. He tried everything, but she kept getting worse, kept turning into some sort of animal. He couldn't kill her. She was already dead. So he drowned her in the lake."

Lupis shifted his gaze at me and I have no idea what type of expression he saw etched on my face. Lupis's eyes watered, filled to the brim with tears. "If there was anything that he could have done to save that little girl, he'd have done it." He slammed his hand flat against the table. "*Do you understand THAT*?"

I scooted backward and gripped the gun.

"What makes us human, Mick?" Lupis's lip curled and his gravelly voice sank deeper.

I jumped up, nearly knocked my chair over, and grasped the pistol with both hands. That's when I remembered what Harry had said earlier when I'd talked to him. *Bring me Lupis Rudolph.*

Lupis stayed seated and leered at me. "It's our soul, Mick. It's our soul that makes us human. That's what the fountain takes away from you. It keeps you alive, but in exchange, it eats your soul. I don't think it always did that, but it does that now. Katie wasn't a bad girl. She was the sweetest little thing you'd ever meet."

Lupis smiled when he said this. "But what drives me crazy is the thought of her down there on the bottom of that lake right now, wrapped in chains that will eventually rust and break, still thrashing to get free. I hope the stories are true, that the lake is bottomless."

I backed up to where the open door hung ajar, my shoes crunching glass and glanced out into the blackness. "Harry!"

"Do you know what the problem is?" Lupis asked.

I didn't answer him. I yelled out the door again. "Harry! Get up here!"

And then Lupis said, "Katie should've died of pneumonia. I should've let her die. Because as long as she's down there, I have to feed it."

CHAPTER 35

"HARRY!" Where the hell was he?

I glanced outside and then back at Lupis, who remained solemn at the table. His lips moved, but he wasn't talking to me. I lumbered farther out the door, wondering if Britney might be close. That is, of course, if Lupis Rudolph wasn't lying.

I looked over at the black surface of Kate's Lake. *Is she really down there, wrapped in chains, struggling to get free?* I shivered and knew that Lupis had not been lying about that part. He'd been too passionate about it. And something about the way he'd told it made me think that possibly…

"Mickey!" Harry's voice strained. His silhouette approached the deck. Damn, I was glad to see him.

"Listen," I said as Harry climbed the steps, leaning heavily on the hand rail as he did so. "Lupis Rudolph is inside here and Britney's in the woods."

"Did Lupis tell you that?" Harry asked.

"Yeah."

"That motherfucker's lyin'." He spat the words, pissed off, his anger as evident as the stink from his rotting flesh.

I glanced back at Lupis. My breath caught when I saw the bastard standing about two feet from me, glaring at me. I spun, but it was too late. His hand shot out and connected with my chest like a jackhammer. I sailed backward and connected hard with the deck railing right across my lower back. The wood gave with a lazy crack and then I was falling, holding the gun in front of me, and looking up through the trees at the stars blinking their eternal carelessness.

I hit the ground with a thud; then rolled to the side and moaned, struggling to breathe as if my lungs were full of lead. Pain raced up my side. My face hurt again and now I had a nauseating ache in my back. This was not a good night for me.

Once on my belly, I lay still, trying to catch my breath. The leaves and grass were cool and it felt good not to move. Ruckus ensued behind me, from up in Bob's cabin.

Harry.

Glass shattered. Crashing furniture, then a deep and frightening growl. I had to get up there. Harry was in there.

Get the fuck up!

I shoved, like doing a pushup with a mountain of bricks on my back, and got to my hands and knees. I still held the gun; thank God I hadn't dropped that. A new surge of adrenaline kicked in and dampened the pain in my side, hip, and face. I was able to move.

I pulled my legs underneath me and hoisted myself up. Another crash blasted from the cabin.

I'm coming, Harry. I tried to yell, but only a warbled grunt escaped me.

I trudged up the deck steps, winching myself along by grasping the deck rail like an injured man leveraging rope to climb a mountain. Another one of those growls wafted out and I guessed it was Lupis, but didn't know for sure.

It's not what he is; *it's what he's becoming.*

Some sort of animal.

There's really no name for it. A brief flash from this morning shot through my head and I remembered the broken-down chain-link fence rotting in the weeds, something that at one time, probably stretched all the way around this place.

What the hell was *this place*?

I stumbled through the door, the gun raised in front of me. Broken shit lay scattered everywhere, the remnants of someone who'd fought desperately and lost.

"Harry!" I yelled.

"Hey Mick." Lupis's voice, deep and distorted. I whirled to see him standing in the corner with one arm wrapped around Harry's chest and the other around his neck.

"I love you, Mickey," Harry said, defeated. "Find Britney."

Lupis snarled and rage swallowed any shred of humanity he may have once had. With a swift and tortuous movement, he ripped Harry's head from his body like stretching a piece of aged taffy until it snapped.

"*HARRY!*" The dream-like feeling was gone, swallowed up in one gulp like a shark devouring meat, and everything was real; horribly and undeniably real. Lupis dropped both pieces of Harry to the floor like discarded garbage, the body crashing in a heap and the head hitting the linoleum with a dull *thonk*.

My gun went off before I realized I was going to shoot. I gripped it in both hands, my arms straight, but relaxed enough to absorb the recoil. Doing what I'd been trained to do.

The first bullet burrowed dead center of Lupis's chest and slammed him against the wall. The second bullet tore through his throat, splattering chunks of red against the wall behind him. Both his hands shot to his neck and his eyes bulged like a dying animal.

He scrambled to get away. I fired again. The 9 MM slug punched him square in the side and he flopped like a rag doll through the glass, which exploded out into the night in shards of reflecting light. And then Lupis was gone.

I gazed at the gaping window. Frozen, unable to move. Burnt gunpowder drifted heavily and my ears rang. I glanced at Harry's corpse and then peeled my eyes away, lowering the gun. He'd asked me to kill him, hadn't he? Even though it wasn't me who did it, this is what he'd wanted. But he'd fought. He'd tried to kill Lupis Rudolph. He'd tried to kill whatever Lupis Rudolph was.

"I'm sorry, Brother." My lip trembled. A strange loneliness swept over me, like waking the morning after a child's death. If I hadn't been such a chicken shit to start with and killed Lupis Rudolph when I'd first seen him.

Find Britney.

Yes, I had to do that. It's why I came back here.

My steps thudded across the floor, echoing lifelessly as I limped toward the door. "I'll find her."

I said it to Harry without looking at him, without seeing the mess of him.

CHAPTER 36

I stopped outside of Bob's cabin and stood there on the steps, wincing. Tears clouded my vision like rain blurs a windshield. I dug my cigarettes out of my pocket and lit one. I can't explain how, but smoking dulls pain, at least it does for me, and helps me think clearer, even through the excessive ringing in my rattled eardrums.

"Where are you, Brit?" I spoke quietly perhaps hoping she'd answer through some sort of telepathy. Desperation will do weird shit to you sometimes. She was gone, somewhere out there in all that blackness.

Lupis Rudolph was changing into something, Mick, don't lose it now, there's still more to do, he was changing, you saw it, don't lose...

I'd shot the bastard. Just like I'd shot whatever the hell that thing was on the trail. That thing that charged at me. *...it's what he's turning into.*

I plopped backward onto the wooden steps, falling hard onto my butt, flaring the pain in my side and back. I grimaced and let out a small moan. I gazed into the darkness like a crazy man, holding a 9 MM Berretta in one hand and a lit cigarette in another. At the end of my rope.

Mick!

What the hell was I even doing here? What would Mom and Dad say? Of course they'd never say anything bad about me, but in my mind's eye, I pictured them lying in bed at night, talking like married couples sometimes do, and talking about me; their alcoholic son who never amounted to shit, not in the grand scheme of things.

"Mick!" Screaming. Was that screaming?

"Mick! *Help ME*!" Holy shit, someone *was* screaming. *Snap out of it, Mickey,* Harry's voice whispered in my head. That voice drowning out all others.

"Mick!"

Britney.

I heaved back to my feet.

"Britney!" I yelled. She was out there, somewhere in that abysmal blackness. *If* it was her I heard.

In the distance, splashes of light cut through the woods. Headlights, thank God… someone driving back here, someone in a truck or some sort of four-wheel-drive. Bob?

"Britney!" I yelled again. My voice sounded strange, to me it did anyway. All this shit going on; those screams, a car driving down here, I'd shot a guy, Harry's body lay in two pieces in the cabin behind me.

And I just stood there, smoking a cigarette.

Harry.

Even in the end, he'd fought to be the savior, still the best, still the strongest man I ever knew in my life.

Then, like a hangover having run its course, that disconnected sense vanished. The world turned topsy-turvy, and righted itself, thrusting me back to the here and now. Strange at first, but then everything started working right, as if my brain and body had somehow gotten out of synch, but suddenly shoved back into alignment.

I dropped my cigarette and ambled toward where I'd heard Britney. I gripped the weapon tight in my hand, my forefinger rested along the cool metal of the receiver. I'd kill any motherfucker that got in my way tonight.

"Semper Fi."

CHAPTER 37

I couldn't see a goddamn thing.

"Britney!"

I lingered on the bank of Kate's Lake and stared at Harry's old cabin. I listened to the noises, listened to the night. I hoped to God I hadn't lost her, that my stupidity and procrastination hadn't resulted in her getting hurt, or worse.

The vehicle drew closer. Its engine revved and rumbled. The bobbing headlights splashed the blackness like an erratic flashlight waving and provided shadowed glimpses of the area around me. It had to be Bob. Who else would be coming back here?

That's a question I wished I'd never gotten an answer to.

The picture of Britney that Harry showed me back in Iraq. *I'll get you two together*, Harry had said as I'd stared, fixated, at the photograph. That's where it all started. That damn picture.

I'd find her.

The muffled drone of the generator in the cellar of Bob's cabin hummed its monotonous tone. The belching engine of the approaching vehicle echoed off every tree, twig, and weed. I closed my eyes and listened for any kind of movement, for footsteps in sticky mud, the rustling of leaves, or breathing.

Something snapped off to my right, like someone (or something) had stepped on a dead twig. I had the gun up in front of me, trained, my finger dancing lightly on the trigger.

"Britney?" I didn't yell, but didn't whisper either.

No answer.

More rustling. An image of Mary's rotted face haunted me. *Don't freak out, goddamn it.* The last thing I needed was to pull this damn trigger and have another regret to drag around my whole life. I had to be sure.

Headlights flooded the area with a soft glow and I saw her, Britney, standing about fifty feet in front of me. Her eyes were wet, streaming tears, and I saw blood leaking from her mouth, dribbling down her chin as if she'd vomited a gallon of it. Both of her hands were smashed against her belly, clamped there.

Blood trickled between her fingers and dripped into the mud. The top of her pants was soaked with it. My God, she's hurt bad!

She dropped to her knees as the headlight turned away, shrouding us in darkness. A garbled cry escaped her that horrified me. Her knees made a soft *splat* against the wet mud along the bank of Kate's Lake.

"Britney!" I ran, but it felt like one of those nightmares where you can only move in slow motion. The slippery mud didn't help things, and I fell after about two steps. I clambered to my feet and lumbered to reach her.

Damn it, don't let her die out here! Not her.

I dove just as she fell forward and caught her; wrapped my arms around her. Her breath strained and her head lolled over against mine, her wet, blood-smeared cheek touched my face. She fell limp and slipped through my grip.

"Hold on, girl!" *Stop the bleeding.*

I couldn't tell if she was still conscious. I hoisted her into my arms, strained to my feet, and stumbled backward, away from Kate's Lake, trying to get her up into the grass where I had a little bit of light to work with from Bob's cabin.

Stop the bleeding, Mick, Sergeant Higgins spoke to me. I didn't want to hear from him right then, but what choice did I have? At least he was here to help. Right now, I wouldn't turn down help from anyone.

I found a flat spot in the grass and let her down gently. The approaching headlights bathed us as the vehicle finally reached the cabin and stopped. I hoped they wouldn't shut their lights off. Whoever *they* were. *Be ready.* I gripped the gun tight.

I glared down at Harry's dying sister. Her hands were still clamped to her bleeding stomach and tears poured from her eyes. I watched the pain engulf her. I saw something, wet and slippery under her hands and knew that it was something from inside her, but had no idea what.

I touched her shoulder. So fragile, so delicate. "Hold on, help is here. We have to get you out of here." If I could get her in that vehicle, who I still assumed was Bob, we could get her back to Gainesville to the hospital. It was the best shot we had. It occurred to me then that I was crying as I spoke to her.

My girl from the photograph.

I pushed a strand of hair out of her eyes and she looked at me. "I'm gonna get you out of here," I said, "Just hold on."

Hope shot through me as she nodded, barely, but noticeable. I dropped the gun next to me and pulled my shirt off. I moved her hands away from her belly and placed my shirt over the gaping wound, then placed her hands back on it.

"Keep pressure on it," I said. She nodded again.

And then it hit me… I had a goddamn iPhone in my pocket! Harry was dead, I had no reason not to call for help.

"I'm gonna call," I said. She touched my leg.

Okay, I thought as I dug in my pocket, *I've got this.* I *will* save her. But don't forget about Mary, or that guy on the trail who'd darted into the woods, and don't forget that vehicle that just pulled in. For God's sake, don't forget that. I still didn't know what side ole' Bob was on. He and Lupis Rudolph could be drinking-buddies for all I knew, which meant Bob would be pissed as soon as he saw Lupis Rudolph was dead. And, what if Bob was some sort of monster too?

Something about that didn't add up, but I didn't have time to think through all of it.

I wasn't taking chances. My thumb hovered over the phone to dial 9-1-1, when a familiar voice called my name. I froze, the skin of my neck prickled. That sense of being in a dreamland returned like the nausea of a gut-wrenching flu.

"Mick!" she yelled.

I whirled and saw Amy standing in front of what looked like a truck; the headlights obscuring any details.

Amy?

Before the question of *what in the fuck is she doing here* coalesced, I saw the shadow behind her, loping toward her as she stood oblivious. It ran like a leopard. I started to scream.

Mary.

CHAPTER 38

I dropped the phone, grabbed the gun, and broke into an awkward sprint toward her.

"Amy!" My voice cracked. "Behind you!"

She was close enough to hear me, but I'd never reach her in time. I faintly heard someone yelling for me to "Drop the weapon," but I didn't care about any of that. I watched in horror as Mary, running on all fours like an elusive apparition through the dust and darkness, charged my wife.

Amy looked behind her, but it was too late. She didn't even have a chance to react before Mary hit her and slammed her back against the side of the vehicle. The truck rocked, metal crumpled, and I heard the dull shatter of the side window as it gave. Amy rebounded and fell face-first onto the ground. Mary leered over her like a lion over its kill.

I had an open shot right then.

I stopped as Mary's foot came up and smashed into Amy's back. I heard the hollow thud as it hit her and I even saw Amy's body, limp and unconscious, jump from the force of the blow. That goddamned rotting bitch was killing my wife!

Mary lifted her foot again and I fired.

The first bullet missed and hit something metal, but the second struck home, directly into Mary's chest. She flopped back and I shot her again, this time blowing part of her jaw off. A strip of boney flesh dangled from her face like a piece of hellish jewelry.

Another bullet slammed into her hip and she jerked sideways.

But that shot had not come from my gun. Someone else was up there.

Mary stumbled and I fired again. So did the other person. One of us hit her in the stomach, doubling her over, only this time she fell and landed hard and then rolled to her side, writhing on the ground.

I scrambled to my feet. "Amy!"

I ran to her.

"*Amy*!"

Someone else yelled too. "Tell Snider to get his ass out here!"

When I reached the vehicle, my brain swam in a dizzying muck, like the choking fog of smoke. I held loosely to the ever-slipping realm of reality, as someone might grasp the handle of a whirling merry-go-round traveling at ludicrous speed. If the world had gone mad, didn't I have the right to let go and be flung to God only knows where? This had to be some kind of freakish nightmare.

She lay before me on her stomach, almost peaceful looking, except that the angle of her head was wrong, crooked somehow, folded under her shoulder in an impossible stretch that caused something inside me to twist.

My Amy.

"Get 'em on the radio," the other person yelled, "I don't give a shit where he's at. Send everyone else out this way too."

That was all background noise to me, even the guy calling for the ambulance and possible MEDI-VAC barely registered.

I collapsed to my knees next to her and slipped my hand over hers, letting the gun drop to the ground.

"Oh Jesus," I said, "I'm sorry, baby." My words were garbled noises. "I'm so sorry."

A splash resonated from Kate's Lake and I glanced up to see someone running toward it. Possibly the person who'd given Amy the ride out here. Mary was gone. The splash I'd heard was her jumping into the lake and this guy, the guy who might be a cop, was chasing her. Mary wasn't dead.

Amy's hand was limp in mine, delicate and fragile, something made of ancient glass. Fuck everyone else on this goddamned earth, this was the only one I loved and I'd take everything thing back I'd ever said or done wrong to prove that once and for all.

Funny how we realize shit like that when it's too late. The question of *what in the hell is she doing here* still danced around in the back of my head and all I could do was stare at her. And hold her hand. Her eyes were open, but I wasn't sure if she was seeing anything. I wasn't sure if she was dead. Her neck was broken.

Suddenly, she blinked.

My breath caught and I whispered, "Amy?"

"You can save her," the voice spoke as the shadow crossed over us. Someone fell against the side of the vehicle, breathing heavy. "It's not too late."

I looked up to see Lupis Rudolph, worn out and wounded, slumped against the side of the truck, glaring at me. His chest heaved laboriously, reminding me of an old gunfighter, mortally wounded, and sputtering his last heroic words before the movie ended. My ears and cheeks grew flaming hot and my throat constricted as my rage boiled, about to explode like a geyser.

"Go to hell," I growled and fumbled around for the gun, not taking my eyes off him.

"Do you want to save her or not?" Lupis's eyes found Amy and then drifted back to me. "We have to get her to the fountain before she dies."

The goddamned fountain.

Visions of Mary's decrepit corpse lurking in the darkness with maddened eyes glaring out from deep shadows settled loosely in my thoughts. But there was another possibility that popped into my head. A thought so pure in its simplicity and yet so complete in its ruination.

Maybe the fountain hadn't worked on Mary or Harry because they'd been dying already. And maybe, just maybe, Mary had gone feral because the brain cancer had already eaten away the sane tissue, leaving nothing but the discarded shell of a person who once was.

Amy was different.

She was young and strong and had nothing wrong with her. The water would heal her because that's what the fountain was for. It would heal her. It would save her. As the thoughts pummeled my brain, an ember of hope ignited like the nova of a dying star, and as it did and as my longing soul accepted the possibility, I ignored the smile spreading across Lupis's shadowed face.

"You said it was stagnate; that the water was bad." I heard myself saying it, but it sounded like it was coming from someone else.

"It ain't stagnate," Lupis said. He took out a pack of cigarettes and lit one. "I was just saying that. 'Sides, it'll work for her." He pointed at Amy. "She ain't sick or anything. The others were sick. My girl, Katie, was sick."

My girl.

I looked up at him. He *owes* it something. He owes the fountain. *Don't forget about that, Mick. Don't forget about what Harry said.* I'm not sure who was saying that in my head, but they were wrong. They didn't know what I knew. Amy wasn't dying next to them.

"I can't move her," I said, referring to Amy. "I think her neck's broken."

"We can't leave her laying here." Lupis exhaled smoke into the air and nodded toward Kate's Lake. "This place'll be crawling with cops here in a bit. That man," he pointed toward the person who'd chased Mary down to the lake and who'd, presumably, given Amy the ride down here, "he'll call everyone he knows. That's Wayne Tillwood, the deputy over in Gainesville."

Wayne Tillwood.

"Wayne!" I yelled.

Wayne spun around, his dark shape by the water's edge held a gun at his side and his shoes made squishy sounds in the mud. "Amy alright?" he asked.

"No," I said.

"Goddamn it. Where's Britney?" Wayne ran toward me, slipping and stumbling up the bank of the lake. "I saw her car when I was pulling in."

"She's over there." I pointed to where Britney was lying on the ground; a small, motionless heap.

He broke into a desperate run toward her and I watched him go. It's what I'd expected and what I'd wanted. Now I had to figure out how to move my wife without killing her.

. . . . .

"Good move," Lupis said, "I didn't know what the hell you were doin' there for a minute. Thought you were bringin' him over here."

I put my hand on Amy's back and felt her breathing. I also felt the rattling inside her, like a water hose with air bubbles rushing through it. Her lungs were filling up with fluid; blood, most likely. Her eyes were wet with tears and blood oozed from her mouth in a steady stream. Her lips were moving, but no sound came out. Her eyes were turned toward me, looking at me, accusing me, begging me.

I brushed her hair out of her face. "I'm sorry," I said, feeling worthless. I'd never been more worthless in my whole life than when I said that. *This is my goddamn fault, all mine.* She was so broken. The woman I loved, the mother of my children. Amy was thinking of them right now. I knew it because I knew Amy.

"Don't lose it." Lupis stuck a finger out at me. "All we have to do, is get her to the fountain."

"I can't fucking move her!" The thought of picking her up with her neck bent like that horrified me.

"You can try. You *have* to try. It'll work with her; the fountain will heal her."

"What about water from the Lake? You said it has some of the same stuff in it?" I stroked Amy's hair.

"It ain't got much, if it does. Nothing that'd save her."

I stared into her upturned eyes, watching her tears flood across her nose and soak the ground beneath her head.

"Look," Lupis sounded impatient, like a frustrated salesman about to give up. "She'll die if you just let her lay here. That's a fact. Your only choice is to try moving her, get her to a place where no one'll find her, and then we'll run back and get the water."

Lupis was right and I hated it. It wouldn't matter if she were in the fanciest hospital on earth, she was still going to die; Mary had already done the damage.

"Okay," I wiped snot off my face. "Where to?"

"I say we take her into the woods with us, we'll put her somewhere along the path so we can move faster."

"How far is it?" I remembered Harry saying it was way back in there.

"Mile or two, I reckon."

Damn it all to hell, we had to go. I my slid my hand under her neck and felt a bulge, hard and bony, against my palm. Nausea danced in my stomach and I swallowed a lump in my throat. I pushed the other hand under her pelvis. "Okay baby, I have to move you. Hang on."

Hating it, I pulled her up to me, hoisting her weight up into my arms. Her limpness fell against my chest, as Britney's had done only a few minutes earlier. Amy glared at me, her eyes wide open, as if to say *what in God's name are you doing*? I looked away.

I hoped to God she wasn't in pain. Wouldn't a spinal cord injury like this prevent pain?

Lupis pushed himself off the ground. "Okay," he said. He ambled around the car and I shuffled along behind him. Amy's dead weight was already clumsy and the muscles in my arms strained to keep her up. I did my best to keep her steady.

I glanced over toward Britney and saw Wayne Tillwood on his knees, bent over her and holding something against her, most likely a bandage or the shirt I'd placed over her wound. I hoped she'd be okay. An old photograph that was never anything more than a fantasy, sometimes a dream, still resides in an old suitcase I keep in the attic. The photograph of a girl that I should never have met.

We rounded the corner of Bob's cabin and Britney was out of sight. We reached the edge of the shadowed trees and I saw the path standing open like a screaming black mouth. Harry had taken this same walk not long ago and for the same reason… to save his girl.

We were hopeless romantics, me and Harry.

Lupis Rudolph disappeared into the blackness, swallowed up. Only the sounds of his scraping feet and harsh breaths escaped the dark. I followed a few steps behind. I swear it got colder. *This is bad, little man,* Chuck Verhey said.

"Kiss my ass, Chuck," I said. Lupis kept walking as if he hadn't heard me.

CHAPTER 39

We were fifty feet into the woods and I couldn't carry her any longer. Amy was small, but her limp weight kept slipping through my arms. I tripped over rocks and God knew what else. Lupis tromped ahead of me.

"Lupis," I hissed, trying not to yell. I pictured Wayne Tillwood hearing me and telling his cop buddies that he'd *heard someone talking in the woods* and then here they'd come. Didn't want that. "Wait up, I can't carry her."

Lupis stopped. "Set her down someplace. We need to hurry up."

The dark shapes of trees loomed in the night like sleeping demons. "Give me a few minutes here."

I couldn't see shit, but spotted a dark clump of trees off to the side of the path, barely illuminated by the moon's filtered light. *Jesus, help me to find her if I leave her here.* I stumbled to a flat spot and knelt down, straining to keep from falling forward. Carefully, I laid Amy on the ground, being extra cautious with her neck. A shiver of fear shot through me as I pictured her dead. I placed my hand on her chest. She was breathing, thank God.

I leaned down and said, "I'll be right back, baby."

Was I going to leave her alone out here for bugs to crawl on? What if Mary found her? *How in God's name did it come to this?*

A cold hand fell on my shoulder and I nearly cried out.

"We gotta go," Lupis said, "before it's too late."

I nodded, glanced back at Amy, touched her face one more time, and stood up. "All right, we need to move," I said. "I don't want to leave her here like this."

Lupis didn't answer, he just started walking. I stood and looked down at the spot where I'd laid my wife and saw nothing but blackness.

. . . . .

Without Amy, I moved a hell of a lot faster, staying right behind Lupis. I shoved at his back and whispered through clenched teeth, "Hurry up!" The image of Amy lying on that ground, in the dark, unable to move, blanketed every thought and throbbed at my temples. My Amy lying there dying accompanied only by the sounds of the woods, abandoned like a child's toy cast out a car window.

I'd get this fixed. I swore I would. Things like this didn't happen. Not in the real world.

Lupis picked up the pace and it creeped me out. He hunkered down, almost as if he wanted to walk on all fours.

Some sort of animal, that's what Lupis said they turned into, *no name for it really*.

I'd forgotten how far a mile was. When Lupis stopped, I plowed right into the back of him. For someone who'd been shot three times, he was solid as a rock; like running into a tree trunk. I stumbled back.

"What the hell?" I said. We were far enough away that no one would hear us back at the cabin.

"Someone's here," Lupis said and held a long, skeletal finger to his lips. "Shhhhhhhhh."

I listened and heard only the bubbly sound of flowing water, not a river, but a small trickling stream.

The fountain.

Lupis ducked and then scampered away; he made very little noise moving through the underbrush. I waited to the sound of my thumping heart and raspy breath. We needed to hurry up. *Someone's here*. What did that mean? *Someone good or bad?* I wished like hell that I knew which one of those categories Lupis fell into. He'd killed Harry, so that made him bad. But he was helping me save Amy, so that made him good. Didn't it?

A dull glow caught my attention, like a dying flashlight. It brightened and the light was strange, almost iridescent, swelling in this abysmal blackness like a bubble at the bottom of some deep ocean. I watched it, transfixed, wondering what it was, unable to move; captivated by its brilliance.

A few seconds passed before I realized it was a goddamn lantern. The shape of someone sitting next to it materialized and I let out a gush of air that I didn't realize I was holding. Just a lantern, a plain old lantern. *Christ!*

Lupis was right; there *was* someone else back here. I crouched to one knee as the light melted away the blackness, never taking my eyes off the lantern or the person sitting next to it. I thought it might be that gigantic weirdo who lived along the bottoms, the one I'd seen dart away along the path, though I had no idea what they'd be doing back here with a lantern.

The image of Amy lying back there in the dark overshadowed my fear and the urgency to get this done, to get some of the water and get back to her, intensified with each passing second. And then I wondered what the hell I was supposed to put the water in to take it back to her? I didn't bring anything and I don't remember Lupis having anything with him either. My heart thundered faster and I glanced around as if I might see a nice shiny jug or a beautiful cup just sitting there. This seemed like something –

"Figur'd you'd show up." The voice cut through the darkness like sharp glass and it froze every thought in my head. I recognized that voice.

Bob. And he *wasn't* talking to me.

I followed his gaze and didn't see shit except for the dim outline of trees reflecting the lantern's dull glow.

"Did you bring anyone with ya?" he didn't yell, but spoke loud.

"You know I don't have a choice," the voice, deep and throaty, echoed out of the blackness and it scared the shit out of me. I stayed crouched, not wanting to be seen by whatever had said that.

"I reckon ya don't," Bob said. "But I'm gonna kill ya if ya get too close, you know that."

"Ya ain't killin' no one," the voice growled. "you're too old now. You didn't stop me last time."

"I didn't know you were back here the last time, Lupis."

Holy shit… that other voice was Lupis! It sounded nothing like him, not even when he'd changed back at the cabin. This was more growly, animalistic, like what a wolf might sound like if it suddenly sprouted the ability to speak.

"Why don't ya just go on back," Bob said. "Ya know it ain't no good. If there's any shred of humanity to ya, go back."

"I can't." Lupis remained hidden. "I don't have a choice."

"We all got choices."

That horrid grimace on Lupis's face as he killed Harry flashed in my mind.

Bob bent down and picked up a shotgun lying next to him, something I hadn't noticed until he picked it up. *I've already shot him,* I thought, *three times in fact, and it didn't do a damn thing*. Bob knew something I didn't. It occurred to me right then that I no longer had the gun that Harry had given me, the one I'd shot Lupis and Mary with. I left it lying on the ground next to where Amy had been knocked down. Most likely, the cops had found it by now.

No matter. I waited for Lupis to make his move. I hoped to Jesus, Mary, and Joseph, he'd hurry the fuck up. I wanted that goddamned water.

"Did ya bring anyone with ya?" Bob asked again and a cold chill shot through me.

"Of course," Lupis answered. "You know I can't touch it."

He's selling me out.

"Tell him to get outta here," Bob said. "This here's between us." He paused a moment, then said, "It ain't that fella's friend is it? The one livin' in my cellar?"

I didn't move a muscle. I didn't even blink.

"The one livin' in your cellar is dead." Lupis's voice drifted from the darkness. "I don't think he was turnin'."

"He was turnin'; he was just fightin' it." Bob clicked the hammer back on the shotgun. "They all turn. Even you did."

I caught movement out of the corner of my eye and noticed a massive creature prowling out of the darkness, slinking toward Bob. It hunkered over, as if struggling to stay upright, its head low. As it weaved through the trees, I noticed the snout protruding and found myself once again reminded of a wolf.

I bit down on the side of my mouth to stifle a scream and slumped back against a small tree trunk. It never looked in my direction, but the hairs on my neck stirred from the gooseflesh breaking out on my body. I wanted to run right then, just turn my chicken-shit ass around and run like a madman back through the woods, most likely gouging an eye or stumbling headlong into the dirt.

I clamped my hand against my mouth and pressed against the tree trunk. I watched in stunned horror as it lumbered toward Bob, who stood there, watching. He didn't seem the slightest bit surprised to see it.

"She would'a become this, my little Katie" the thing said, "That's what I keep tellin' myself. That's why it's better for her, where she is." His words were hard to understand, like hearing a recording played on slow speed. In some reality, I understood that this monster was Lupis Rudolph, but my brain wouldn't embrace it.

There's really no name for it.

"Yep." Bob still hadn't raised the gun. I wished he'd start shooting. "Only she'd've been worse cause she was sick."

The creature didn't say anything, but crept closer. Bob never so much as flinched, as if he saw shit like this every day.

"It'll be different this time," the Lupis-Rudolph-thing said, "This one ain't sick. We can save her."

Oh my God; he was talking about Amy.

"The water's bad," Bob said.

"It ain't bad; it's the people drinkin' it that's bad," Lupis's voice rose and grew angry.

In one fluid and shocking movement, Bob lifted the shotgun up to his shoulder and fired. Lupis flopped backward as the shot echoed through the woods, hitting him dead in the chest. I wondered if people back at the cabin heard that. I wondered if Amy heard it.

Lupis crashed backward and then charged again. Bob aimed and fired. And fired again. A semi-automatic shotgun. Lupis wailed and I heard him running through the woods, trying to escape.

And then everything stopped. An eerie silence descended on me, almost unnatural. The echoing of the shotgun blasts lingered in my ears. Lupis had not expected Bob to be sitting back here. And neither had I. I'd pictured a little pool of water that we'd walk up to and fill our... whatever the hell we'd find to fill... and be gone. Instead we ran into Bob.

"You can come on out," Bob yelled.

I gawked at him, shocked that he spoke. He gazed in my direction.

"I got him." Bob loaded two shells into his gun.

Goddamn it. I couldn't just sit here, hiding behind this tree. Amy was waiting for me.

"C'mon now," Bob said. "I know you're there."

For Amy. *I love you.*

I stood and stepped out from the trees, moving slowly toward Bob with my hands out to my sides, open, to show I wasn't armed. I wondered if the Iraqi soldier I'd killed had thought the same thing when he stepped out of his hiding-place carrying the stick with his white T-shirt tied to the end.

Bob leaned the shotgun against a stump. "It's alright," he said, "I ain't plannin' to shoot ya."

Relief settled into me when he set the gun down. "I don't know what's happening here," I said.

"I wouldn't expect you to." His eyes narrowed to slits as I drew closer. "This shit's been goin' on for decades, probably hundreds of years."

"What shit?" I stopped. If he decided to go berserk and grab the shotgun, I wanted time to react.

"This shit."

I stared at him, waiting for him to elaborate, and he only stared back at me with an expression that reminded me of someone who'd been asked to reveal their deepest and darkest secret.

He shook his head and asked, "Why are ya here?"

It made no sense to lie to him, yet I had an urge to do just that. "I need some water." The lifeless words fell out of my mouth and melted into the darkness around us, consumed by something ravenous and hidden.

"That's the shit I'm talkin' about," Bob spoke through clenched teeth. "This goddamned water."

I debated telling him I didn't give a shit and that I needed it, now.

"Ya know, the government even found out about this place a long time ago, built a big-ass fence 'round it." Bob waved a hand in an arc as if I had no idea what building a fence around us meant. "Guess they got tired of it or somethin' cause they didn't stay. Guess they realized the same shit we did." He shrugged, then added, "I personally think them two government guys drank the water and never left and it was so top-secret, nobody else knew it was here. One of the guys you shot on the trail." He pointed a pudgy finger at me.

I remembered the rotting, chain-link fence I'd seen this morning while walking with Britney. I also remembered the creature that had charged me earlier. I even recalled the jerk of the gun in my hand as I'd fired. I licked my sore lip as he pulled out a pack of cigarettes, and lit one. "Long story short, this here ain't no fountain of youth, not by a long shot."

Crazy as it sounds, seeing Bob smoke; I decided to have one too. It fit the occasion, I suppose. My nerves were shot.

"You know what this place is?" Bob asked.

I shook my head. How long would I listen to him drone on? I kept picturing Amy back there lying by herself in the dark and that I needed to get back to her right now.

"This here's the fountain of death. You seen what it does to people. It turns 'em into somethin'."

"My wife, Amy." I heard my words like listening to a conversation from an adjacent room. "She needs some of that water. She's in the woods; she's dying."

"Ain't you listenin'," Bob hissed, "I said it's bad. This water ain't gonna save her."

But it would.

No, it won't, little man.

Yes, it would! Amy wasn't sick, like the others had been. It might work. "Look." I blew smoke into the air above me. "I want to try. If it makes her bad, like Mary, I'll kill her."

Bob laughed. He actually laughed at me, the old sonofabitch. "Yeah, right."

I brought my cigarette to my lips and took a nice long drag. My rage blossomed like an ember smoldering dangerously close to something explosive. Funny how it pisses us off when people see through our bullshit.

Bob's face straightened and the lantern cast an eerie glow that made his eyes look sunken, like pits in his skull. "That thing I shot just now, did you see it? Lupis?"

I could charge Bob, tackle him and then beat the shit out of him. My heart kicked into higher gear, but I kept my cool, for the moment anyway. "Yeah." As I spoke, I quickly scanned the ground, searching for a stick or other weapon of opportunity I might need in order to get past him, to get back to my Amy. "I shot him too. Back at the cabin. He killed Harry."

"Well," Bob lowered his gaze. "That *thing* was my Great-Uncle. It was his daughter, Katie, who drank some of this water and so did he."

I hadn't connected the dots earlier that Katie had been Lupis's daughter. "He told me about Katie," I said. I spotted a rock not far in front of me that, if the shit hit the fan, I thought I could get to and hurl at Bob before he could shoot me. *Just keep him talking, little man.*

You know my plan, Chuck.

Bob nodded and cast his gaze over me, staring into an abyss, lost in thoughts that only he could see. "I wasn't even born when all that happened with Katie. My daddy told me to watch this place, that there weren't nothin' good about it. And, he told me to watch out for Uncle Lupis."

I'm coming baby, I thought, *just hold on, I'll be there*. He was trying to talk me out of it, out of taking the water. I took a small, shuffling step toward the rock and asked, "So you've been living back here your whole life, watching this stupid fountain?"

"Yeah," Bob suddenly looked tired and smaller somehow, as if he'd deflated from a massive breath he'd been holding. "I've only seen Uncle Lupis about ten times. I've shot him three or four times when he brought people back here. I didn't know he brought your friend back here. I swear I didn't know that." He spoke as if I blamed him for everything wrong in the world. Sorrowful was the word that came to mind and my anger cooled. "If I'd known, I would've stopped him and then none of this would'a happened with you."

Hearing him say that made me realize he *was* the good guy. And he'd failed.

Like I'd failed Amy.

"Ya see," he said, "this place is strange and not only 'cause the water keeps you alive. It also makes you pay it back. This here is more than a place," Bob glanced around again. "It's a presence of some kind. Something that owns you once you give in. That's what happened to Uncle Lupis; it owns him. Now he owes it for taking the water from it. Probably why your friend had me call you out here, come to think of it. He owed it." His eyebrows furrowed as if that idea had just occurred to him.

The idea started to materialize, that the fountain was not some scientific anomaly, but rather a haunted lake, when something rustled behind me, something big, and I whirled. Bob grabbed his shotgun. But it ran away from us, crashing through the trees, getting farther away.

"What the fuck is that?" I asked.

"That'd be Uncle Lupis, most likely," Bob said. "Prob'ly won't see him for another year or two."

That thing knows where I left Amy.

He'd been there when I laid her along the path. *Christ almighty.*

"I gotta get to Amy," I gasped, feeling sick.

"Where's she at?"

"Along the path. I couldn't carry her all the way back here."

Bob grabbed his lantern and I said, "I have to get some water."

"Let's go to your wife," Bob said. "You don't want none of this here water. It'll only make things worse."

My wife will die because of me. Because of me.

Because of *me.*

She's not sick. The water will work and I didn't care if she was a little different afterward.

"I have to," I told Bob.

Bob begged me. "I ain't gonna let ya."

"Please." Something inside me slipped, as if a snake, coiled deep in my brain, were startled awake, slithering, devouring, and with each juicy bite it took, less of me remained. "She's not sick. She'll be okay."

"She'll be okay if you let her alone," Bob said.

Would Lupis Rudolph kill Amy? I'd find the mess he left of her; her insides strewn about the forest floor like dirty laundry.

My daughters. *Daddy, what happened to mommy?*

I launched myself at Bob. He raised the shotgun, but not fast enough. I reached him just before he pulled the trigger and drove my shoulder into his chest. He caved easily, falling backward, and dropped the shotgun. I slipped on the muddy rocks and fell, landing painfully on my left side, the side where Jessie had kicked me in the ribs.

Bob collapsed with a painful grunt. His lantern crashed next to him and then exploded into a ball of fire as the casing shattered and the kerosene ignited. I gaped in horror as he flailed, as the flames engulfed him like an insatiable beast.

I scrambled awkwardly to my feet and stomped on the flames, doing my best to put them out. Bob arms and legs slowed to jerky movements and charred clothing drifted off of him like fleeing insects. "Oh Jesus," I cried while staring at his blackened mouth hanging open; frozen in a silent scream. "I'm sorry." My blubbery voice sounded alien and it frightened me.

I didn't mean to kill him. I only wanted to knock him down and get the gun. That's all. I needed the fucking water! Why didn't he let me have the water? Why, goddamn it, couldn't anyone understand this?

Off to my left, within a few feet, the water bubbled and trickled.

The fountain.

I shuffled away from Bob's sizzling body, the thick taste of smoke coated my mouth, and I limped toward the water. A small round hole in the rock floor, about the size of a car tire, roiled with water filled to the brim, like air was escaping from somewhere beneath the surface. I stepped closer, mesmerized. Tall walls of rock surrounded me, like a roofless cave, and the fountain looked to be right in the center of a hollowed-out hillside.

I *felt* it, a small vibration in my chest, like a deep and sustained chord from a hellish instrument, it resonated, and I sensed whatever this place was. *It's a presence*, Bob had said. Yes, a presence. Alive and knowing, it drew me to it. If I took that water, I'd take a part of it with me; a part that would always be hungry.

A part that would never stop eating.

But Amy's not sick. She isn't. She's injured, but not sick or dying as the others had been. So what if I took some of it with me? I'd still have Amy. The price would be worth it, no matter what the price was.

Daddy, what happened to mommy?

I don't remember taking the last few steps; I knew that I stood next to it, my feet right on the rim of the small hole where water sloshed, circled and begged. I imagined the taste would be sweet, like nectar, and it looked so clear, so refreshing. It was so clean, in fact, that I knew by drinking it, it would wash everything bad from inside me. And it would make Amy better.

I dropped to my knees next to it. How do I get it out? How do I get it to her? I could suck in a mouthful and try to hold it as I walked back down the path, hold it until I reached Amy. But that was a shitty plan. What if I accidently swallowed it? Or didn't get enough? I looked around me, seeing nothing. Then an idea popped into my head. I reached down to peel my shirt off and my fingers hit the bare skin of my stomach. My shirt was gone. I'd taken it off to cover Britney's wound. My pants? Or…

I twisted and looked behind me at Bob, at the site of the charred top half of him.

CHAPTER 40

I'll never forget those few minutes. Perched on the edge of that fountain, gazing down into it. I wondered where I'd end up if I jumped in and started swimming down that hole, through the tunnel.

When I woke up this morning, I thought about that moment which now seemed so long ago. In a way, I was glad Harry died. I didn't want him to see me, to know what I'd done.

Standing on the edge of that fountain with Bob's dirty, unburnt socks in my hand was the last chance I had to do the right thing. In fact, I remember gazing down into that small pool of swirling water and thinking…

. . . . .

…don't do it.

Was that me or someone else thinking that? The sinister presence I'd sensed earlier swelled, like the stench of death as you drew closer to where its source lay rotting, and the hairs on my arms tingled. The stench of Bob's roasted corpse lingered and I was faintly aware that I heard crickets chirping again.

Get away from here, little man, Chuck Verhey boomed in my head and for the first time in my life, I heard fear touch his voice. He was terrified of this water because it was going to kill him if I drank it. I leaned my head back and laughed at that thought.

"You'd love it if I ran away from here, wouldn't you?" I said it between guffaws, hoping Chuck heard the contempt etched deep in my words.

I waited, but Chuck didn't answer. Strange that he'd spoken at all.

Daddy, what happened to mommy? Their sweet little voices. *Daddy, what happened to you?* A cold tear trickled down my cheek.

They'd understand, some day. They'd understand that I didn't have a choice.

I held Bob's shotgun in my left hand, and his dirty socks in my right. His dirty, stinking socks were my back-up plan. I'd felt like a shit at first, peeling them off his feet. His body was charred black, even his face, and the hair on his head was gone. His arms, chest, and legs still smoldered. Smoke drifted in wisps from his body, like the steam from cooling blood, but I paid it no mind. *Guess the water won't help you,* I thought, *it doesn't bring people back from the dead.* If you stop and think about it, it was his own goddamn fault for not giving me the water. It didn't have to come to this. I tried to be nice about it. I begged him.

Thank God, his feet and legs weren't burned. I needed his socks. I tore them off one at a time and was pleasantly surprised that they weren't old and thin with holes in the heels and toes. Hell no, 'ole Bob must have made a trip to Walmart because these socks were thick and soft. Perfect.

You're messin' up, Smith, Sergeant Higgins screamed in my ear. *You're messin' up and you better goddamn stop!*

"Kiss my ass," I said. Holy Christ, I'd ever told Sergeant Higgins *that* before. It felt good, liberating! I laughed out loud again, only this time my laughter sounded crazy and it scared me.

Gripping Bob's socks in my hand, I lumbered back to the fountain. I can't remember if I'd been laughing still, but I might've been.

She's waiting for you.

A dull hum, sort of a fuzzy, vibrating sound, dug into my ears and then morphed into something different, something that pulled me toward that water, like standing in front of a large magnet while wearing a thick, metal necklace. I thought I heard screaming, off in the distance, but I wasn't for sure. It might have been in my head.

I dropped to my knees and laid the shotgun on the ground next to me. Instant relief surged through my legs. Everything hurt. I leaned forward, bringing my face toward the swirling surface. Just before my mouth touched the water, I had a horrid image of something down there below the surface, watching me. I closed my eyes, unable to stop now, unable to do anything but drink from it.

The cool water touched my lips and I filled my mouth, and I swallowed.

Wait, wait, wait, you might be saying. *I get it, but I wasn't expecting that.* Well, see, remember when I told you at the beginning of this story that I blame my wife for what happened?

Now you know why I blame her.

I hadn't meant to, I wanted a mouthful to take back to Amy, but I'd swallowed out of reflex. I was so thirsty, so damned thirsty. The cool water raced down my throat and hit my stomach in a refreshing slosh and it felt good. So thirsty. I gulped another drink. And then another.

Finally, I sucked in a mouthful and held it. That awful hum suddenly stopped and so did the vibration. The only sounds were the crickets and the bubbling water. I sat there in the woods, alone. The darkness thickened and I was scared, terrified in fact, and I wanted out of there. Everything that had happened up until then started to become a blur, like a dream that faded quickly after you woke up.

Time to move. I couldn't hold the water in my mouth forever. I dipped the socks into the pool, soaking them good, and lifted them out, soaked and dripping. This was my back-up plan. I had to reach her before they dried.

I grabbed the shotgun and stood up, breathing heavily through my nose, feeling like a person about to puke with my cheeks puffed out and my mouth full of liquid. I glanced around and for one brief and horrible moment, I was lost. I had no idea where the hell the path was and panic reared its ugly head. It was blacker than a coal-miner's ass out here; I couldn't see shit.

Where was the goddamned path?

I turned in a full circle, my frightened eyes wide. Everything looked the same.

And then, directly in front of me, a lighter patch of darkness where the moonlight shone through the trees. My path. The relief was so profound, I wanted to cry. I started walking as soon as I saw it, making my way up a short embankment, and plowing my way towards Amy.

On my way, baby.

My eyes burned and my heart raced and I fought the urge to run.

. . . . .

I reached Amy quicker than I expected. Things were starting to work in my favor and a wave of peace brushed over me, like things might be okay. Luck was on my side.

I found her right where I'd left her. The moon rose up and shined, as if God himself had clicked on a flashlight to show me the way.

I laid the shotgun on the ground next to her and got down on my hands and knees, and touched her, feeling her chest still moving up and down. Her face was hidden in shadows, so I reached out with my fingers, finding her lips and bent down as if to give her a goodnight kiss. I let what little water was left in my mouth spill out into her. Then I placed the socks, which were still soaked, over her mouth and squeezed. I heard water dripping out and I cupped my hands as I squeezed, making sure I hit the target.

She swallowed. I heard her swallow. Not once, but at least three times. Little clicks in her throat, a weak whimper, and I wept as relief washed through me. I squeezed the socks harder to get every drop and with it a sense of dread crept into me, like a skeletal insect twisting inside me, growing restless, and I clenched my teeth.

After I'd squeezed out every drop, I tossed the socks and stroked her hair and sobbed next to her.

"It's gonna be okay, baby." My tears flowed. Oh my God, I loved her so much.

I sat up and gazed in the direction of Bob's cabin. Through the trees between here and there, lights, most likely headlights, splashed through the woods, fighting through trees and leaves. I wondered briefly if they'd heard the shotgun blasts from Bob's gun. Surely not or they would've come running.

I imagined the place was crawling with cops by now, all looking for Mary. And me. And Amy. What would happen when they found Harry in that cabin? Would they keep looking for us?

I hoped Britney was okay.

I turned back to Amy. "We gotta stay back here for a while." I wished she could answer me. I suddenly felt so alone without her to tell me we'd be okay. That this all would turn out okay like she'd tell me sometimes when we'd run short on money, or when we'd decided to buy the house a few years back.

Or when I'd quit drinking and fought through those first few months.

I lay down on the hard, damp ground and wrapped my arm around her. I never thought in a million years that I could fall asleep. I didn't know what would happen or how to tell if the water worked. I was thinking about that when I drifted off to sleep to the sound of her labored breathing.

▪ ▪ ▪ ▪ ▪

A bird chirped and something rustled in the leaves behind me, like a scampering chipmunk. My eyes snapped open and I squinted against the bars of sunlight filtering through the trees.

The water.

Amy.

I twisted around to look at her, but she was gone.

CHAPTER 41

Three weeks have passed.

I've been staying at Harry's old cabin and I have to say, it's not bad at all. Mornings are my favorite. I've always loved peaceful mornings, even in Iraq. Amy and I used to camp in the mountains a lot when we were first married, and those crisp mornings drinking coffee made over a fire were the best. We stopped doing that stuff after the girls were born, but I missed it. I didn't realize how much until I stayed here at Harry's cabin. We'd start doing that kind of stuff again.

I called my in-laws the day after getting the water for Amy and told them we decided to stay in Indiana for a few more days. I'm pretty sure they knew I was full of shit, they sensed something wasn't right. For one, I called *them*, which, in all our years of marriage, I'd never done. Amy's parents and I don't hate each other, but we aren't drinking buddies either. I called them again about a week ago. Amy's mom had started crying, asking where we were and saying she wanted to talk to Amy, *right now*! I hung up on her then tossed my phone into Kate's Lake. Amy's too.

I knew her parents loved our kids, and they'd take care of them as long as they needed to, even without me asking. Her mom and dad probably had every cop, FBI agent, and the entire Colorado National Guard out hunting my ass. It was just a matter of time before I'd have to face the music.

I'm sure Amy never told them exactly where she'd gone since she left Colorado in such a hurry. That's the part I hate thinking about, the part that will haunt me for the rest of my life. Amy caught a flight out of Colorado two days after I'd left; the day after Harry's funeral. She'd known something was wrong with me, she'd known I was drinking and she was coming out to get me.

I know this because I've got six voicemails where she said it. If I'd have just checked my goddamn messages!

. . . . .

I don't know why in the hell you're not answering, but I wanted you to know my plane landed about an hour ago and I rented a car to drive to Gainesville. I should be there in an hour or two. I'm going to Harry's mom's house. I love you.

I erased four of her messages, but I kept that one. The others were quick snippets of information. *I left the girls with mom and dad. I'm flying out there, you'd better not be drunk.*

I had no problem erasing that one.

The two I kept, I wanted to hear again and again. I don't know why. Maybe the desperation in her voice, the realization of the love inherent there. Or perhaps I kept those two because I remember what I was doing when she called and left those messages.

The other message said: *I went to the police station, Mick. A guy named Wayne Tillwood offered to help. He said he knew you and that you were with Harry's sister.* She'd hesitated right then, leaving a brief silence that I'd forever wonder what she was thinking about. Then she continued, *Anyway, he said that she'd gone out to that cabin at Kate's Lake and since you weren't at your motel Wayne asked if I wanted to go out to Kate's Lake, he thought you might be out there with her.*

She muffled the phone likely by holding it against her chest or clamping a hand over it, but I still understood her as she asked Wayne how far away the place was. He mumbled something back, and then she came back on; *we're about forty-five minutes or so from there. Goddamn it, Mick. Call me if you get this. I'm scared and I feel like I'm on a wild goose chase here. I love you… I don't care what's happened.*

I'm pretty sure that's the message I got when I first walked down that dark lane to Kate's Lake, right before I saw Mary trying to put on the lipstick.

Sometimes the irony of life is so poignant. I'll never stop thinking about those voice-messages, even when I know it does me no good, that's the one thing that drives the stake through my heart, and it's the void in my chest that I can never fill.

. . . . .

I woke up this morning, early as usual, and sat out here on the porch for about an hour in Harry's old rocking chair. It shocked the shit out of me when Britney showed up. She'd apparently borrowed a four-wheel drive from someone. One thing I've noticed here lately is that I can hear shit from a mile away. It's like I've got super-hearing now. I'm chalking it up to nature, being out here in the fresh air. It does a body good.

There've been several people come back here the past couple of weeks. A lot of cops and when they show up, I hide in the woods and wait for them to leave. That's another thing I've noticed I can do here, I can *sense* things. Like this morning, I knew it was Britney coming out here. Don't ask me how, but I did. And, when she got closer, I knew someone was with her. To be downright honest, I smelled them. I swear I did. And whoever rode with her wasn't a threat. Most likely, someone along for the ride to keep her company. She must've been scared to death to come back here after everything that happened.

A dark gray pickup truck emerged from the trees, easing down the lane toward Bob's cabin. I stayed put in my rocking chair, not caring if she saw me… in fact, I was hoping she would.

The truck rumbled to a stop in front of the porch. Britney rode in the passenger seat. I recognized the driver immediately, but felt absolutely no emotion toward him, Britney's ex-husband, Jesse. He sat there behind the steering wheel, glaring at me. He hated bringing her back here to me. Strange what love can do.

She climbed carefully out of the truck, most likely still recovering from that horrible injury she'd gotten from Mary. The stench of fear, thick like the rot of dead flesh, infested the air. I smiled, trying to ease her trepidation.

She folded her arms and stopped at the bottom of the steps, leering at me like I was someone she didn't know.

"Mick?"

"Hi, Britney." Strange saying that, as if we hadn't spent those two days together and drank beer out on that deck and came back to Kate's Lake the morning after.

She asked, "Are you okay?"

I saw myself saying yes, that everything was fine, but the words that came out were, "No. But I will be."

She hesitated, still looking at me in that strange expression. "You look different. What's wrong?"

I didn't have a clue what she was talking about. I shrugged. "I don't know. I feel great, no thanks to him." I flipped a hand at the truck and Britney shifted her gaze to the ground. She knew.

"Mick..."

"Sorry, just sayin'." I didn't know what to say. I didn't know why she was there, frankly. "You want to come up here and have a beer?"

Harry had left a lot of beer in the fridge, along with several bottles of Jim Beam, Jack Daniels, Old Granddad, and even a full bottle of Old Crow. I hadn't touched the Old Crow yet, that was some rot-gut shit if there ever was any. But I'd finished the Jim Beam and Jack Daniels already and was about halfway through the bottle of Old Granddad. It wouldn't be long.

"No thanks." She shuffled her feet, glanced around her, and said, "I knew you'd be back here."

"How'd you know?"

"Your stuff is still at the motel. Wayne said they never found you or your wife and that they've called your house in Colorado several times trying to get a hold of you. He must've talked to your mom and dad or something yesterday... he said it's turning into a missing persons case."

"And you thought I'd be here?" I asked, not trying to sound like a smart ass, but for some reason, thought I might have.

She nodded.

"You gonna tell anyone you saw me?"

She shook her head.

"He probably will." I nodded at Jesse.

"I told him not to."

I shrugged, still not knowing for sure how she'd known, intuition perhaps, and then dropped it. In the grand scheme of things, I didn't give a shit. If the cops came back here, I'd know it; they couldn't sneak up on me.

"What'd they say about Harry?"

Her eyes were dark, as if she'd seen many sleepless nights. "They said Harry had been dead for a long time, that someone had killed him back at that cabin a while ago. They've searched everywhere for Bob, but still haven't found him. They think he left the state and is hiding somewhere." Britney smiled on that last part, she knew part of that story was bullshit, but she didn't know how much. I considered telling her that Bob was a crispy-critter way back in the woods, but then thought better of it. The less she knew the better for her.

I smiled and nodded. "Part of that's right. Bob's definitely hiding somewhere, but not here."

"What about Harry? You said you talked to him that day." She pushed a strand of hair behind her ear. "Was he really here?"

I wondered how honest I should be. I didn't want to start talking about Lupis Rudolph, monsters, or the fountain of youth. That would spawn a whole list of things and pretty soon every cop in Indiana would be back out here.

"Yeah," I finally said. She deserved that much at least. "He was here. I don't know how, but he was alive. He was sick though. I mean, real sick."

Her eyebrows crinkled and I thought she might cry.

"He didn't want you to see him. I told you that."

"What about that girl, or that thing that attacked me? Was that Mary?"

I nodded and gazed out over the stillness of Kate's Lake. The early sun glistened off the water. Beautiful.

"Is she dead?" The desperation in Britney's voice broke my heart so I told her what she wanted to hear.

"I think so," I said. "She drowned in the lake." For all I knew, I was right. I hadn't seen Mary since that night I shot her.

Britney stood there for a long time. I got the impression she wanted to leave and I sensed her anxiety as she got more and more agitated, like waves of electricity. She cupped her elbows in her hands, still folded across her chest. The silence grew awkward.

"Why don't you quit staying back here?" She asked. Her voice quivered.

"I can't." That was the truth.

"Why not, Mick?" Now she *was* crying. I didn't look at her. I didn't need that shit right now.

"I just can't, that's all."

I kept my gaze trained on the lake, staring at it, lost in it. I waited for her next question, wondering how many she'd ask before I had to spill everything and tell her all the details. But, to my surprise, the next thing I heard was the door to the truck slamming shut and then they were leaving. She didn't look at me and kept one hand next to her face, as if hiding behind it.

I was glad she left. I hoped she'd never come back. I had stuff to do here, stuff that might take a long time.

I decided right then that if Britney *did* come back, I'd tell her everything, all the gory details. I could've told her about Amy and what had happened to her. Then told her about Bob and about my run-in with him and how I'd accidently (and I'd stress that) killed him. Then I would tell her about the fountain.

Tell her about the fountain.

I needed to tell her about that. A yearning to tell her, like a wolf craving meat, I'd have to give in eventually. And I could show her, walk her back there and *show* her. The thought of doing that filled me with a desire greater than anything I'd ever had before. Even though she'd left upset, something told me that she *would* be back, might be a few days, or even a few weeks, but she'd be back. And we'd go see the fountain together. I'd show her –

A rustling in the bushes behind the cabin caught my attention. I rose from my chair and peered into the woods. There she was, my Amy, hiding there in the trees only a few feet from the edge of the porch, staring at me. Her head hung at an awkward angle, but I'd gotten used to it. Even the flaccid skin and clumpy hair no longer bothered me. She was alive and that was all that mattered.

She would get better.

I've seen her a couple of times the past few weeks, usually at night. I haven't been able to get close though, she's real skittish. The other night, I woke up to the sound of something walking around outside on the porch. I eased out of bed and tiptoed to one of the windows and gently pushed back the curtain. She sat in a rocking chair, right next to the one I was sitting in earlier this morning. I'd left a shirt out there (one that had been Harry's when he lived here) and I noticed Amy had wrapped it around herself and she was just rocking, staring out at nothing. It was dark and I only saw the back of her head, but it had been wonderful.

The fact that she's this close to me without running off is a huge step forward. Her eyes look better too. They're still glazed over, staring into nothing, but she's facing me. She sees me! Her stench doesn't bother me either; in fact, I don't think it's as bad now as it's been before. That had me worried for a while.

"Just a second," I said. My heart galloped with excitement. I'd been leaving stuff out for her to eat and I knew what she liked, but I had to run inside and get it. I hoped to God she wouldn't run away while I was in there. I opened the screen door and hustled inside. I'd killed a squirrel last night and had it lying on a plate on the counter. I grabbed it, plate and all, and ran quickly back outside.

Amy had moved up onto the porch. I'm pretty sure she was waiting for me.

I took a cautious step toward her, then stopped and set the plate down, never taking my eyes off her, and then backed away slowly. "There you go, baby," I said. I couldn't contain my smile or the tears floating down my cheeks.

A few seconds passed and neither of us moved. Then she squatted, grabbed the squirrel off the plate as if it were a handful of cotton-candy, and bit into it with ravenous joy. The sound of her eating disgusted me, but we'd get past that. The happiness swelling within me was enormous. I fought the urge to run to her.

As I watched her, I said softly, "I love you, baby."

We'll meet again
Don't know where
Don't know when
But I know we'll meet again some sunny day

Keep smiling through
Just like you always do
'Til the blue skies
Drive the dark clouds far away

- Vera Lynn

ACKNOWLEDGEMENTS

Here we are again, reader, closing out another story. I do hope you enjoyed this one as much as I loved writing it. As you can imagine, I leaned heavily on my own experience in the Marine Corps in developing Mick's character. Alcoholism and PTSD are two very real things and quite often, they're related. Many of our Marines, soldiers, sailors, and airmen must contend with this very real affliction and though I used it as the basis for my made-up story, I do not take this subject lightly.

I do need to make some clarifications on the differences between my own experiences and Mick's so as not to put myself on a pedestal I don't deserve to be on:

The story eludes to Mick as a veteran from the war in Iraq. You can conclude by the timeline that Mick would have served around the 2012 to 2013 timeframe. I served in Desert Shield/Desert Storm from 1991 to 1992 and I was never in the Iraq conflict that started in 2001. Mick is also portrayed as being Marine Corps Infantry. Though I served with the infantry, my job was a truck-driver (what we in the Marine Corps would call a 3533. Motor T, baby!).

I modeled Harry after one of my best friends in the Corps named Jerry (JT) to whom I dedicated this book. We lost contact years ago but I still think of him. The times we had. The places we traveled. The trouble we got into. I hated the Marine Corps when I was in, but part of me has missed it ever since. I miss the friends, the camaraderie, and the adventures. A time when it was okay to live on the edge. *Semper Fi, brothers*.

Writing a book is the easy part. Editing and publishing it is a whole other ball of wax and one cannot (or should not) do it alone. I must thank the following people:

My wife, Tammy, for putting up with me through all this (and for reading *Kate's Lake*).

The whole team at Black Rose Writing for publishing my book.

Michael Maher who was once again, my original beta-reader and who influenced much of what ended up on these pages.

Catherine Payne for the development edit which was crucial to identifying and fixing the glaring plot holes I had in there.

Mike Herzog for your continued support, teaching, and feedback.

The Bottoms is a real place (not in Indiana) and though I changed many of the details to fit my story, a few people will recognize that name and place; those of us who grew up at "the club" (Beth and Sheryl, you know what I'm talking about).

I want to especially thank Nancy Jones. Nancy is a retired English teacher who I met in the driveway of my house! Her feedback on *Kate's Lake* was huge and this story would not be what it is if it wasn't for her. Thank you, Nancy.

ABOUT THE AUTHOR

David Odle spent four-years in the Marine Corps as a motor transport operator serving from 1989 – 1993. David is pictured here in Saudi Arabia during Operation Desert Shield, 1991.

David discovered his love for reading and writing at the age of thirteen. David is the author of the Urban Fantasy novel, *Markus,* and is currently working on his next novel.

NOTE FROM THE AUTHOR

Word-of-mouth is crucial for any author to succeed. If you enjoyed *Kate's Lake*, please leave a review online—anywhere you are able. Even if it's just a sentence or two. It would make all the difference and would be very much appreciated.

Thanks!
David

Thank you so much for reading one of our

Occult / Supernatural novels.

If you enjoyed the experience, please check out our recommendation for your next great read!

Absolute Darkness by Tina O'Hailey

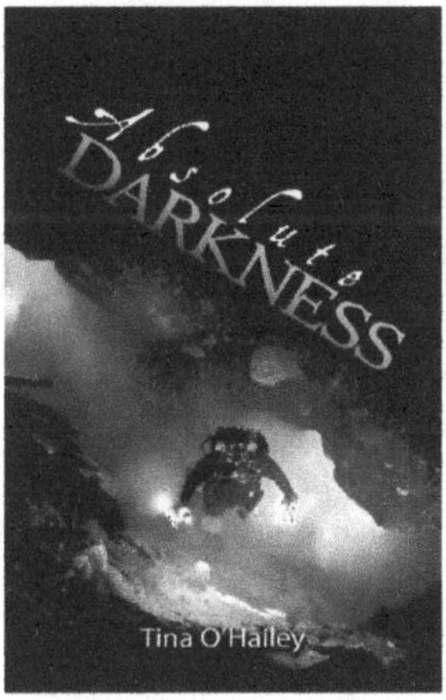

"Tina O'Hailey nails it. She has a great talent, a gift. Character development is exceptional, the scenes are set so carefully that I found myself immersed in each."

–Ken Bangs, author of *Guardians in Blue*

View other Black Rose Writing titles at www.blackrosewriting.com/books and use promo code **PRINT** to receive a **20% discount** when purchasing.

BLACK ROSE writing™